"A new talent just hit the urb
a genuine gift for creating dangerously hilarious drama."
    —*RT Book Reviews* on *The Accidental Demon Slayer*

"With its sharp, witty writing and unique characters, Angie Fox's contemporary paranormal debut is fabulously fun."
    —*Chicago Tribune* on *The Accidental Demon Slayer*

"Angie Fox has done it again. In the latest adventure featuring the fabulous demon slayer Lizzie Brown, Fox deftly creates complex characters with a gift for gab, weaving multiple storylines together to create sidesplitting encounters that are both romantic and suspenseful."
    —*RT Book Reviews* on *The Last of the Demon Slayers*
                                            (4½ stars!)

"*The Accidental Demon Slayer* is a delightful new paranormal romance that is hilarious, exciting, suspenseful, dangerous, and an adventure ride of action from start to finish. The characters are eccentric, the writing flows great, and the storyline is original. I adored every page of this outstanding debut novel and I hungrily look forward to getting my hands on Angie Fox's next book."
                                            —*Fresh Fiction*

MORE . . .

Also by Angie Fox

Immortally Yours
Immortally Embraced

immortally
ever after

angie fox

St. Martin's Paperbacks

5248 5579 9/13

IMMORTALLY EVER AFTER

Copyright © 2013 by Angie Fox.

For information address St. Martin's Press, 175 Fifth Avenue, New York, NY 10010.

ISBN: 978-0-312-54668-7

Printed in the United States of America

St. Martin's Paperbacks edition / September 2013

St. Martin's Paperbacks are published by St. Martin's Press, 175 Fifth Avenue, New York, NY 10010.

10 9 8 7 6 5 4 3 2 1

*To my intrepid friend and critique partner,
Kristin Welker, who first suggested pranks
in the minefield.*

acknowledgments

Special thanks to Stephanie Takes-Desbiens for an early read and some great advice.

The comic and the tragic lie inseparably
close, like light and shadow.

—SOCRATES

chapter one

I rearranged the best poker hand I'd had all night and stared at the grinning sphinx across the table.

Frank Sinatra's "Luck Be a Lady" had a tinny sound on the ancient record player behind him.

Jeffe squirmed his muscular lion's body, his tail whipping up a decent breeze.

I fingered a pair of sixes and fought back a smirk. The sphinx couldn't bluff to save his life. His tail always gave him away.

And my cocksure attitude had cost me the last two hands. I straightened in my camp chair and fought the urge to fiddle with my nose.

The army-issue lantern flickered above us, casting uneven light.

"Would you like to bet more?" he asked, practically bouncing. He shook out the thick, tawny hair that framed his sharp, humanlike facial features. "I would be most interested in your stash of Junior Mint candies." He turned to the preening vampire on my left. "And your collection of Justin Bieber albums."

Marius went red. "I do not—"

Jeffe nodded in approval. "It is glorious music. Very bouncy. Whenever you play it or sing it, all the sphinxes gather."

The pale, hook-nosed vampire stood, toppling his chair, his eyes blazing red, fangs out. "I do not listen to Justin Bieber!"

The sphinx stared at him. "Okeydokey. Too bad you will not bet. You would not beat me with that hand."

Marius had left his cards facing up on the table. He sank down, a shock of hair falling stylishly over one eye, his arms crossed over his chest. "I fold," he snarled.

I glanced at the only other player in the game— Marc, my boyfriend. He winked at me before tossing his cards on the table. "I know when to quit."

Yeah, right. Maybe at cards.

I focused on Jeffe. "It's just you and me, cowboy." I blew out a breath and rearranged a two of spades that was doing me no good.

Marc ducked behind me to take a look. "You've already bet all your ice cubes for the next month."

"Don't remind me." Ice was hard to come by where we were stationed. The mess hall issued three a day. Three. To think, I'd been an ice-cube whore before I'd been sent to this godforsaken desert.

Marc leaned close. I could feel the heat rolling off him. He was a shape-shifting dragon and they always tended to run a few degrees warmer than most.

His warm breath tickled my ear. "I don't think the sphinx can lie."

"He's got to get a bad hand eventually." I hadn't seen anyone pick up the game so fast.

Jeffe tossed his mane over his shoulders. "I was born under a lucky star, and the cracks on the pads of my feet mean good fortune. Would you like me to show you?"

"No," I grumbled, trying to concentrate.

"Full house!" The sphinx laid his cards out on the table, clearly unable to stand the suspense for a second longer.

I groaned and tossed him my two pair, glad I at least kept my Junior Mints. Jeffe had already won a back rub, half my Tootsie Rolls and my I'm Not Really a Waitress nail polish. Maybe there was something to this lucky-star business.

Since we'd taught him how to play Five Card Stud, favors and loot had piled up in Jeffe's tent like spoils of war. Case in point, right next to him he had a box of hot chocolate packets, three lemons, werewolf hair conditioner, a bicycle, and a brand-new pair of loafers. Jeffe didn't even wear shoes.

Good thing we didn't have any money to blow. Well, we did, but it was useless. There was nothing to spend it on where we were.

Marc stretched, sliding his hands through his spiky blond hair that was forever in need of a cut. He gave me a quick peck on the head. "I'm going to look in on my bypass patient."

I glanced after him as he grabbed his cup and headed out the door, glad he hadn't made a big production of kissing me. I couldn't say the same for the way he'd laid one on me in the mess hall this morning. Or yesterday morning when he caught me coming back from rounds.

It was strangely embarrassing. Or it could be that I was just bad at relationships.

Maybe it would be different if Marc and I actually had a real conversation from time to time. Talk, laughter, it used to come easy back in Louisiana before the war, but now, it was like we had nothing left to say.

The only thing we ever talked about was work. Half the time, public displays of affection seemed like they were more about proving our relationship than about us.

See. Look. We're okay.

I fingered my cards. Maybe I was just tired. We were, after all, in the middle of an eternal war.

The younger gods had revolted against the older gods. Again. They'd been fighting since Rome was a tiny town where everybody knew your name.

The gods battled over women, treasure, cities. They destroyed said women, treasure, and cities. Pretty soon, they forgot what they were fighting about. It didn't halt their obsession with war.

Our only hope came in the form of prophecies that could bring peace. They centered around a "healer who could see the dead." Me. It was tricky because I had to keep it a secret. My particular gift was outlawed by the gods—probably because I *could* change things. If they learned who I was, they'd have me killed . . . or worse.

Still, life had been better since I'd managed to finagle a cease-fire back in the fall. It was spring now, not that you'd ever know it in limbo.

I'd been ready to give everything I had for that peace. There were only two people who knew my secret. Marc and Galen of Delphi, the special ops soldier who had put everything on the line for me.

Galen and I had shared three sublimely delicious, hot and frantic months, then his duty called, and he left. I had to struggle on with no closure and no answers. Sometimes I wished I'd never met him.

It hurt to think about Galen. I wondered what he was doing, if he was all right. The alternative was too painful to dwell on for long.

I had to believe he was using the fleeting peace for good. My colleagues and I were doing our best on this end.

We'd set up a temporary clinic in our MASH camp. Instead of putting soldiers back together, we were offering preventive checkups to creatures who'd never had good medical care before. We delivered babies, we vaccinated against basic diseases like tar fever and horn rot. We even performed some pretty complex surgery. We were making life better instead of simply preventing death. It felt good.

"Want to go one more?" I asked the grinning sphinx, gathering the cards. Heaven knows why I bothered.

Jeffe shifted from foot to foot. "Yes. Yes, I do. But, oh, how do I say this?" His eyes darted toward the door. "I think Dr. Belanger wants you to follow him."

No he didn't. At least I didn't. I was having fun with my friends. If I left it would stifle that little part of me that just wanted to breathe.

I shuffled the cards, just like my dad taught me. "He's checking on a patient."

Marius gave me a long look. "Marc might need a second opinion."

Jeffe nodded vigorously. "You should go after him."

What? Were they afraid I'd win back Marius's Poly-
nesian fertility statue? I didn't want it.

I did a one-handed double cut and sprang the cards
back up. They didn't even notice. "Marc is perfectly capable of handling a bypass on his own." He was a heart
surgeon, for God's sake.

The door creaked open and Holly poked her head in.
Curly tendrils escaped her ponytail clip. "I just saw
Marc leave and Petra wasn't with him." She straightened. "Oh, there you are," she said, as if she were surprised to see me.

"You people are starting to creep me out," I told her,
managing a swing cut. Holly saw, but she had a funny
look on her face. Then it hit me. The camp rumor mill
was working overtime. I gave her the hairy eye. "What?"

"It's nothing!" she protested.

And my name was Steve. "Marc isn't doing anything
crazy, right?" He tended to be rash at times. It was
enough to drive me up a wall, especially when it worked
for him.

My friends sat in uncomfortable silence. "Come on,"
I prodded, my eyes sliding over to Marius, who had
taken a sudden interest in his fingernails.

Rumors didn't merely run through this camp, they
galloped. "Okay, fine. I don't want to know."

If Marc needed my help, he'd ask. Or maybe he
wouldn't. It was hard to tell with him these days. The
entire relationship was beginning to feel like that time
I shrank my favorite sweater in the wash and stub-
bornly insisted it fit.

Still, nothing in this camp stayed a secret for long.

Jeffe shook his head, talking to himself, watching me. "It hasn't happened yet. I don't know why it is not yet."

I banged the cards down. "Out with it." I glared from Jeffe, to Marius, to Holly, who had found a fascinating knot on the wall.

"Now you really screwed up," Marius grumbled at Holly.

"The rumor is that it's about a wedding!" Jeffe said, unable to contain himself any longer.

Holly gasped. "Jeffe!"

"Whose wedding?" I asked. "Is it Kosta and Shirley?" No wonder she'd skipped poker tonight. They'd only been together for a little while, but they'd sure pined enough.

Jeffe's shoulders sagged. "I did not think of them. I was thinking of you."

"Ha! No." I grabbed up my cards again. "Marc is smarter than that."

Jeffe choked on a hair ball.

"Breathe," I told him. "There's no way Marc is proposing." When we'd first dated, back in college, he'd hinted around at it so long, trying to figure out what I'd say, that I was afraid I'd have to ask him.

Holly turned with a start as Marc leaned his head in the door. "Hey, guys."

I jumped a foot. "Hey, yourself."

He didn't *look* like he was up to anything. Just your typical strong, gorgeous doctor boyfriend. Then again, he hadn't been gone long enough to check in on a heart patient.

The deck dug into my fingers as I held on for dear life. Was nine o'clock too early to go to bed?

All four of them were grinning at me.

He wouldn't dare. We weren't wide-eyed medical students anymore. We were in the middle of a war.

Shake it off.

If I bought into every camp rumor, I'd think the officers' club was built on an ancient Egyptian burial site, the mess hall hamburgers were made with swamp monster meat, and the mechanics were going to do the full monty on Saturday night.

Besides, if I was going to marry anyone, it would have been Galen. And he was gone.

Marc opened the door wide. "Let's take a walk, Petra."

I sat frozen on my camp stool. "Now?"

Every single one of them was nodding at me.

Hell. Now the rumors would really start. Knowing this camp, they'd have a betting pool set up on the sex, weight, and birthday of the baby before we passed the infirmary.

I stood. "Sure." I could do that. I'd faced down wild imps and soul-sucking Shrouds and even a pair of giant scorpions who'd wanted to eat me. I could handle a bit of gossip. I knew Marc. He wouldn't rush this.

I tried to smile at him as I ducked out the door, but Marc looked nervous. Jeffe wasn't the only one who couldn't bluff.

Get a grip.

It didn't mean anything.

A line of sweat trickled down my back. Ten years ago, when he and I lived in New Orleans, I'd stumbled across an engagement ring in his dresser. He must have been planning for days to ask me. Weeks, maybe. He'd never managed to pull the trigger back then. And there had been so much less standing in the way.

He gazed down at me, his deep green eyes glittering. "I found something interesting in the minefield."

"Fine." Good. I rubbed at the tension in my neck. The minefield was rife with pranks. Maybe Marc had set up a new one. Or maybe it was the first leg of a little walk he had planned. I didn't know.

Still, I didn't feel like taking chances. I cleared my throat. "Are you positive you don't want to get a drink at the officers' club?" I asked, a little too cheerfully.

"Since when are you a big drinker?" he chided, leading me down the darkened path.

It was never too late to start.

The night air was chilly as we walked the paths through the low-slung tents of the MASH camp.

A group of mechanics passed us going the other way, calling out their congratulations. I pretended not to notice.

Stomach churning, I focused on the torches lining the walk.

We'd talked the new gods into a generator for the hospital, but, otherwise, they insisted we go old-school with lanterns and anything else we could set on fire. Because, you know, we were the progressive side.

Marc handed me a torch as we left the path and headed up through the unit cemetery, stopping at the edge of the minefield.

Now, the minefield wasn't loaded with actual explosives, at least I didn't think so. It was our junk depot, so full of broken-down vehicles, half-wrecked buildings, and machinery parts that the bored among us had seen fit to rig it with practical jokes. It was pointless and immature, but that's why we liked it.

"Are you sure this is a good idea?" I asked. Not just because I wasn't great at relationship talks. But also because this was the minefield. At night.

"What are you afraid of?" Marc teased.

"You want a list?"

I didn't like to wander too far from 3063rd. I was a doctor, not a soldier. And even though the minefield was on the edge of camp, the wards weren't so strong out here.

Imps stalked the desert outside camp, along with lots of other cursed creatures that I didn't like to think about. Like giant flesh-eating scorpions. Yes, Galen had saved me once, but I wasn't keen on pushing it.

Plus, with the cease-fire signed, the army was cleaning house and dumping a scary amount of new junk in here.

Marc nudged me along. "Let's go."

We could barely see three feet in front of my torch.

A bloodred slice of moon shone above as I buttoned my rust-red flack jacket.

Maybe I'd get hit with a bucket of pickled eggs and have to go home.

Marc was way too confident as we eased past the wrecked ambulance at the entrance.

I squeezed in my stomach as far as it would go and inched between a gutted Humvee and the shell of a burned-out guard tower. I took a second look. That wasn't even ours. "This is such a bad idea."

"I know," he said, taking my hand. He kissed me at

the wrist, his lips brushing my sensitive skin. I went a little breathless.

Damn the man.

"I didn't mean it as a compliment." I looked out over the twisted, darkened path ahead of us. We were definitely headed somewhere. You'd think if it was the latest, greatest prank, he'd at least be telling me about it by now.

I ducked away from him, edging around a musty-smelling archway, avoiding the trip wire strung across it.

He followed, grinning.

"You're enjoying this too much," I said.

He tilted his head. "You're not enjoying it enough." I felt the rough tug of my torch as he slipped it from my fingers and propped it up on a pitted, half-falling-apart hospital gurney.

He pulled me close, his lips bent to mine. "Here. Let me show you what I mean." He kissed me once, twice, his mouth teasing me. His warmth washed over me as he nibbled at my lower lip.

Heat flushed through my body, along with fear. I felt like I was agreeing to something, without having any of the facts.

Besides, we had to keep our guard up out here. Gently, I pulled away.

He watched me intently. "Is there something wrong?"

"No," I lied. "Nothing." He should be everything I wanted. I slid my hands up his well-muscled arms, over his chest, and felt his beating heart. He was a good person. It should be enough.

Somehow, it wasn't. I'd been seeing Marc for less

than three months. Sure, I'd been ready to get engaged ten years ago, before we'd been separated by war, before they'd told me he was dead. It had been enough of a shock to see him alive and well. I was just starting to get to know him again.

It wasn't as if we could still pretend we were naïve residents back at Tulane and that the last decade had never happened. It had and now both of us had changed.

"Come on," he said, leading me forward, waiting a second while I reached back for the torch. "I worked hard on this."

I offered up a quick prayer that he was still talking about a prank.

We walked until we came out of the side path and onto the main one. We waited a moment before emerging.

Father McArio lived just down the way, supposedly for the peace and quiet. I knew it was because he liked to minister to the lost souls that lingered just beyond the wards.

I didn't want to wake him, or more to the point, be in a position where he was asking where I was going with Marc. The rocks just beyond the minefield were a huge make-out spot.

Marc took my hand and silently tugged me deeper into the darkness, toward the rocky plain beyond. Damn it.

Unlike some couples, we didn't need to go to the rocks in order to be alone. Marc and I shared a tent. That was enough of a commitment for me right now.

Marc had never been as much of a risk taker back in New Orleans. Now that he was stuck in the wilds of limbo, that had changed. Lots of other things had too.

Give me a few years and I might be able to figure him out again.

My nerves tangled as he led me onto a path that lay just beyond the largest outcropping of rocks. We'd never been this way before. Sweat dribbled down my neck. I was aware of every single step as my boots crunched against the rocky soil.

He led me down into a hidden enclave. It was cooler than above, as each step took us farther from the surface of the desert.

We found ourselves in a low, rocky clearing. I planted my torch in a holder near the edge.

Marc continued on to a large stone slab at the center. Shadows danced across the hard planes of his cheek and jaw.

The fire caught a dark red wine bottle and two glasses. I blew out a breath. I could do this.

He reached down and withdrew a wrapped black bundle. A grin tickling his lips, he unwound it to reveal a single, red rose. The soft petals were just beginning to open.

I was taken aback by the completely unexpected beauty of it. Nothing grew in the dusty red soil of limbo.

"Happy birthday," he said, holding it out to me.

Relief and gratitude whooshed over me. My birthday. "It's not until next month." I didn't care.

He shrugged a shoulder, obviously pleased. "I couldn't wait."

I brushed my fingers over the delicate petals, smelled the sweet fragrance. I hadn't seen a flower in eight years, since I'd left home. "How did you get this?"

His eyes shone with pleasure. "It wasn't as hard as finding this."

Marc pulled a small red box from his pocket and I froze. It looked just like the box I'd found in his dresser when we worked together at Tulane.

He'd been ready at that time to give me a ring. And then he was kidnapped by the gods, brought down here to fight an eternal war. I'd lost him.

And now?

I was afraid to move, terrified to think.

Please let it be a necklace. I'd love a necklace. I'd wear it everywhere. I'd never take it off. I'd cherish that necklace until I went old and gray.

He stood over me, his expression earnest.

My heart stuttered and I felt my desperation rise as he bent down on one knee and opened the box. It held the simple diamond solitaire from so many years ago.

I squeezed my eyes shut.

"Hey." He touched my hand. "Look at me." When I did, I saw the worst thing of all—hope, happiness. His sincere belief that this was a moment he'd want to cherish. I still couldn't believe this amazing man was kneeling in front of me. "I know I only just found you again, but Petra, I love you. I can't imagine life without you." He stood, a smile tickling his lips. "Will you marry me?"

Hell and damnation.

I would have. I should have. But that didn't matter now.

Yes, he'd been my first love and I'd been overjoyed to find him again, but I'd *just* found him again.

I wet my lips, realized I was shaking. He'd been

gone for ten years. Now we were in the middle of a war. We couldn't expect it to feel like it used to feel.

Or maybe I was just a complete commitment freak. Marc was a good man. He was smart and considerate and he had that annoyingly beautiful adventurous streak. He came from a warm family, a loving home. And he wanted to re-create that here, as much as we could. I loved him. There was no reason not to want to be with him.

For the rest of my life.

"I can't." I said it quickly, before I lost my courage. My head buzzed and it almost felt like someone else saying the words.

He sat back, shocked. "Why?"

I froze as my brain searched frantically for an explanation. There was nothing either one of us could say that would make this right.

God, I wished he would just get up off the ground.

My eyes filled with tears. Marc was loving and strong and smart and, I hiccupped, gorgeous. He was perfect on paper. But that didn't mean I should marry him.

I owed it to him, and to myself, to take a step back from this. For now, at least.

My fingers trembled as I gripped the stem of the rose, like a lifeline. It snapped in half. "Damn it," I said, focusing on the broken stem, unable to look at the man in front of me. "I'm sorry," I said, as if that would somehow make it whole again.

But it was broken.

Pebbles rained down from the ledge above. It took me an extra second to even feel them as they landed on our heads and scattered at our feet.

I wheeled around to see Horace the sprite. He was about half the size of the average man, with golden wings fluttering on his heels and at his shoulders.

"Finally." He exhaled, planting his tiny combat boots on the stone slab. "Do you know how hard you were to find?"

Marc stood, eyeing Horace. "Not hard enough." His eyes were guarded, his expression stony.

"Hurry," the sprite said, ready to take off again. "It can't wait."

I tried to wrap my head around whatever Horace wanted. "What's the matter?"

"Two critical cases," he said, his pointy ears twitching. "Both stabbed. Most likely poisoned as well."

I didn't understand. "Did the attending on call send for us?" They should have been able to handle two casualties.

Marc and I needed to focus on what had just happened. I owed it to him to talk this through, to try to explain why I'd put a bullet in his heart.

Horace shook his head so hard that glitter rained down. "The attending surgeon is unaware. Absolutely no one can know about this."

It was unheard of. "Why not?"

Horace's wings trembled as he hovered above us. "It's Galen."

chapter two

Cold shock washed over me. "Galen is gone."

He'd cut all ties. Never mind that I was madly in love with him. I'd never felt for anyone what I'd felt for Galen. He was everything to me. Hell, probably the reason why I couldn't say yes to Marc.

Once upon a time, I'd been ready to promise Galen anything. And he'd walked away.

Horace frowned. "Not anymore." The sprite tugged on my sleeve. "Hurry."

God. Two critical cases. Stabbed. Possibly poisoned.

"Is there something I should know?" Marc asked, studying me.

"There is," I said, dreading it with every fiber of my being.

"Now!" Horace demanded.

"Right," I said, as we took off after the darting sprite. Soon. I'd tell Marc soon.

My pulse pounded and my legs felt like rubber. Galen

was mortal because of me. He was injured, possibly dying.

Shit.

I couldn't imagine a world without Galen in it.

Marc stayed with me, next to me, as we cleared the rocks.

Goose bumps skittered up my arms as we dashed into the minefield. We ducked past hulking skeletons of buildings and dodged piles of debris on either side of the path.

The last thing we needed was to trip a booby trap. Horace darted in and out of the mess. "What happened?" I called out. "Why is it a secret?" Worry clawed at me. Just what kind of trouble was Galen in?

Horace's flight trajectory wavered as he glanced back, his face pinched with worry. "I don't know. He'll only talk to you."

"What the hell?" I missed a step and would have gone tumbling to the ground if Marc hadn't caught me.

Get it together. Galen needed me. That was the only thing that mattered right now.

In a few minutes, I'd be face-to-face with the man I thought I'd love forever. If I made it there in time. I was such a mess.

I didn't know how I was going to pull this off. Why couldn't Galen see Marius? Rodger? They'd be more objective, more clinical. They could talk to him without the anticipation, the fear, their heart pounding in their ears.

Galen had insisted I leave his memory behind and that I love again.

My stomach dropped into a large, black hole.

And so I had.

I skirted a beat-up VW bus, my foot catching a trip wire in the dark. Horace screamed as the door flew open. Hickey horns shot out like crazed bats. Half animal, half plant, their spindly bodies writhed and their sucking appendages waved like the legs of two dozen octopi.

One landed hard on my back. Before I could react, Marc swiped it off, knocking it into Horace, who already had two on him.

"Run!" the sprite screeched. "Leave me!"

I started to go, but Marc pulled me back. "What'll they do to him?"

"He'll live," I said, urging Marc to follow. Horace would just look like he'd been making out under the high school bleachers.

We rushed out of the minefield and down through the cemetery to the MASH 3063rd. The low-slung buildings usually comforted me. Now I was acutely aware that every supply hut, tent, and torch post we passed brought me closer to Galen.

I blew out a breath, determined to get a choke hold on my emotions as I headed for the OR, with Marc at my side.

He didn't know Galen had been my one and only lover besides him. I glanced up at Marc. Now certainly wouldn't be the time to tell him that.

"Don't worry," he said, his breath coming in harsh bursts as we passed the recovery tent and rounded the corner toward surgery. "I've got your back."

God. I'd broken his heart and he still wanted to help me. I was insane for not being able to feel more for this man. Had the war hardened me that much?

Jeffe stood watch at the entrance to pre-op. He wore his guard's collar and the earrings he'd won from Holly at poker last night. Somebody should tell him modern guys didn't wear dangly pearls.

"None shall pass," he thundered. "Except for you, Petra," he added happily.

No way. "There are two casualties," I said to the cross-dressing sphinx. "I need Marc in there."

Jeffe held up a paw. Darned if he didn't have the matching bracelet. "Galen of Delphi's orders are—"

Not worth anything if I was going to save his hide. "The handbook says you have to listen to me," I insisted, thankful for military protocol for once in my life.

Jeffe tilted his head. "You actually read the handbook?"

"Told you I'd get around to it eventually," I said, starting past the sphinx.

He blocked me, baring a lion's mouth of teeth and two sets of razor-sharp claws.

Fuck. "Don't you even think about slicing me with one of those."

Jeffe's snarl dropped. "It is just that it is a secret that Galen is even here and I'm not allowed to tell anybody but you and Horace." He ducked his head around me. "And now he knows." He gestured at Marc.

Yeah, well, Marc was about to find out a whole lot more. "We don't have time for this."

Marc rubbed at his temples. "What if I defeat you?" he asked. "Quick. Ask me a question."

The sphinx perked up. "What is the nature of man?"

"An easier one," Marc snapped.

"How hard would it be to strangle a sphinx?" I mused, not really expecting an answer.

"Oh, I know." Jeffe brightened. "Are you getting married?"

My heart stuck in my throat.

"Not today," Marc growled, shoving past him.

I followed, wincing.

"What?" Jeffe asked as he let us pass.

"Come on," Marc said as he pushed open the door to pre-op.

I followed him. "I wish you'd just get mad." Anger, I could deal with. Guilt was something else.

We stopped at the long sink by the entrance to the OR.

Marc handed me a flat, orange bar of soap. "I'm not going to get mad at you," he said, scrubbing hard with his own bar. "I'm going to talk to you. Something's holding you back and I need to know what it is if we're going to move past it."

I'd always tried to do the right thing, but these days, I wasn't sure if I knew what that was anymore.

Anticipation hammered at me and, on its heels, shame like I'd never felt before. I dug the soap against my skin, as if I could scrub myself numb.

Marc was watching me. "This Galen of Delphi. Do you know him?"

In the biblical sense.

"He was a patient of mine before," I said, not exactly lying. "He stayed in camp and a lot of us got to know him."

Extremely well.

To the point where every instinct I had screamed at me to rush to Galen, to see how badly he was hurt.

But we didn't have that luxury. He needed me to keep it together. For years, I'd prided myself on my cool detachment. Galen seemed to be the only one who could strip me of it in an instant.

Marc watched me, worry sharpening his features.

When he spoke, his tone was even, well thought out. "Let me handle this one. We'll tell this Galen that you can't treat him."

The last thing I needed was Marc protecting me from Galen. "Thanks, but I've got it."

He didn't respond, but he watched me ominously, as if he could sense a threat.

He was right.

Without nurses, we helped each other into our gowns and masks before hurrying out into the OR.

Galen stood against my table, bloody and bruised. His expression was hard, his black special ops uniform torn, exposing a muscular shoulder.

Despite the dirt and the gore, he was strikingly beautiful.

I knew his strength and his power. I'd seen the scars slicing over his chest and abs, the old ones white against his deeply tanned skin, the new scars pink and raw. Once upon a time, I'd been the one to comfort him, to touch him.

He was fighting for every breath, most likely battling poison, as he cradled a gorgeous woman. She might as well have been naked as she swooned all over him in a minuscule bikini top that did nothing to hide her thrusting nipples. He had one hand wrapped around her bare midriff, the other tangled in the gauzy skirt that was cut all the way up to the vee between her legs.

I couldn't have been more shocked if he'd started fucking her right then and there. "Who the hell is she?"

His eyes caught mine. "Her name is Leta."

I didn't realize I'd spoken out loud.

He was close to passing out, but he clung to her as if he'd never held anything more precious.

"I need you to save her," he said, almost desperate.

My pulse pounded in my ears. "I will," I promised automatically. It was the only thing I could do.

chapter three

"Help me get her on my table," I said, as Marc and I pried the woman from Galen's arms.

His impossibly blue eyes locked with mine. Naked excitement rushed through me. I could see the love there, the longing.

Get a grip.

Most likely, it was for her now.

"Well, good thing I brought a friend," I remarked as I adjusted the large silver light over my table.

"Petra," Galen began, as if he too hadn't expected the raw shock of being together again.

"What happened?" I asked, schooling myself, assessing her condition. One thing was certain—she wasn't regular army.

His expression hardened. "We were attacked crossing the lines. Short daggers and three-headed hounds."

Marc joined me. "She's got a bite on her neck."

I glanced back at Galen. "He's about to fall over."

Galen grimaced against the pain. "I took a few

hits. It wouldn't have been anything if I were still immortal."

I examined the gash on his arm. "Yes, well, it could kill you now."

His eyes blazed at me, bloodshot and hard. "Save her, Petra."

"We need to give you a shot," I said, tamping down my emotions, finding the syringe in my cart.

Galen gripped my shoulders as he struggled to stay upright. I staggered sideways under his weight. "Let him do it. You said you'd save her!"

"Fine," I ground out, as Marc took hold of Galen, steadying him.

"Punctured carotid," Marc said, as if he couldn't quite believe we were switching places. Me either.

Since when did patients dictate treatment? They hadn't, until Galen of Delphi came along. His years in special ops had made him way too used to giving orders.

And my weak heart made me listen.

Marc half lifted, half shoved Galen as he collapsed onto the table.

Hades. We'd gotten here just in time.

The poison was tearing through his system, eating away at his vital organs. And he was right—this time, he wasn't immortal.

Marc worked with quiet efficiency.

It drove me crazy that I couldn't control this, that I couldn't help him.

I took stock of the woman on my table.

"My name is Dr. Robichaud. You're safe with me." I didn't even know if she'd heard me. Her almond eyes were wide, her olive skin pale.

Her neck showed round, biting scars along with fresh puncture wounds. She'd been shackled with some sort of collar that drove spikes into her flesh. She had to be a shifter. Kept against her will.

Holy hell. "Are you from the old army?"

Galen had brought a hostile into camp. Sure, we sometimes treated the enemy—before putting them under guard. But I doubted that's what Galen had in mind.

Shit.

We were harboring the enemy.

We could be executed for this.

She stared at me, glassy-eyed. I needed a chart, damn it. I needed to know what I was dealing with, and what I could give her.

"Are you a werewolf?" I asked, frustration rising as I inspected the tears in her larynx. If she were human, she'd be dead.

I glanced to the table next to me. Galen convulsed as Marc gave him 20 cc's of toxopren. The shot was as big as a horse tranquilizer and neutralized poisons. It also burned with a fire that made grown men scream.

If it had been anyone else on the table next to mine, I would have called for backup, screw the consequences. Galen had no right to bring me into this. I didn't know what he was thinking—secretly harboring a soldier from the old army.

It was his sheer dumb luck that I trusted him implicitly.

I was such a fool.

Shaking my head, I covered her lower body with a blanket and reached for a clamp of sterile gauze. "Suction," I said, out of habit. I didn't have a nurse.

The blood seeped out as fast as I could wipe it away. Whatever had tried to take a bite out of her neck had nicked her carotid artery. I stitched up one hole. Two. There had to be at least one more. I couldn't see with all the blood. My own pulse hammered in my ears. I needed to stanch the flow. I needed to stitch. I couldn't do both at the same time.

This secrecy might just kill her.

But if I called in help, chances were I'd be signing her death warrant.

Sweat and steam gathered under my surgical cap. "Marc?" I called, unable to keep the worry from my voice.

"He's not responding," he said, his voice sharp. I knew that tone. Death usually followed.

Heat tore through me and it took every fiber of my being to stay with my own patient. I promised him I'd save her.

Her heart rate monitor let out a pulsing, high-pitched warning. One hundred eighty beats a minute. She was losing too much blood.

I stanched the bleeding. Found another hole. Stanched the blood. Lost the hole. Her very life seeped through my fingers.

Alarms screamed as her vitals plummeted.

And then I saw her spirit begin to rise.

"Goddamn it!" I snatched for the adrenaline on my cart. It should have been ready for me. I should have had a nurse. Hands shaking, I prepared the shot.

Galen had risked too much bringing her here. It was impossible to work like this.

And it was my fault. I should have called a halt to this the minute I saw how serious her condition was.

If anybody killed her, it would be me.

Limbs molten, I plunged the adrenaline into her battered artery.

Her spirit faltered. She bent over her body, watching it for a long slow moment. Then she continued to rise.

I pulled the shot out, tired, defeated, and sick with the whole damned thing. It was too late. I'd failed her and Galen. "Leta," I said, remembering her name, angry at her, pissed as hell at myself, wishing to God I'd been quicker, better.

She lifted her head at the sound of her name. She was beautiful, with pronounced, sculpted features and lush lips that fell open when she saw me watching her.

"You can see me," she said, breathless as she drew a hand down her long neck. The scars from her collar were raw and pink against her pale skin, which was surprising to say the least. Normally, spirits manifested without injuries. Her pain must have run deep enough to reach her soul. I shuddered. I'd never seen anything like it.

Marc came up on my side as she began to rise. I shook my head and pulled off my mask. "It's too late."

The spirit clamped a hand over her mouth and let out a small shriek. "You're her!" Leta whispered.

Jesus Christ on a biscuit.

Marc exhaled sharply. "This woman's a dragon." He pulled down the blanket covering her, exposing a winged mark at her hip.

Leta's soul paid no attention, her focus on me. "You're the one I've been dreaming about!"

I stared at her, shock warring with complete and utter what-the-hell as Marc climbed up onto the table. He yanked at the waistband of his scrubs to reveal the dragon symbol on his hip. He positioned them together— brand against brand.

She was dead. I didn't understand it. Besides, her brand looked different. They had to be from separate tribes or species or something.

He pressed against her and murmured words in a language I didn't understand. The air thickened.

Her spirit hesitated.

He touched his chest over his heart, *reached inside himself,* and drew out what appeared to be a glimmering strand. It was so thin and light I could barely see it.

With great care, he placed whatever he'd drawn from his own heart over hers. It disappeared into her skin, as if it had never been there at all.

I didn't know what he was doing, what I was seeing.

"Petra," Marc uttered, as if he were in another world, "stitch her now."

"She's flatlined," I said, ignoring my own words as I dragged my cart to the other side of the table. She'd stopped bleeding. Her heart was no longer beating. Hands shaking, I wiped the blood and found two puncture wounds I'd missed.

Throat dry, I focused on my work. Not on her spirit hovering above me. Not on Marc, whispering to the dead woman as ancient magic wound around them.

Tinges of blue fire flowed between them, through them for all I knew. They tickled my fingers as they seeped from her wounds.

My stomach knotted. I was afraid to look directly at them, terrified of what I'd see.

I thought I knew Marc. But I had never witnessed this side of him.

"She's stitched," I said, double-checking her neck. Even as I did, it seemed as if her flesh were trying to heal, to close over the wounds.

Marc brought his mouth to hers and breathed.

Her eyes flew open and she jerked. Her spirit stared at him, then at me before she was sucked back down into her body.

The heart rate monitors screamed. Her heart rate was at thirty. Forty. Fifty. I started CPR.

Marc grabbed my wrist. "Don't."

"You can't be serious." I took her vitals. They were too low. But they were climbing. It was impossible.

Still, she should be dead. I watched in shock as she climbed back into normal range and the machines quieted.

"Blood pressure ninety over sixty," I said, my throat parched, my own heart threatening to pound right out of my chest.

What the hell had happened here?

She was living, breathing.

She'd survived. No thanks to me.

Focus on the job. She'd lost a lot of blood. I hooked her up to an IV and checked her vitals once again. Normal. Un-freaking-believable. I dressed her neck. Then I couldn't help but glance back at Galen.

"He's hanging on," Marc said, slowly lifting himself from Leta, still whispering to her.

I checked on Galen. Marc was right. He'd done a good job. Now we just had to hope for the best.

Galen squeezed his eyes, didn't open them. "Will she be all right?" he rasped.

"Yes," Marc answered.

Galen winced, as if the effort to speak were too much. "Thank you."

I turned my attention back to Marc. "You have to tell me what you did." Maybe not right now, but soon.

Leta clutched at Marc, her fiery red hair tumbling down her back. She seemed to resent him pulling away and reached up at him as far as she could.

Marc's voice betrayed his bitterness as he held himself over her. "She's been kept as an animal for too long. She needs the touch of a human dragon or she could lose control and shift."

"Go." I was only grateful she had him, because we didn't have any shape-shifting dragons on call, and she would have been dead before I went checking her body for dragon marks.

I sighed despite myself. Too often, we worked with limited information. Sometimes, it cost people their lives.

In bits and pieces, Marc extricated himself from Leta's grasp. Still holding her hand, he wheeled her into a private recovery room.

I wound a length of clean gauze and dipped it in warm water. Marc had neutralized the poison in Galen's system, which had been the biggest threat. But Galen was bloody and still in his flack jacket. It was heavy and black, etched with a Ken rune on the left shoulder. It was the mark of a warrior, the symbol of flame, sex, action, and heroism. I'd seen every bit of it firsthand.

Not that I needed to be thinking of that.

I wiped his face, his neck. I focused on the gold commander's star at his collar as I slowly unbuttoned him.

How many times had I done this when we were together?

Only back then, as my fingers slipped each button free, I was anticipating him as a man. Now that was over.

It wasn't the fact that he was ordered to go. I understood that. I'd always known that was coming. It was that he chose to cut me out so completely.

I was almost disappointed when I saw he wore a Kevlar vest underneath. It was ridiculous. Of course I was glad he'd had added protection. Still, my fingers itched to touch his chest, if only to see that he was solid and whole.

I slid his jacket off and saw his shoulders had taken the brunt of his enemies' fury.

"Oh, Galen." I sighed. It slipped out, like the words of a lover.

Which was pointless. I didn't know why I couldn't shut down, stay clinical. I was a combat surgeon, for Christ's sake.

It was over between us. Now would be a good time to keep that in mind.

I eased him out of his Kevlar vest. Old scars ripped across his well-muscled chest. He had a slice on his side. One near his hip. I focused on cleaning the wounds and felt every one of them as I stitched and bandaged them.

He reached for me. "Petra," he groaned.

I soothed his hand away and rested it on the table. "We'll talk in the morning."

I finished bandaging Galen just as Marc returned.

He looked tired. "I have Leta in the isolation room of the ICU." He crossed his arms over his chest. "It's the best way to keep her under wraps." He glanced at a spot on the wall. "I'm having Shirley work up a new ID for her."

Oh, no. "You have Shirley involved in this now?"

We didn't need to be putting the company clerk in mortal danger. Galen had to take that woman and get her out of here.

"She'll require at least two days in recovery," Marc said.

I sighed. He was right. Optimistic, even. Two days was the minimum if everything went smoothly. Dragons healed fast, but they weren't immortal.

"We might as well stash them both together," I said, gritting my teeth as I went back for Galen. I moved him out through the back of the OR and through a small hallway into the ICU.

"At least I got a chance to check on my heart patient," Marc said, as I led Galen past the one occupied room and into the one next to it. Leta was resting peacefully. The room wasn't large, but we made it work.

Marc stood next to me as we examined what we'd done. "He needs to rest."

"Good luck with that."

Marc shot me a curious glance. "We should head back. Morning rounds start early."

It was the last thing I wanted to do. I couldn't keep

on pretending with Marc, not after his proposal tonight.

I followed Marc to the door, reminding myself that this had nothing to do with Galen.

Still, a small part of me hurt as I closed the door behind us and saw him take her hand.

chapter four

Marc and I walked across the darkened compound. It was late. Torches burned low, flickering unsteady light across the path in front of us.

We could see our breath in the frigid night air. He was close enough to put an arm around me. It was what he usually did. But he wouldn't tonight.

I was glad, because I wanted to keep my distance but would never have had the heart to say no again. I dug my hands into my pockets. "That dragon in there. She said she dreamed about me."

Marc snorted. "She was delirious."

I hoped.

He focused straight ahead, refusing to look at me. God, I had about eighty things to say and I didn't want to talk about any of them.

"About your proposal," I began, bracing myself. I needed to lay it on the line, no matter how hurtful it would be.

He stopped. "Look, I get it." Torchlight caught his

rigid features. "It was too soon." He cast a frustrated glance out into the dark before piercing me with a steady gaze. "I just don't want to lose you."

So he felt it slipping away too.

"Marc," I began, wishing I could control this or him or—anything. I was grasping desperately onto the ledge. My fingers were slipping and I knew it. There was nothing I could do to keep from tumbling over. "It's not like it was before." I could see in his eyes that he knew. "I realize we can't expect it," I said quickly. "It's hard to explain." Maybe I'd stayed in this relationship for the past three months because I couldn't explain.

"So let's talk," he said, in a way that made it half inviting, half challenging.

My head hurt to think about it.

God, this had been so easy before. Back in New Orleans, before this war and our separation and everything else. But now things were never easy with Marc.

I took his hands. They were as unsteady as mine. "This is supposed to be the simple part, where we're in love and everything is perfect and right. It's not supposed to be this damned hard." Unless it wasn't right. He had to recognize it too. "There's something missing."

A muscle in his jaw clenched. "We'll work it out," he said, as if declaring so would make it happen. "Come on," he said, taking my hand, walking me back to the tent we'd shared since peace had begun.

I probably should have pulled away, but it didn't matter now. His proposal had brought everything to a head. Maybe we could have gone on pretending for a few more weeks, months. Hell, I was willing to bet some people did it for years. But now it was over. I didn't want to pretend anymore.

We arrived at our squat, red hutch. It felt almost foreign as Marc held open the squeaky wooden door.

Inside it was pitch-black. Which, okay, of course it should be. It had to be after midnight. But it wasn't only that. The tent was like a cave.

I watched as Marc lit a single lantern on the desk next to our narrow cot. It was always dark in here. We kept the light-blocking shades down. Marc insisted it was too bright when I lit more than a lantern.

"Talk to me," he said, easing down onto his elbows. He patted the place next to him.

I stood, motionless. Afraid of what I had to say next.

"I think I should stay with Rodger and Marius for a while." They'd been my roommates before all of this.

"Petra." He stood quickly, the lantern banging onto its side before he righted it again. "We're not in a good place. I get it. But sometimes, you have to take a chance."

His arms closed around me and I reached for him too. I held him tight, my face buried against his strong chest. He smelled spicy and warm. God, I loved the way he smelled. I loved him. But I didn't love him enough. And I couldn't keep doing this. I sniffed, forcing myself back, willing him to understand. "That's not the answer."

I was all for commitment, persevering, fighting to make things right. But when all we had was the fight . . .

He looked as lost as I felt.

"Stay," he said.

I nodded, holding him close.

He eased us down onto the cot within the stifling silence of our tent. He held me as if he could protect us both from what needed to happen.

We fell asleep that way, tangled together, with the bed made and our boots on.

I wished with all I had that I could love Marc the way he deserved. But that night, even as I slept, I dreamed of Galen.

My mind took me back to the room where I'd left him. He stood by the bed, wearing a black T-shirt that stretched tight over his powerful arms and chest. Black fatigue pants hitched over his waist and hugged his thighs. I knew exactly where hair dusted his lower abdomen. I'd memorized the place where the muscle on his hip curved down toward his cock. I had run my tongue down it and tasted the salty skin there.

I wanted to do it again.

Fire licked through my veins.

Galen showed none of the injuries that had almost killed him tonight. No, he was sinfully potent, with that same jaw set too wide and a face that was all angles.

Galen was too rugged, too intensely built to be considered textbook handsome. No, he was more than that. He was brutally and unapologetically male.

The single lantern cast the left side of his face in flickering light—generous lips, sculpted cheekbones, and the intense look of a soldier who knew exactly what he wanted.

It was precisely how I'd remembered him.

And it was dangerous as hell.

The corner of his mouth tilted into a grin. "I knew you'd come back."

I did too. On a certain level, this was unavoidable. "I couldn't stop thinking about you."

I wanted to be embarrassed by the admission. I should have been. But all I felt was an intense desire to touch him. Only I couldn't move. I couldn't think beyond the pure lust spreading from my core.

He closed the distance between us. This time, I didn't back away. He caught the nape of my neck, his fingers tangling in my hair as he drew me close. I bumped up against the hard planes of his chest, my legs tangling with his. His hot breath scalded my cheek. "Tell me you want this."

Slick, warm pleasure pooled in my veins. I notched up my chin. "I'm not running."

He huffed at that, a small push of breath that promised all of the things we'd had once and lost.

The emptiness of it burned. My fingers curled into my palms, the nails digging into skin.

"Shh . . ." he whispered against my lips. His voice moved over me like a touch, and just like that, I had the insane desire to lick the sweet spot below his left ear.

He dragged me close and his mouth descended on mine. His kiss was hot and urgent, born from pent-up longing and regret. I kissed him back with everything I had as I clutched at his shoulders, ran my hands over his broad back, whispered my fingers through his short, thick hair.

His body tangled with mine, hard and insistent as he drew me tight. We clung to each other, kissing, touching, worshipping each other the only way we could.

I remembered the taste of him, the gentle stroke of his blunt, battle-hardened fingers. It was like coming home.

He kissed my neck, his teeth grazing my skin, igniting sparks of sheer lust. His hands traveled up my sides and caught under my breasts. I gasped as his thumb grazed a nipple.

I lifted my arms like a child as he stripped me of my tank top. I wasn't wearing a bra and I watched his eyes darken with desire as he took in my bare breasts. God, I loved that look. Only Galen looked at me that way.

"I almost forgot how beautiful you are," he murmured to himself. If I didn't know better, I'd think it was pure wonder coloring his voice as he bent to take my nipple into his mouth.

He laid me down on the bed, but I barely felt the mattress beneath me as Galen feasted on my breasts. I wrapped my legs around his hips. I needed him closer, I needed more.

His blue eyes caught mine and I watched him lave a nipple as his other hand found the tie of my scrub pants. He tugged it open, skimming his fingers under my panties to where I wanted him most.

"Holy hell, Galen."

It was too much, and at the same time, I needed more—craved it like air.

"Tell me what you want," he said, finding my slick center.

God, I was on fire. I ran my hands along his chest, flicked a nipple, and watched him gasp. Heard him groan as I tasted it.

I writhed my hips against him, but damn the man, he didn't move.

No more teasing. No more talk. I needed him. Now. Hot and naked and inside me.

He watched me like he wanted to devour me whole. "Say it, Petra." He teased my opening with his fingers. Fucking-a—he was still fully dressed.

I shoved myself up on my shaking elbows. "Get naked. Now."

He stood in one fluid movement. Jesus, he was incredible. "Why?" he asked, satisfaction warring with desire as he yanked off his shirt and dropped it on the floor. He shook out his shoulders. "What are you going to do to me?"

I had no words.

Eyes on me, he tugged open the top button on his fatigue pants, like he was ready to tear it off. "Tell me," he ordered, as he ripped open the next button. His hand moved lower still, baring those gorgeous abs, that thin line of black hair that traveled straight to his cock.

My throat went dry.

I could see the outline of his cock, raging hard against his fatigues.

One more button.

He stopped, the muscles in his neck corded, his body straining to hold back. Waiting.

Trembling, I slipped my thumbs under my panties and slipped them off, along with my scrub pants. I let my knees fall open, baring myself to him.

He let out a low groan in the back of his throat and for a second I thought he was going to snap. Then again, this was Galen. The man knew no limits.

I licked my lips. I wanted to tell him to fuck me, to shove himself inside me and ride me, make me come. But I wanted more. Shyness crept up on me as I said the words. "Make love to me, Galen."

His eyes widened and the sheer tenderness on his face took my breath away. And then he was on me, the delicious weight of him on top of me as he shoved off the fatigue pants and fit himself against the core of me.

He braced himself over me, grinning like a madman.

"What?" I asked, finding it was contagious.

"I love you."

Warmth flooded me. How I needed those words. How I wanted him.

I brushed my lips against his once, twice.

He shifted and I felt the tip of him against me. "Always," he said, driving home.

I wrapped my legs around him, holding him close as he began to move. Sweet heaven. There was nothing more perfect than the feel of this man inside me, over me, his hot hard length owning me. No one but Galen made me feel this way—so whole, so honest, so scorchingly alive.

I kissed him, straining to meet his thrusts. His hands were everywhere. So were mine, stroking, touching, loving.

"Galen." I gasped against his mouth, kissing the edges, kissing his chin. "Don't stop." Ever. I didn't . . . "I don't want this to end."

He nuzzled my neck, stroking my thigh. "It doesn't have to."

He hooked a hand under my knee and drew me wider as he pushed himself achingly and beautifully deep.

"Stay with me." His lips ground against my ear.

Always.

He pushed harder. Any second, I was going to shatter.

"More." I reached behind him and cupped his heavy sack.

"Gods!" He thrust hard, tumbling us both over the edge.

I came undone, the pleasure of it rocketing through me. I clung to him, like I'd never let go. Feeling everything this man was and could be to me. I didn't want it to end.

The next instant, I was alone, naked in the desert. The cool night air swept over my body like an icy touch. I raced to my feet, cold shock flooding me. Goose bumps raced up my damp skin as I moved to cover myself.

Galen was gone.

I woke with a start, blind in the night, before the light from the single lantern slowly came into focus. I felt as trapped and alone as I had in the desert. Or maybe it was still the dream. I sat up slowly, feeling Marc shift on the cot behind me.

He was awake. He caressed my hip, as if it were a question.

"I have to go," I said into the darkness.

Marc didn't protest as I slipped out of the tent. It was too early to show up at Rodger's with my things, but still, I had to get away. I showered and changed into a fresh pair of scrubs.

Dawn was breaking as I detoured on the way back from the showers and went to go check on our patients. With any luck, Galen had gotten some rest last night as well—although I hoped to God his dreams weren't as vivid as mine.

Jeffe remained outside the intensive care entrance, looking as fierce as he could while wearing my hot-pink I'm Not Really a Waitress nail polish.

When I eased my way inside, Holly sat at the small ICU desk.

She stood, eyes wide, when she saw me. "Why didn't you tell me Galen was back?"

"Shh!" She'd probably meant to whisper, but it came out like more of a shriek. The ICU was smack-dab between Recovery and the OR, and noise traveled. "He got in last night," I said, voice low, eyes flicking to the doors that led to the other rooms. "Marc and I treated him."

She moved to my side. "I can't believe nobody told me."

"I know. It's a first, right?"

"So what happened with Marc?" she asked, reaching for my hand. "Oh." Her eyes widened as her fingers tightened around mine. "Did you give it back?" She cringed. "Is this because of Galen?"

I snatched my hand back. "No. And no."

She eyed me. "You can't leave me in the dark on this."

"Watch me." I reached for her trademark candy jar and came up with air.

She dug into her pocket and handed me a Laffy Taffy. "Defensive much? I just want to help."

I got that. "You're here, aren't you?"

She crossed her arms over her chest. "Jeffe found me last night, said it was a matter of life or death that I switch shifts."

In this case, he wasn't exaggerating. "Thank God for

small favors," I said, unwrapping the candy, "and gambling debts."

"I would have done it anyway." Holly leaned in closer, as if the plywood walls had ears. "Shirley could have been a little more creative with the names. I mean really—John and Jane Doe?"

I bit into the tart cherry-flavored taffy. "By the time the paperwork is processed, they'll be gone."

"What's going on in there, anyway?"

Nothing I wanted to explain. I stuffed the wrapper into my pocket. "I can't believe you and Shirley are in on this now."

Galen needed to take that woman and get her out of here.

Holly moved to the other side of the desk and retrieved the charts. "She's been asleep most of the time," Holly said, her eyes flicking to the door. "He's a handful."

"Tell me something I don't know," I said, accepting the charts and girding my loins.

With any luck, we'd have them out of here soon.

Unless Galen had other plans. When that happened, the man was a brick wall.

I paused for a second outside the door, charts tucked under my arm, as I centered myself and assembled a mask of careful neutrality. I'd mastered the look in my years as a medical professional. Too bad Galen could see through it in about two seconds flat. No doubt he'd been listening to everything Holly and I had said. At least she'd resisted the temptation to ask me how I felt about seeing him again.

I pushed the door open, half expecting to see him

standing next to his bed, like in my dream. For once, I was glad to see him flat on his back in a hospital bed. He sat slowly, his pecs flexing as he pushed himself up. Naturally, he wasn't wearing his gown. In fact, I was willing to bet he was buck naked under that sheet.

Don't think about it.

"How are you feeling?" I asked, going for inane chitchat as I placed the charts on a rolling cart and unwound the stethoscope from around my neck.

He watched me, as if he knew what I was thinking. "I'm better now."

My gaze flicked back to his chest and I remembered how I'd tasted it in my dream.

Stop.

This was lunacy. I shouldn't want Galen. I was stronger than that.

I did my best to remain clinical and I might have even pulled it off. There was no point in lingering as I checked the bandages on his shoulders, his side, and on his hip. Yep. Naked.

I took his vitals. No need to focus on the way his touch rocketed through me.

He'd obviously seen some action even before he'd received his most recent wounds. There was a fresh pink scar across one shoulder blade, another slice on his arm.

I itched to touch it, to make it better.

It wasn't my problem anymore.

I wished he'd never come to camp, with *her.* I didn't do this emotional shit and I sure as hell wasn't the type who could seesaw back and forth. I'd seen enough drama and loss to last me a dozen lifetimes. I'd lived it every day for eight years and I didn't need a fucked-up personal life as well. I'd done my level best to forget about Galen and I couldn't wait to get back to it.

So why had I come here early? Alone?

Because I was an idiot, that's why. Galen made me do stupid things like think too much and talk too much and *care*.

His eyes caught mine. He touched my arm and I stilled as the heat of it wound through to the very core of me. It was such a familiar feeling, and I hated that I craved it. "Thank you for saving her."

I shook my head and pulled away, resisting the urge to rub at the spot. "Thank Marc. I almost killed her."

I made the notations in his chart and then moved to her. I didn't want to wake her up, so I read over the night notes for a minute. I could feel his presence soaking the air behind me.

He cleared his throat roughly. "I'm glad you were here," he said to my back.

I squeezed my eyes closed, then forced myself back to what really mattered, or what I could at least control.

Holly's blue scrawls were harder than usual to follow. I started over.

On one hand, I was glad that he could call on me during desperate times. But the other part of me screamed at how unfair it was that he thought he could cut me out of his life and then just slam back into camp like nothing had happened. Back into my dreams.

He'd endangered us all.

And he had no right to look at me the way he was right now, like nothing had changed. Like he'd never left.

He tilted his head, a faint smile playing over his lips. "You look good, Petra."

I fought off a wave of longing. I didn't want to have this conversation, like we were old friends who happened to run into each other.

"I'm not doing this," I said tightly.

He'd been more than my lover. He'd been everything to me. He was my life. And he'd walked away when I'd needed him most. He'd willingly cut me out, blocked off all communication. Pretended I didn't exist.

He'd messed with my head so badly, I couldn't even commit to a man who loved me and *did* want to be with me.

And so I focused on the situation instead of the man.

"Why did you bring her here?"

For a split second, he looked vulnerable. The muscles in his jaw flexed. "I needed to keep her secret—and alive." He gave me a level look. "This is important."

"But I'm not important enough to tell me what's going on."

He gritted his jaw. "It's classified."

I tucked the charts under my arm. "I'm out of here."

The words rushed out of him. "I don't want to put you in any more danger than I have."

That stopped me. "Too late."

He sat up straighter, winced. "What happened to you?"

I returned his look with a hard stare of my own. "You don't get to ask me those kinds of questions anymore."

He watched me, as if he could see *into* me by sheer force of will. "I heard you moved on," he said, his voice tight. His mouth twisted at my surprise. He crossed his arms over the wide planes of his chest. "You know how hard it is to keep a secret around here."

Heat rushed through my veins. "Marc isn't a secret." I wasn't about to tell him how everything had gone wrong. I needed to leave, to run, to let this be over. I notched my chin up. "Marc asked me to marry him."

"Good." He swallowed hard, staring straight ahead.

My face warmed. I couldn't believe I'd said that. But I wasn't about to open any doors with Galen. "You told me not to wait for you."

He simply nodded.

It was over between us. It had been since Galen ended it all those months ago.

"I still love you," Galen said quietly, as I pushed out the door.

I kept walking.

chapter five

I tossed the charts onto Holly's desk and headed outside. Blood pounded in my veins and my head felt like it was going to float away.

He had no right to pull me into his emotional shit.

Before I met him, my love life was blissfully simple. I had none. Now it was a goddamn fucking soap opera, and a shitty one too.

I stalked across the crowded courtyard and made a beeline for my tent. God, I hoped Marc wasn't there. Still, if I was going to break down, I sure as hell wasn't going to do it out here.

He still loves me. What the fuck was I supposed to do with that?

Sure, he might want me, but he certainly couldn't be with me. He couldn't love me, hold me, laugh with me. So, basically, his love was a false promise, a tease.

I dug my hands into my pockets and squinted against the morning glare. I didn't feel cared for, I felt played.

Shouts sounded a split second before a group of

maintenance workers nearly ran me over from behind. "Watch it!" I stumbled forward. Could anybody give me a break this morning?

I'd just braced a hand on the supply depot when a gaggle of clerks picked that moment to come pouring out like it was on fire.

"This is it. This is it." One of them grimaced, giving a hard shake to my shoulder as she passed.

Oh, geez. My stomach gave a twirl. I'd already had enough excitement to last me the rest of the war.

"Cool it," I protested as a petite yet forceful secretary trod on my foot.

"Sorry!" she called, joining the throng of people heading south.

A burly sergeant rushed past, the one I'd treated after he'd started a locust plague a few months back. "You." I grabbed him by the sleeve. "What's happening?"

His meaty face and bald forehead shone with sweat. "The war has started again."

I dropped my grip.

"They say it's worse this time."

I pinched the bridge of my nose, trying to take it all in. "How could it be worse?" This was war. We specialized in blood, death, and destruction. We had a monopoly on misery.

I joined the crowd, some of us running now.

We'd had peace for such a short, precious time. It wasn't fair. It broke my heart to think it could be over so fast.

We jogged past the maintenance and supply tents, kicking up the red dust on the paths. The grit worked its way into my eyes and up my nose. I rubbed my face on my sleeve.

The crowd bottlenecked about fifty yards down, at the mess tent. It stretched long and flat under the limbo suns. To the right of it, a maze of personnel tents unfolded into the distance.

"Come on." I halted at the back of the jostling line. At least everyone was in as much of a hurry as I was.

A collective gasp rose from inside the tent and a few people on the outside started pushing and shouting.

"Just what I've always wanted to see," grumbled a voice behind me. "A riot."

I turned to find Captain Thaïs. He was my least favorite doctor in camp and not just because he was a demigod asshole. Thaïs had almost killed me a few months ago. He'd made an insane attempt to incinerate the enemy and hadn't minded in the least if he got me too.

He had no conscience, no soul, which meant the gods had carted him off to jail for about five minutes, before pardoning him.

I didn't even want to share the same air. Thank God the mechanics had taken things into their own hands. Lazio had unbolted the mess hall doors from their hinges and tossed them aside.

Worked for me.

The crowd surged and pretty soon the entire mob of us made it inside. The television blared the latest from the Paranormal News Network, or PNN—all immortal news, literally all the time.

It was our version of CNN, with a few obvious exceptions.

The only TV in camp was a 1970s cabinet model

that my enterprising colleagues had bolted to the make-shift stand on the far right wall.

They'd pushed back all of the tables so that a crowd at least twenty deep flooded the hard-packed ground in front of it. But really, there were people everywhere—on the tables, sitting on the serving areas, standing on chairs along the far wall.

I wormed down the side, along with about four dozen other people. The air inside was hot, and getting worse by the second. At last, I saw a little bit of room on the floor, a few feet in from the serving area.

I about groaned out loud when I saw Thaïs had the same idea. "Isn't there a segregated demigod viewing area up front?" I asked, edging him out and diving in next to a group of nurses.

"A demigod goes where he pleases," he said, getting elbowed by the crowd as he took the last available spot—next to me.

Lovely.

It was hard to even hear the television over the din of the crowd. A young-looking reporter with curly brown hair swallowed hard, as if the camera itself were about to attack him. "This is Zach McKay. Stone McKay is on vacation."

"Ah, nepotism at its best," I said, trying to edge Thaïs's knee out of my space.

He gave me a sour look. "You're just jealous because you come from a family of nobodies."

Quite the contrary. I was perfectly happy to go home and stay out of this.

The reporter stood at the top of a dusty red stone battlement. His eyes darted to something offscreen, then widened as he returned his attention to us. "I'm here at New Army Base 8C, which this reporter believes will soon be under attack."

The camera rolled over hundreds, if not thousands of our soldiers in their brick-red uniforms as they readied the cannons and took their battle positions.

Truly? I rolled my eyes. The penalty for spying was death-by-dragon incineration. Yet PNN had a reporter imbedded with our army, sending live footage of troop movements.

It seemed there was no secret as large as the ego of the gods.

The picture shook as we heard a distinct rumbling in the background. The reporter wet his lips. "We'd like to apologize. My camerawoman is on her first assignment as well. Our sources indicated that the armies would not be advancing for some time."

Thaïs growled under his breath. "Is he kidding? We never should have submitted to a cease-fire to begin with!"

I resisted the urge to elbow him in the ribs.

The wobbly camera panned over the desert beyond the fort, where the air itself seemed to shimmer.

"Did you catch that radiation?" the reporter half whispered, like it was a secret between us and about three million other viewers. "This is all happening live. We are in quadrant 133.9A where the new god army is defending the Setesh Wastelands. As you can see, there is energy building in the desert. The gods can transport a battalion or less with no impact to the air whatsoever. Any more, and you get glimmers of it like we're seeing right now."

Thunder rolled over the desert, the skies darkened, and suddenly at least three battalions of old army soldiers appeared out of thin air. Artillery at the front. Behind them, massive black dragons stomped and fought at their restraints. Then, finally, endless rows of ground troops in old army tan.

The young reporter looked like he was going to be sick.

Explosions boomed and the camera fell to the ground, stuttering black-and-white snow.

PNN cut to a stick-thin blond woman behind the PNN news desk. She clutched her powder-pink-taloned hands in front of her and seemed shocked to even be there. "We're back in the studio while we deal with . . ." She paused so long I wondered if she forgot where she was. "Technical difficulties."

Her eyes widened as she listened to her earpiece. "Is that the only crew we have out in the field? It is the only crew. Okay. I apologize. We'll try to get them back." She did her best to buck up and rally, her expression going stern. "Our sources had made it quite clear that the gods had retired to Shangri-la, for their annual mortal death trials and skiing tournament. Obviously, the old gods had other things in mind."

She wiped a shock of hair from her damp forehead. "I'm former intern Valerie LeMux, filling in for Stone McKay, who is, I'm sure, returning from vacation as we speak. In the meantime, let's go to commercial and we'll see if we can get Zach back for you." She gave a shaky, five-second grin, then opened her pink-glossed lips and let out a high-pitched, keening wail.

I didn't blame the banshee one bit. I'd have screamed too, if I thought it would help.

The camera lingered for a few moments until it abruptly cut to a commercial for the Basilisk of the Month Club.

I turned to Thaïs. "Nobody was ready for this? We're in the middle of a war." A temporary cease-fire was just that—temporary. What part of that had these people not understood?

For once, the demigod and I were in complete agreement. "Oh, we're ready," he said, eyes wild.

"I hope." I mean, I thought we were. We'd stocked up on supplies and made sure gremlins didn't make off with the generators. We were up a doctor, thanks to Marc, although I didn't know how we were going to keep his dragon girl or my ex hidden if we had massive casualties in the ER.

Thaïs crossed his arms, thinking. "The Setesh Wastelands are about thirty miles north of us, which puts them close to the 8033rd."

We took their overflow, along with the 7964th. I hoped our sister units had kept their supplies up and their people focused.

The soldiers around us cheered as an ad came on for *The Real Werewives of Vampire County,* a new reality show set in Malibu of all places. Heaven knew why anyone cared about a spoiled werevulture and her clique.

PNN came back on and the camera focused on a nervous-looking Valerie. At least she'd combed her hair, although it seemed she'd begun to chew at her talons. "I'm Valerie LeMux, filling in for Stone McKay. Junior reporter Zach McKay is live in the field. In case you're just joining us, the old army has broken the cease-fire and launched a surprise attack on the new army stronghold in the Setesh Wastelands. From what we understand, the new army took this ground six months ago, as they routed the old army at the Mountain of Flames."

The camera cut back to the curly-haired reporter. "Zach McKay here and I've made it to the highest battlement of Fort 8C," he yelled over the pounding, screaming sounds of artillery fire.

Okay, he wasn't just new. He was insane.

At least he had some fear. I could see his microphone hand shaking. It sounded like sonic booms going off behind him. "As you can see, old army bombs are pounding the wards just twenty feet from this fort." The camera panned to a wall of dense black smoke as searing artillery fire blasted into it.

His face fell for a moment, and then he rallied. "Normally, either side would resort to a glorious field battle to hold this land. This fort was built because the desert floor in this area of limbo can be six feet thick in places—sometimes less—with the natural risk of digging a hole straight into Hades. And as openings into Hades are, by nature, quite unstable and prone to unleash demons, it seems the new army opted to construct aboveground defenses."

The camera panned out to show the inside of an immense fortress, constructed from desert rock. New army archers and artillery lined the battlements, while infantry amassed on the ground. The soldiers looked hard, focused. They had to be scared.

Zach's microphone hand shook even more. "It truly is a marvel of engineering for them to not only mine the rock, but bring it here and set it up between two natural obstacles. We have the bottomless sand pits to the east and the glass desert of the Furies to the west. I'm told that is less than an inch thick in places and not very good to walk on."

We weren't going to get casualties. These people were going to be incinerated.

The reporter wiped at the sweat streaming down the sides of his face. "I think it's safe to say that the old army strategy will be to blow holes in the floor of our fortress, effectively sending us into the abyss for good."

Thaïs grinned

My blood went cold. It *could* get worse than blood and guts and regular death.

Instead of being a positive change, a time of hope, the cease-fire had made the war even more grisly.

How could these people place such a low value on life? The gods were immortal. Surely if they needed thousands of years to live and have children and *be*, they could at least try and fathom why some of us would want a simple lifetime. A fucking chance.

The new army had positioned their people straight over Hades. And the old army wanted to open holes and send their troops directly at them.

The cub reporter straightened as a commander worked his way through the lines. "Colonel. May we have a word?"

The crusty solider kept going. "No."

Screeches pierced the air and we watched as black dragons launched straight at the camera.

"The wards are down! The wards are down!" Zach hollered. Black dragons shrieked straight overhead. "They're huge!" Cannons fired. Artillery tore through the dragons. I'd seen blood before, but I'd never seen a living creature torn apart.

I watched in horror as they shifted into desperate, bloody men and women, and fell to their deaths.

And holy hell—they were wired with explosives. Dragons streaked straight for the command center, the artillery, the elite forces on the ground, exploding on impact, killing and maiming.

The crowd around me went stone-cold silent.

The camera shook. I tried to see through the blackened smoke rising from the stronghold. They were kamikaze bombers. Dragons. I couldn't believe it.

Soldiers ran, regrouped, jumped from the fortress, and scrambled into the sand as they burned.

The PA system in our camp crackled to life: *Attention. Attention all personnel. All on-duty surgical staff report to the OR immediately. All off duty, sit tight. You're next.*

The mess tent was quiet as death for a split second. Then tables rattled and chairs groaned as anyone who had anything to do with the OR headed for surgery.

Thaïs knocked against me and I didn't even care. I was used to violence, tragedy. I just didn't expect to get a front-row seat—or for it all to start again today.

Bodies crowded together as we bottlenecked at the door. I was shorter than most of the people around here and the mass moved against me with claustrophobic fervor.

The air grew thicker, hot.

I shook it off. At least I knew I'd make it out of the mess tent alive. No telling what the start of the violence meant for Galen. He'd be heading back into battle as a mortal.

"Hold up!" someone ahead yelled.

I ran smack-dab into the soldier in front of me as the crowd ground to a halt.

"What is it now?" Thaïs grumbled.

PNN droned above the crowd.

"In breaking news, a new prophecy is being handed down right now by the oracles."

I stared at Thaïs for the first and perhaps only unguarded moment in our lives. "Now?" They wanted to screw with us *now*?

He looked as shocked as I felt. It used to take weeks for the oracles to deliver a prophecy. It gave me time to prepare.

I edged past him, toward a chair that had toppled in the fray. I turned it upright and stepped up above the crowd. I wasn't the only one. Person-by-short-person, heads popped up like gophers.

Valerie was saying something, but I couldn't hear because the crowd noise had started up again—on-call people trying to get the hell out versus backup medical like me who had to see exactly what was going on. The crowd jostled against my legs.

PNN cut to a shot of people camping out up on a mountain. There were hookah vendors, dancing girls, and tents full of tailgaters.

"Disgusting." Thaïs grunted next to me. "Ever since

Hermes tweeted the location of the hidden continent, it's been a goddamned hippie party."

We watched a pink-suited PNN reporter struggle against a conga line as she tried to get in her live shot.

Thaïs made a lewd gesture at the screen. "There are condos going up on the far side of the mountain, for gods' sake!"

"Pipe down." He was not my new TV-watching buddy. Besides, I wanted to hear.

PNN cut to a shot of the three oracles emerging from their cave and onto a platform overlooking the sea.

There was Radhiki, in a bloodstained sack, wearing huge round sunglasses that covered half of her face. She looked more like a Real Housewife than a feared oracle as she stared out into the ocean.

There was Lu-Hua, her stick-straight black hair arranged in layers and streaked with blond highlights as she held up a large femur bone.

There was Ama, with bloodred paint smeared over her ebony cheeks, wearing a glittery gold tank top and a censor's rectangle covering her girly parts.

Lovely. Even the oracles had gone Hollywood.

Ama hissed as the camera panned in on her face. Her eyes rolled up in her head as she began to hum.

A hush fell over the crowd, and our mess tent, as we waited for her to speak. To tell us what came next.

Hell, I'd be willing to do just about anything to prevent a tragedy like the one we'd seen today.

Her lips quaked as she groaned. *"The healer who can see the dead . . ."*

Her eyes flew open and I nearly sidestepped off my chair. She began panting, gaze unfocused. *"The healer will uncover the bronze weapon,"* she snarled.

Hell. Not that thing again. I didn't know whether to slink to the floor or scream bloody murder. I'd had enough of the bronze dagger to last me a lifetime—quite possibly three or four.

Ama snarled. *"With it, the healer shall arrest the gods."*

Oh, sure. Why not go up against the gods?

Ever since I'd been forced to yank it out of Galen's dying body, the bronze dagger had brought nothing but fear and damnation. I'd had to deal with it while it followed me around. I'd had to use it to fend off soul-sucking Shrouds. The thing had practically stalked me outside of a hell vent.

I was so glad when the goddess Eris swiped it. I thought I'd finally gotten rid of it. But no. I was never done with the bronze dagger. At that point, I was convinced the bloody weapon would follow me to my grave—or worse—put me in it.

But I'd do it. I'd take up the dagger again. I'd do it for every kid out there on the battlefield right now. Every soldier injured and fighting for life. As well as the ones who hadn't made it.

Ama collapsed onto the ground, spent.

Oh, well, wasn't that nice? At least somebody could relax around here.

A healer who can see the dead will uncover the bronze weapon.

When? Why?

The least she could do was give me some fucking detail.

Grim, I eased down from the cafeteria chair and made my way out of the tent. No doubt I'd find out soon enough.

chapter six

The yard was clogged with casualties, and I could hear more choppers on the way. I stopped to triage a burn patient. They'd packed dressings on his chest, neck, and on the right side of his face. His left was criss-crossed with so many scars, I could barely tell what he was supposed to look like.

"Hang in there, soldier. I've got you." I eased back the gauze in a few spots to see what we had. Second- and third-degree burns, a mix of mottled black and red oozing wounds.

An out-of-breath EMT drew up next to me. "We've given him glucose and saline."

"Good." He was losing a lot of fluids. The gauze was soaked. I took a closer look. He was swelling fast. I kept my face carefully neutral as my heart sped up. "He's going to lose that airway."

The soldier watched me, his eyes hard with pain and fear.

We didn't have much time. I stared daggers at the

EMT. "Give me a trach tube. Now." Before he dilated to the point where we couldn't get it in.

"We're going to get you through this," I said, focusing on the soldier. He was a corporal. Infantry. I glanced down at his neck. His dog tags were gone. Damn it. Was it too much to ask that I actually know about my patients?

A cool shiver ran through me as the ghost of my former nurse shimmered into focus next to me. Charlie looked like a teenager, too skinny for his rusty red army scrubs. "They're in his left pants pocket."

I really hated when Charlie showed up. But in this case, I hoped he was right.

One way to find out. I winced. "I'm sorry to do this." The soldier's combat fatigues were bloody and torn. Trying not to grimace at the pain I knew I was causing, I slid a hand into my patient's pocket.

"You got it," Charlie said, reaching down to help, his hands passing right through our patient. My fingers came in contact with metal. "Jimmy Zern," he said. "He's a shifter. Twenty-two years old. Blood type A positive."

I slid the dog tags out and flipped them over in my hand. Damned if he wasn't right. I clutched the tags and pointed to the nearest nurse. "Get me three hundred cc's of morphine."

The soldier was in obvious distress.

The EMT returned with my trach tube. My patient was starting to gasp.

I glanced at the hard face of the EMT. "You didn't give this patient a painkiller."

His eyes flicked up to me as he positioned the soldier's head. "I'm not allowed to anesthetize immortals in the field."

"He's a shifter," I snapped. Gods be damned. We couldn't wait.

My patient gasped and gurgled as I inched the tube down his throat, without the benefit of morphine. I felt his pain. It was suffocating both of us.

But we got the tube down. He could breathe.

"Ready?" I asked the EMT as I handled the legs and he took the shoulders. We hoisted the corporal onto a stretcher and rushed him inside.

A half-dozen nurses had turned the walk-in clinic into a makeshift burn unit. They'd cut off his clothing and bandage the burns. We hooked the corporal up to a ventilator and assigned him to a twenty-four-hour watch. He should make it. At least he was in good hands.

Our base commander, Colonel Kosta, barreled past me, sterile hands up. "If you're done with him, we've got about five dozen of his friends out front."

"Tell me something I don't know." I scrubbed up for surgery and made it out onto the floor in time to help with a mass influx of close-combat injuries—artillery shot, metal-weapons wounds.

From what I could see, it had been a massacre.

The operating tent was packed. I had a table by the front, near one of the big fans. You'd think that would be good, but all it seemed to do was blow hot air around.

By my third patient, I was getting a massive headache and an intense urge to run away and jump in the nearest tar pit.

Marc had the table in front of me. He stepped away

as an orderly took his patient to recovery. "How are you doing?"

"Good." Which was a ridiculous thing to say in the middle of the latest bloodbath.

Still, I didn't need to worry about Marc understanding, at least when it came to this.

My goggles fogged at the edges as I worked on a particularly dicey shard of glass that had severed a lung in three places. At least that was how many I'd found so far.

Nurse Hume stood to my right, assisting.

Marc made his way to my free side. "Hey," he said, under the clattering chaos. "You need a break?"

"I'm okay."

He didn't budge. "I'm not giving up on you."

I glanced up, locked eyes with him. "Don't do this. Not now." I wasn't about to give him false hope.

Hume suctioned. "There."

I looked to where he was pointing and saw another shard of glass. I extracted it, holding it up for Hume and Marc to see. "Do you realize how close to the abyss he had to be to get this kind of a wound?"

Marc shook his head. "What are you talking about?"

That's right. He hadn't seen PNN. "Let's just say the old army has invented a whole new brand of horror."

Complete with dragon suicide bombers.

"Christ," he said, keeping an eye on his table. It wouldn't stay empty for long.

"Over here," Hume murmured, suctioning near another shard.

Damn.

It was like they were multiplying. I was thankful again for the anesthetic we'd developed for immortals. It was impossible to imagine doing this surgery while the poor kid on my table was conscious.

Nurse Hume handed me a retractor.

I tried it, realized I needed something smaller. "Get me a McAndrews clamp," I said to Hume.

While he went off to look, I took over siphoning the wound. "We have a new prophecy," I said, voice low, eyes on my patient. "The surgeon who sees the dead gets her fricking bronze dagger back. Again."

I glanced up at Marc, expecting shock, coming up way short. Hell, maybe he was surprised. It was hard to tell with the surgical mask covering his face. Still, he looked way too calm. "Did you hear me?" He especially should recognize my own particular brand of hell.

No one knew about me and my ability except for Marc, and Galen. And now Leta. Shit. This was getting better and better.

He exhaled hard, the breath tenting his surgical mask. "Don't borrow trouble."

Oh, that was rich. "Because the oracles have been wrong before." I located another sliver of glass and tossed it onto the tray.

"You're looking for problems," he ground out.

I didn't have to. They found me all on their own.

Marc leaned close. "If you want to stew about something, start thinking about how we're going to keep our special guests a secret now that recovery is flooded."

"Thanks for that." I couldn't wait to get them out of here. "Why the hell did he ever come back here with her?"

Marc's eyes were guarded. "She's a fugitive," he said, heading back to his table. At my surprised look, he added, "Leta explained everything."

"Nice," I muttered as he went to inspect the X-rays they were posting for him.

Galen wouldn't tell me squat. Meanwhile Marc got explanations from the dragon who'd died on my table.

I focused on stitching together torn muscle. Classified, my ass. At least one of them had had the decency to fill us in after we'd risked our necks.

We finished surgery in just under eighteen hours, which in truth was quicker than I'd expected. Dawn was beginning to edge through the high windows of the surgeons' locker room as I peeled off my cap and tossed it into the bio waste bin.

My ponytail was half falling out and my eyes felt like sandpaper. I didn't care.

I plunked down on the bench between the rows of lockers and just sat.

There was a time I thought I could beat this war—that the things I did to make the prophecies come true would make a difference. Now, I didn't know.

I'd worked so hard, bled soul-deep to help bring about that cease-fire. And for what? It was hard to see if it had been a true time of peace or simply a delay of the inevitable. War, suffering, death. I didn't know how to escape it. Or if we even could.

I shoved to my feet.

Marc hadn't even wanted to hear about the bronze dagger, as if that would make it go away.

It galled me, the way he refused to acknowledge what we were dealing with.

He was too cynical. This war had hardened him as well.

I shucked off my surgical gown. Oh, who was I kidding? There was a time when I'd felt the same way. Like I could be logical, practical, and all of this would go away.

Ha. I wadded the gown and tossed it into the biohazard bin.

Now I felt too deeply, for people and things I shouldn't feel for at all. I didn't want to dive back into that mess, but trying to handle everything on my own sucked.

No matter how hard I tried not to admit it to myself, I knew Galen would understand about the dagger.

I yanked open my locker and pulled out a PowerBar and a half-full bottle of water.

He'd wanted to protect me when the knife had first started showing up in places it shouldn't. Galen had insight, answers—even if they were based on an insane faith in me and my abilities.

Maybe I didn't miss him so much after all.

I tore through my PowerBar without tasting it. It was fuel, nothing more. And if I slowed down, I might fall over. That was the problem with marathon surgery—my body wanted to crash, but my brain was still going a hundred and eighty miles an hour.

There was no way I was going to sleep. And anyway, I needed to check on Galen. No telling who had walked in on him during the chaos of the last eighteen hours.

Grabbing a clean mask, I took the shortcut through surgery, half expecting to be called over to assist. But

there were no more patients waiting and the only surgeons left out on the floor—Kosta and Rodger—had
eyes only for their patients.

When I pushed through the double doors to the ICU,
a new nurse sat at the desk.

"I'm here to see Jane and John Doe."

She finished making a notation in a chart and slid
her pen behind her ear. "They're in quarantine."

Nice touch.

She checked her list. "Beds 2Q and 3Q."

Quarantine. So they'd been separated then. "Thanks."
My heart pounded and my palms began to sweat.

Don't think of the dream.

Or sex.

Or the way our bodies slid together so perfectly.

It hadn't been so long ago that I'd lived that dream.
I'd had Galen in my bed every night. I remembered
every kiss, every touch. Vividly.

Lord have mercy.

I took the back exit out of recovery, to the flat strip
of land before the rise of the hill where we landed our
evac helicopters. Six small red tents stretched out in a
row, with the requisite ten feet between them.

Each was big enough for one patient, and me when I
crouched over.

This was so dumb, but I did it anyway. "Knock,
knock," I said, easing inside 3Q before I lost my nerve.

Galen's eyes flew open and he was up in an instant,
sword in hand.

"Whoa, hey!" He was keeping a short sword under
his pillow? That blade was at least two feet long. I held
up my hands. "It's me."

At least he was wearing boxers. That and nothing else. The walls of the tiny tent closed in around us.

He'd been lying on his side, curled slightly. I used to snuggle back into him when he did that.

"Just the woman I wanted to see," he said, his voice thick with sleep . . . or perhaps something else. That's when I noticed he had two swords pointed at me . . . in a manner of speaking, at least.

"Are you going to put that thing away?"

He quirked a brow. "Which one?"

The man had absolutely no shame. "Both."

Merde. I'd tried to tell myself that I was checking on him, making sure he was safe and well hidden.

But the truth was, I'd wanted to see him. I was starting to need him. And if I wasn't careful, that desire would flay me alive.

The muscles in his shoulders bunched as he eased the steel blade back into its hiding spot.

This was such a bad idea. I didn't know what I was doing. I was strung out and tired and I needed . . . "Sorry," I said, scrubbing my hand over my face. "I shouldn't have come. It's been a rough twenty-four hours."

"Sit," he said, gesturing to his rumpled bed. When I hesitated, he gave me a resigned look. "I'm not going to try anything. I know you're with—" He gestured, unable to even say the name.

"Marc," I said quickly, feeling my ears redden at the tips. God, I was such an idiot. "I think I just needed to know you were here."

Which was crazy because he wouldn't always be there. He couldn't.

A pained expression crossed his face. "I missed you too."

"Galen—" I stood there, unsure what to say next.

"Don't worry. I'll back off." He shook his head, saying almost to himself, "Every time I see a damned carton of blueberries, I think of you."

I hadn't eaten one since. And they were my favorite.

But I didn't dare tell him that.

He sighed, running his hands through his short, clipped hair. "I didn't set out to barge into your life and cause problems. I thought I could fly under the radar on this one." A muscle in his jaw twitched. "I was wrong."

"No." I planted my back against the tent pole, trying to find the words. This was a man who did what was right. He followed his conscience, even if it got us into trouble. He could regret the situation, but as far as who he was . . . ? "I'm glad you could come to me."

He wasn't my lover anymore. I'd never hold him again at night or tease him in the morning. But I could be with him in this. For whatever time we had left.

He watched me, his face carefully set. Hard.

"How will you get back?" I asked, more than ready to turn my mind to something else.

"I'm special ops," he said. "I'm good at sneaking around."

Yes, well, I hoped he wasn't planning any heroics, not when he couldn't shrug a shoulder without pain. Like it or not, he was human now.

"We'll be out of your hair once Leta is stable enough to travel," he said, as if he hadn't nearly died on my table. "Until then, we need to lie low."

Maybe I wasn't so good at all of this black ops thinking, but, "Why can't our side know anything? Are you hiding from them too?"

"For the time being, yes," he said matter-of-factly.

Holy smokes. It wasn't as if I were overly loyal to the new army, but still, the man had no fear.

I didn't know whether to throttle him or give him a high five. "What are you, the Lone Ranger?"

He shook his head slowly. "I'm just trying to make a difference," he said, as if that were it.

"What happened?" I asked, not expecting an answer.

"She was my mission," he said simply. "I acquired her near one of the old army outposts."

He sat on the cot, and this time I joined him.

He rested his forearms on his knees. "She's a special breed that the old army is trying to weaponize."

"Lovely."

"Yes. Let's just say our side is very interested in the program they're developing. I was sent in to extricate, or exterminate if necessary."

"Galen—"

"I wasn't going to do that," he said quickly. He scrubbed a hand over his jaw. "Still, getting out of there was rough. Leta was weaker than our reports suggested. And she fought me. They'd clipped the membranes on her wings back to the bone so she couldn't fly. She couldn't even shift back into a human. By the time I'd gotten her to the edge of the containment area, we'd been spotted."

"I'm glad she went with you." It must have taken a lot of trust. Galen was good at that, at getting people to believe in him.

"She didn't have much of a choice," he said tightly. "You saw what the old army does to their dragons."

I'd witnessed them harnessing the dragons back in one of their camps. And I'd seen them use the dragons as weapons on PNN. I could hardly get that image out of my head.

"They keep them like animals." I'd seen it. And I'd been horrified at the complete and utter lack of humanity. I just hadn't realized how widespread it was.

The lantern light played over his sculpted cheekbones, the firm line of his jaw. He was harder than I remembered, more raw. "If a dragon isn't useful in human form, the old army fits them with a collar that forces a shift. They're used exclusively as animals—for communications, scouting"—his lip curled—"and weapons."

My stomach turned at the thought.

Galen traced a hand over his arm, his blunt fingers trailing over deeply tanned skin. "Leta is one of the rare shifters who has the gift of telepathy."

I sat back, stunned for a second. "I'm surprised they didn't kill her outright."

Telepathy would be a priceless commodity around here, where all communications were controlled by the gods.

His eyes caught mine and held. "That's what I wondered."

"Telepathic humans are hunted down." Like me. Not that I'd ever met one, but I heard the stories.

His mouth tightened. "When I informed my commander I was going in to get her, he ordered restraints."

Okay. "Well, she could have been dangerous."

"A collar," he added.

Oh, hell.

Yes, the old army was brutal in general, but I'd seen for myself what our side was capable of—murder, torture, eternal damnation.

I scooted closer. "Well, you can't just keep her here."

"I don't trust our side to do the right thing."

I didn't either. I touched his leg. It was stupid on about ten different levels, but I needed that contact, that connection. His muscle tightened under my fingers, but he didn't move away. "What are you going to do?" I asked.

His expression was steely. "I don't know."

Hades, this was such a mess.

He coiled under my touch like a cobra ready to strike. "She's been hiding her power," he said, "to the point where she's not even sure it's there anymore. But if she can find it again, nurture it, she'll be able to communicate with any and all dragons, and likely most anyone she wants. She could be a powerful asset to the new army. If we don't use her for experiments or dissection."

I didn't save her life to have somebody cut her apart. "Does she suspect?"

"If she's smart, she does."

I slid my fingers up his thigh, held it. "But she could use her power for good."

This time, he moved away. "With the right people behind her, yes. I'm trying to figure out what we're facing so we know where to go when we get out of here.

"She doesn't trust me, not all the way at least. She seems to have a special bond with Marc."

It had pained him to say it. He shook it off, refocused. "I think we're part of a bigger plan."

"Naturally." I didn't like where this was going.

He gazed at me like he could see into my soul. "The new prophecy proves it."

"Wait." I broke away from him, at once missing the intimacy we'd always shared. "That's going a little far." I mean, really. "You can't expect me to be turning up a dagger, while hiding a dragon, and you."

The corner of his mouth turned up. "I'm used to lying low."

"No." I wasn't strong enough for this. Yes, I admired Galen's faith, but I wasn't sure it meant I had to risk everything for him and his kidnapped asset. And for what? I had no idea how to make this work out right.

Only faith.

He gave me a knowing look. "I can see the wheels turning."

I snorted. "Don't tell me you're enjoying this."

"I missed you," he said quietly.

It was too much—his nearness and his touch and, well, him. "I'm not yours."

Not Marc's. Not anybody's.

"I know," he said simply. But he didn't let up. "We can brave this, Petra. I'll still do whatever it takes to help you find peace."

Jesus Christ on a pogo stick.

"Yes, well, what if we get caught this time? What if they discover you and Leta and they figure me out too? We could wait a hundred years for a prophecy to come true. What if the bronze dagger never shows up? Worse, what if it does? I have no control and no guarantees and I never signed up for this."

"Anything else?" he asked.

I sighed. "Can you be with me on this? Maybe try and freak out too?"

"No."

At least he was honest.

I ducked back out of his tent, more frustrated than when I'd gone in. But at least I wasn't alone anymore.

chapter seven

Marc wasn't home when I made it back to my tent, which was good. I didn't want him to have to watch me move out.

Or worse, help.

At least I was doing something to take charge of my life. Something that didn't involve dragons or prophecies—or Galen.

Luckily, my friend Rodger wasn't busy. Or if he was, I didn't notice. I'd found him halfway to the mess tent and informed him I was moving back in with him, and that I needed him to help me grab my things.

After all, what is it they say about good friends? A good friend will help you move, a true friend will help you move the bodies. I thought back on what Galen had told me and hoped I wouldn't be testing Rodger any more than necessary.

My breath hitched when I spied one of my books on Marc's desk. It would be the last time our things were together like that.

Rodger stood behind me while I lit the lantern. "Why is this place always so dark?"

"Not the time, Rodger," I said, sliding my footlocker out from under my cot.

"I'm just saying." He shrugged, picking up the footlocker as if it weighed nothing. "It's like a crypt in here."

I opened my duffel bag and tossed in a few loose books and some shoes. I crammed my shower kit in and stuffed my pillow under my arm.

It was for the best. Marc and I couldn't keep going on like we had.

"At least you'll get to see more of Galen," Rodger said, taking my duffel and hooking it over his shoulder.

"No," I said, grabbing my snack box. Hell, aside from my bookcase, I was already packed. Or—a niggling thought stuck in the corner of my mind—maybe I'd never really unpacked.

"This doesn't have anything to do with Galen," I said, as we made our way outside. It truly didn't. What I had with Marc was broken. We both wanted to fix it, but that didn't mean we knew how.

Outside, the heat of the desert stung me. I sighed and glanced out over the endless wasteland. Hell, if I had to guess, I'd say Marc had proposed in order to fix it. If we'd been able, we might have even had children in order to try and make things right.

We'd keep going down that path because we were too afraid to get off it.

Rodger and I trudged side by side. What had happened was awful. But at least it had forced me to take a hard turn.

Right off the edge of a cliff.

No, I refused to think that way. I had my werewolf buddy and the rest of my friends. I had a job I was good at.

I didn't need a man or a relationship to make me feel complete. That in itself was freeing.

I'd learned a lot, grown more than I ever imagined.

We drew curious looks as we made the trek to my old tent. "I feel like I'm moving back in with my parents."

Rodger grinned at that. "At least I didn't turn your former spot into an exercise room."

No, he hadn't. When we made it back to my old place, I saw he'd removed my cot completely and had installed cement-block shelves.

I glanced at him. "Not that I'm picky about where I sleep, but . . ."

"Bah, I can change it back. Take a load off," he said, dumping my footlocker and duffel just inside the hutch door.

He didn't have to ask me twice. I stretched out on Rodger's cot while he banged around. How was it that his pillow was better than mine? I raised my head a little. "What about you?"

We'd be back on in five hours, maybe less with all the cases we had in Recovery.

"Super werewolf strength."

Now he was just being nice.

"It won't take long to get your side back together," he said, grunting as he hefted. "Want me to make it dark in here?"

"God, no." Let there be light.

And shedded fur balls in the corners.

I closed my eyes, smelling the tar swamp, listening

to the familiar bubbling out back. It hurt to know that things were never going to be the way they had been with Marc. But at the same time, it felt good to be home.

Five hours later, we were back in Recovery. The place was packed. Burns were excruciating, physically draining, and ugly in so many ways. Beds full of bodies lined both sides of the long, rectangular room.

We'd squeezed temporary cots in between, and the hall in the middle was jammed with doctors, nurses, orderlies, and even the entire bar crew from the officers' club, who had shut down in order to stock supplies and offer nonmedical help.

As soon as Rodger and I walked in the door, there were nurses handing us charts on the most critical cases. Marius arrived as soon as dark fell. And it was well after that before I could even inquire about the corporal I'd found yesterday in the yard. I hadn't seen him among the men, but at this point I wasn't even sure if I'd recognize him if I'd tripped over him.

I was washing my hands, rinsing the slick burn ointment away, sterilizing myself for the next case.

Nurse Hume stood next to me. "What's his name again?" he asked.

I tried to remember the dog tags. "Zanas, Zara?"

"Zern," he said. "The were."

"Yes." The one who'd gone without painkillers.

"He died."

My heart squeezed. "Oh. Okay."

Goddamn it.

This needed to end. The sooner the better. It was all up to me and I had to wait around for a fucking knife.

We worked another six hours before we had everyone settled for the night.

The lights flickered and dimmed until the room was bathed in shadows. Blue lights lined the walls, illuminating individual patient areas enough for us to monitor them while they slept.

I knew I should go talk to Marc. I'd caught him watching me a few times. Still, I wasn't sure what to say to him. I didn't want him to think he had a shot when there wasn't one.

Ending it with him had been the right call. It was hard, but it was also a relief.

Unlike my breakup with Galen, which had shattered me to the core.

I handed a chart off at the nurses' station and lingered on that thought for a long moment. What would it be like if I could actually have Galen in my life?

A familiar voice from behind startled me. "A word, doctor?"

I turned and the air left my lungs in a whoosh.

Galen stood there, at the front of Recovery. He had gauze wrapped around his head and over the lower part of his face, like some kind of Bedouin sheikh on a desert hike.

"What are you doing?" My whisper was about nine octaves too high as I glanced down the line to see if anyone was watching.

He stood in front of me as if he had nothing to hide. He drew close, far too confident for his own good—or mine. "You haven't been by to see me today."

"I've been busy," I said. That's when I noticed he'd also stolen a shapeless examination gown, as if that would hide his power, his raw masculinity. I hoped his ass was hanging out. He deserved it. I planted my hands on my hips. "I thought you'd wait for me."

He frowned. "You thought wrong."

"Come on," I said, leading him to an area just off the nurses' station. I closed the door to a room that held four private examination rooms.

The curtain screeched as I ripped one open and ushered him into a six-by-six area with a bed.

"This is good," he said.

Good, my ass.

It was even darker in here, the blue lights set low. I clicked on the portable medical lamp and we were flooded with light.

My tongue hit the top of my mouth when I took a good look at him. I could see his ridged chest against the thin material. And my heart did a little flip-flop as I spotted the sheen of sweat at the hollow of his neck.

He was the only man who could make an examination gown sexy. And I was going to lose my mind if I didn't get a grip.

He touched my arm and my skin burned at the contact. "Have you gotten the dagger back?" He leaned closer than he needed, realized it, and pulled back.

"No," I said, cheeks heating under his scrutiny.

"'No' to the touch or 'no' about the knife?"

"Either. Both. Take your pick."

He blew out a breath. "Damn it. I need to know what's going on."

"Nothing." So far. "Of course, that's usually when things go to hell."

"That's why I'm here."

"You can't fix everything," I reminded him.

His jaw tightened. "Want to bet?"

I shook my head. "Let me see your bandages." I led him to the narrow bed, ignoring my body's reaction to him in the small space.

Bad idea, I realized too late. He was wearing a one-piece exam gown. How the hell was I supposed to do my job without—oh, my.

I cleared my throat. "Let me just slide the top over . . ." his massive biceps.

He bent his head as I reached for the ties around his neck. I wondered why he didn't try to make it easier, and then I saw the way his hands were fisted at his sides.

I slid the gown down over his broad shoulders and chest, my body tightening in response. The cloth caught at his waist, just below his washboard abs, and I made sure it stayed there.

"Stop," he said, reaching for me, almost as if he were in pain.

"What?" I asked, tucking the gown under his thighs, realizing too late that I was touching him way too much.

He was hard. All over.

I refused to look.

Or to think about the way my skin flushed or how my core had gone molten. I could still be professional about this.

Distant.

Even if the man, not to mention his mere presence, took up every inch of the small exam room.

I traced my fingers along the edge of the bandage at

his chest, and examined the pink, puckered skin. Then I did the same for the cuts to his arms and shoulder. They were raw, but he was healing nicely. "You look good," I said, refusing to think about the way I was touching him.

My elbow brushed his arm and I yanked it back like I'd just touched fire.

Galen was wound just as tight as I was.

"When I was hurt in the escape, I didn't know if I'd ever make it back to you." His voice was thick, his eyes just as blue as I'd remembered. "I've never been this beat up before."

"You're mortal now." He'd given up his demigod status for me.

The intensity of his gaze nearly undid me. "It's worth it."

Now I knew why I'd fallen headlong into disaster for this man.

I smiled and ruffled his hair. "I don't know. I think I'd take the superfast healing."

He tilted his head into my hand. "I preferred the megastrength. You haven't lived until you can bend spoons."

"That was one way you never tried to woo me." He'd preferred blueberries, long walks, and saving me from killer scorpions and soul-eating Shrouds.

He nodded slowly, his face a mask of concern. "So you're saying spoons would have made the difference."

I tossed an exam glove at him and he caught it.

He grinned, sobering as he shook his head. "I never planned for it to turn out this way."

Neither one of us had. The prophecies came with terrible costs. He was trapped and so was I. There was nothing we could do about it as long as this war raged.

"I know it's wrong, but I can't stop believing in us," he said. He touched my cheek, let his fingers trail down my jaw. "It can't end this way."

I didn't have the heart to tell him it must. It had.

He'd never lost faith. Galen always believed, even when I'd found it so hard.

He drew my hand down into his. "When we were escaping, I took Leta across four quadrants. Through enemy lines. Then we hit an old army unit twenty miles from here."

I'd known the armies were advancing. This was war. But I'd had no idea they'd gotten that close.

"You were the only one I could trust. I don't believe in accidents," he said, his back rigid, his features taut. "I was meant to come back to you again. And now the knife has returned—"

"Not yet," I said quickly, as my brain struggled to take it all in. I couldn't think when I was around him. That was the problem. "I don't know when that dagger will show up." Just like I hadn't expected him. In fact, "The bronze dagger should have been here by now." It had never been reluctant to harass me in the past. Unless . . . "What if I screwed up? Didn't see it? Oh, God. What if it's loose somewhere in camp?"

He seemed amused at that. "You can't lose an enchanted knife."

He was one to talk. "You ever had one before?"

"No."

"Then don't go telling me about cursed daggers."

He let out a small snort and I considered it a victory. I missed this. Him.

There was a time when I would have given anything to get over Galen of Delphi. Now, I wasn't so sure.

"You can't avoid it forever," he said pragmatically.

"The knife or you?"

"Both." The corner of his mouth quirked. "Believe it or not, I'm trying to comfort you."

"Then maybe you should put on some clothes. Like a parka."

He gave me a cat-ate-the-canary grin. I had a sudden urge to kiss it right off his face, like I would have when we were together.

He had an odd look, as if he knew, before shaking it off. "I admit that every time you've had the dagger, it's been hard. Hell, it was hard on me to give it to you."

"Considering I pulled it out of your chest." My fingers itched to touch the spot.

He was so close I could almost count his individual eyelashes. God, I could feel the heat rolling off him. "It's like Father McArio said. The dagger is a tool." The tips of his fingers caressed the top of my hand. "It's an insane test every time the knife comes up. But we've succeeded." He closed a hand over mine and I felt it down to my core. "We've changed things."

I slid my hand out from under his, used it to shove my bangs out of my eyes. Wouldn't you know, I instantly regretted losing his touch. "No we haven't. The gods are still fighting. What good is a cease-fire if it only delays things for a while?"

He looked at me, steady, sure. Hades, I'd missed that. "We stopped fighting for the first time in seven hundred years. That's all the proof you're going to get right now. You know the rest is faith."

My heart warmed and suddenly it was all too intimate, too real. "Thanks," I said, feeling my eyes go moist as I let go of some of the worry. I studied my fingers and the red dirt floor of the tent. "I needed to hear that."

Out of the corner of my eye, I saw his deeply handsome features clouded with tension. "You know I'd go to hell and back for you."

I snorted. "Let's hope it doesn't come to that."

He hesitated, which was very unlike him. "Holly says you're no longer with Marc."

My throat felt tight. "Holly has a big mouth."

He watched me, the pure affection in those deep blue eyes nearly undoing me again. "This is our second chance."

"Galen—" I didn't need him winning me back. Or Marc thinking he could change my mind. I didn't need either one of them right now. All I'd gotten in the end had been heartache and pain.

Luckily, he didn't push it.

"It about killed me every time I heard a prophecy. Wondering what was happening to you, how you were handling it."

Yes, well, he couldn't have it both ways. He couldn't look at me like that after he cut off all contact. "I wasn't the one doing special ops missions with no immortal protection." I hadn't gone dark. I hadn't left. "Galen, where the hell did you go?"

It pained him, I could tell. He blew out a hard breath, instantly bringing a hand to the bandage on his side.

Oh, this was ridiculous. "Let me see."

He squirmed to avoid me. "It's fine."

"You'd say that if your arm fell off."

He stopped fighting while I checked him out. "I never wanted it to end the way it did." He paused, then sighed. "They sent me on a special mission to assess and acquire old army assets. Command wanted to see if and how they could be turned."

"Tell me about it."

He glanced up. He was sitting on the edge of the bed, his hands folded. "It was top secret and everything about my life was about to be scrutinized for security purposes." His jaw tightened. "Especially the incident where I ran off to the rocks with you."

My cheeks warmed at the mention of our lovemaking that night. The world had been going to hell, but everything with Galen had been so right.

"I'd done enough to draw attention your way," he said, as if I hadn't just been picturing his insanely irresistible body naked and ready for me. "If I was ever the one to expose you." He shook his head. "It's terrifying."

"I can hold my own." Or had he forgotten how I'd stood up and fought with him? I'd also done a damned good job after he'd left.

He ran a hand through his short hair. "I'm not going to discount what you went through, but you have no idea of the horrors that are out there. That's a good thing. It's my job, my duty, my reason to exist to keep you as far away from that sick terror as I can."

He was a soldier. He faced the monsters so people like me didn't have to.

Never back down. Never surrender. It was written on every fiber of his being. "I refuse do anything to expose you, Petra." His body was ramrod stiff. "If that means losing you, then I'm willing to make that sacrifice. For you. Only you."

The unfair awful truth of it was, he was right. I'd had to sneak around quite a bit to fulfill the last three prophecies. Hell, I'd had to go AWOL. I never would have survived, much less succeeded, with the eyes of the new army trained on me.

My gut twisted as his words sank in. "I'm sorry."

He shook his head. "I don't want your regret."

"What I meant is I forgive you."

He closed his eyes for a moment, letting it sink in. "I'm glad."

I groaned, wrapping my arms around my chest. "What are we even doing?"

He shook his head. "Let's not talk about that now."

"You're still leaving." He'd never tried to hide it.

"I'm needed," he said simply. "The work I do saves lives, it provides valuable intelligence—resources." He glanced around the tiny examination suite. "Somebody's got to keep you living in fine style."

"Rodger's thinking of installing a hot tub next to the tar swamps."

He held his hands out. "You see? My sacrifices are worth it."

God, he was too good. I tilted my head. "I hate it when you get all noble."

"It's my curse," he said, his face light until we both

realized what he'd said. He had been the demigod of truth and nobility. Now he was a man, like any other.

Wait. That wasn't right either. He was an extraordinary man, one who saw the good in people, and in me. He'd almost died trying to protect me. He'd given up his immortal life to be with me and I'd never forget that.

I reached for him. "Good thing I have a weakness for noble men," I said, before I could hit the edit button. He stilled, his thigh tensing under my hand.

I remembered exactly what it was like to have him, how sexy he'd made me feel. How loved. He'd been my partner in all things, for the short time that I'd had him.

It could never be the same as it had been between us, but I found myself desperately wanting to pretend, if only for a little while.

His body had always fit perfectly with mine.

I fought off the rising desire, even as a traitorous thought formed at the back of my mind: *We are alone. No one would know.*

He was practically naked. And he was hard underneath the thin material pooled at his waist. He thickened even more as I stared.

I could have him one more time. Then I could give him up.

He'd been gone so suddenly before that I'd never truly had the chance to say good-bye.

It would be so easy to touch him, to relearn every aching inch of him.

He wouldn't stop me.

His features were hard, his body strung tight. "This Marc, he's the one you had lost before we met, isn't he?

The one you were going to marry." He visibly flinched on that last word.

The mention of Marc's name cooled my desire. "Yes." This was good. I had to remember where I was.

He gave a sharp nod. "I'm glad you found him."

"So am I." Marc was a good man, and I was glad that he was with us, instead of trapped behind the lines of the old army.

But Galen had shown me what it was like to have everything. I couldn't settle for anything less.

"What happened?" he rasped.

I felt my voice waver and before I could stop it, I said, "You."

I had a split second to marvel at the sheer wonder on his face before his mouth slanted over mine. Nothing had ever felt so right. He slid his tongue in my mouth, tangling with mine. I pressed up tight against him, needing him like air.

This was what I wanted. It brought tears to my eyes to realize I could never truly have him.

That I was setting myself up for an even bigger fall.

He groaned and deepened the kiss, or maybe that was me.

He held me close, the gown crumpled between us, his body leading mine. In another five seconds, I'd be flat on my back, under him.

It was all too much. It wasn't what I'd planned. But I burned for him in a way I could never have imagined before Galen entered my life.

I couldn't think, didn't want to as his hands slid up my sides under my scrub top. His roughened touch awakening every inch of my body.

The curtain screeched back and I stiffened. Naked, Galen leaped to his feet, body braced from years of military training.

Marc stood frozen in horror, holding a box of doughnuts from Frank's Fish Market in New Orleans. It had been our place. Our private, decadent escape. I didn't know what he'd had to do to get them.

They were a rare and precious treat.

He dropped them.

I don't even think he noticed. "I thought you might need a break," he said, sounding as shocked and hollow as I felt. I'd never meant for Marc to see this. Us.

"Marc, I—" There was nothing I could say that would make this right.

He took in every detail of my disheveled, passion-soaked state before he turned and left.

"Marc, wait!" I started after him. He slammed the main door. "Damn it." I stopped, sick to my stomach. "He doesn't deserve this." I knew I should go after him, but I didn't want him back. I just hadn't wanted it to end like this.

Galen retrieved his gown from the floor. "It's better he knows we're together."

Wait. No. I straightened my clothes, tried to calm my raging body. "We are not back together." Yes, I loved him and I needed him and I craved just one more time with him. But he knew as well as I did that he was leaving. Our situation hadn't changed.

"I just had a weak moment." Or five. At least he was getting dressed again. "Let's get one thing straight. What just happened here was a one time temptation, not an open invitation to take what you want."

He had the nerve to look shocked. "You wanted it too."

"I did," I said. There was no use pretending otherwise. "I wanted you one last time."

His fury rose. "Thanks for letting me know."

"What else did you expect?" I asked, heading for the door.

"How about a goddamned chance?" he snapped.

I spun on him. "You're the one who ended it." He'd ripped my heart out. I wasn't going to set myself up for another fall like that.

I turned back for the door. My heel slid, and I skidded two feet on the gooey remains of a jelly doughnut. My favorite.

"I was wrong." The raw note in his voice struck me to the core.

I wanted to go to bed and never wake up again. I glanced back at Galen, determined to keep moving. "Right or wrong, I'm smart enough to know what I can't have."

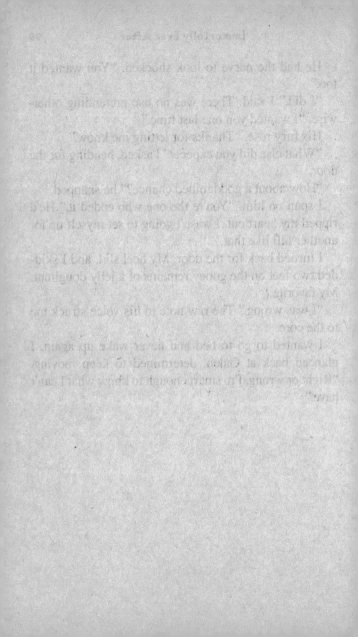

chapter eight

I slammed the door on him and ran straight into more trouble. Only this time it was named Marius. He could have used super vampire speed to get out of my way, but of course he didn't.

"Watch it." He raised his chart over his head and turned so that I smacked into his side. "First Marc and now you." He sneered, dusting himself off as if I carried Moldovian fleas.

A wide-eyed Holly rounded the nurse's desk. "What happened?"

"I don't want to talk about it." I'd wounded Marc more than I ever could have imagined. The prophecy didn't make sense. Galen was pissed off and hiding in the back and I didn't see how I could get him out with all these people around who knew him.

I'd had it with him and this war and these people and there wasn't a damned thing I could do about it.

Thaïs nudged me out of the way as he went to sign in. "Get out of my way. You're off shift."

Yeah, that made it perfect.

I rubbed at the back of my neck. I didn't even know what time it was.

Thaïs hummed to himself. It was both peppy and annoying at the same time. "What is that? The BeeGees?"

"Sycion lyre quartet." He signed his name with a flourish. "This dump is about to change for the better. HQ has finally seen fit to send investigators to this camp."

I about choked.

"Why?" Holly blurted.

Thaïs looked smug. "To bring law and order, no doubt." His mouth quirked. "I hear they'll be looking for spies."

More like a special ops soldier who had gone off the reservation.

It took everything I had not to glance back at the room that held Galen. I wondered if he could hear what was going on, if he knew the danger.

Marius drew up to his full height. It was rare to see the vampire spooked. "How soon?"

Thaïs grinned. "A day. Two at most."

We had to get Galen out of here. I doubted he'd go without Leta. She'd need at least that long to recover. Even if the squad from HQ hadn't arrived yet, Galen and Leta ran the risk of crossing paths with them on the way out. The limbo desert didn't give you too many places to hide.

I'd never met an investigator, but I'd heard the stories. Whole squads of soldiers, complete departments at HQ, hell, I'm sure entire MASH units as well, brought in for questioning and torture.

Because why not, right? How better to get answers than by bringing around an angry manticore or three in order to tear off some arms and legs? Or if they miss and lop off a head, whoops, those mortals sure are fragile.

They'd take entire companies of soldiers, tie them to boulders, and roll the men downhill. At least it was flat around here, which meant they'd probably bring out the hot coals. Answer questions while your feet burn. My toes clenched at the thought. If they liked what you had to say, you'd get to answer follow-ups—while your feet burned. If they didn't like your responses, you just burned.

I stood frozen by the desk as Thaïs and Marius began rounds.

Holly drew up next to me, panicked. "Is Galen still back there?"

"Cover me." I didn't know how I was going to get him out. The big jerk.

Steeling myself, I pushed open the door. The room was dark. "Galen?" I whispered as loudly as I dared.

We had to move fast.

"Galen." I flipped on the overhead light.

The exam rooms were open and empty, save for the one at the back. "It's only me." I ripped open the curtain to exam room two, but he was gone.

I burst out of the room. "How did he do it?"

"What?" Thaïs barked from a nearby patient's bed.

"Nothing." I shared a glance with a worried Holly as I scrawled my signature on the status sheet.

I banged out into the night. The sun had barely set, which meant everyone was out enjoying the 1.5 minutes we got between the blazing heat and the evening freeze.

Focus. I had to get a hold of myself.

I was so intent on heading to see Shirley that I nearly got run over by two mechanics on a motorcycle. They shot out between the secondary supply tent and Recovery.

"Watch it!" one of them called as the contraption screamed past, spitting rocks and engine exhaust.

"Shove it up your—" I choked back the last word as Father McArio breezed past me from behind, his purple stole flapping in his wake.

He raised his water bottle. "Evening, Petra."

Just the man I wanted to see. If anyone had a bead on this camp, it was Father McArio. "You have a minute?" I called after him. And why was it that a sixty-seven-year-old priest was outgunning me?

"Later." He turned to walk backward. He was in his usual army pants paired with a black clerical shirt and collar. The dust swirled around him, his cheeks red from the sun. "I have a few critical cases in the ICU."

I knew exactly who he was talking about. No problem. "Go." As if he needed my permission. I headed for Colonel Kosta's office on the other side of the OR. Shirley may have taken the job of company clerk in order to ogle her immortal Spartan boss, but she was also one of the first people to know what was going on around here.

But she wasn't in her office. She'd left the lanterns blazing. A single fan blew at the papers on her desk. Most of her official documents were weighted down by various staplers, tape dispensers, and coffee mugs. The rest blew in circles on the floor.

When I looked closer, I could see Kosta wasn't in

either. The door to his office stood open. Every lantern was lit.

Not good. I ran a thumb along the door frame. These two didn't keep banker's hours. And they didn't just leave the office open like this. Something had pulled both of them away pretty quickly. And I had a sinking feeling I knew what.

"Petra!" Horace zipped up behind me and nearly gave me a heart attack.

His face was stern, his cheeks flushed. "A pair of level six investigators are here from headquarters," he said, loudly enough to catch the ear of a few clerks walking past.

Bureaucracy, my butt. They sure didn't waste any time. "I was hoping Shirley knew something."

"Who do you think is meeting with them?"

I about choked. "They have Shirley answering questions?"

He trembled slightly. "Not yet. You know exactly what this is about."

I steered him inside and closed the door. The normally busy office was silent as a tomb. "Don't assume anything." Maybe we were lucky and some nut had started a revolution.

He sneered, his voice a tight whisper. "They're looking for an AWOL special ops officer."

I kept my voice neutral and my face blank. "He's gone."

"Interesting." Horace wrinkled his nose. "Because just this morning, I found a stack of pennies on my altar."

I was going to kill Galen.

He always did have a soft spot for the little god. And he never stopped to think that the rest of us didn't always take the time.

Horace glared at me. His narrow face flushed, his bulbous nose had gone red. "Spill it. Why is he still here?" His eyes widened. "You didn't seduce him, did you?"

"What? No." Marc had walked in before I could. I tried not to wince, focused on the obvious. "Did you see his injuries?"

It wasn't as good of a protest as I'd hoped.

Horace wasn't in the mood. "He promised me he'd be gone in a day."

And Galen had promised he'd find a way to be with me forever. We could all see how that had worked out.

Jeffe snarled from the doorway to Kosta's office and my heart gave a little lurch.

"What are you doing in there?" Horace snapped.

"I am under orders to guard this room," Jeffe snarled. The sphinx turned his attention to me. "I saw Galen on the way here. You stay away. He is too good for you."

That might be, but, "I have to warn him."

"Galen knows about the investigators in camp. He saw before you did." The sphinx bristled. "Whatever you did made him very sad," Jeffe lectured.

Yeah, well, I didn't need any opinions from a guard sphinx when it came to my love life.

"Hah!" Horace snarled. "You see? You're rolling your eyes. What are you two doing?"

I felt my face redden with the memory of that kiss. What I'd give for five minutes, consequences-free, with Galen of Delphi. "I don't roll my eyes," I reminded the sprite. Especially over Galen. I was a professional.

Horace's wings beat hard, scattering papers at my feet. "Spare me. It's disgusting. You get that exasperated infatuated look about you whenever he's around. I've watched you for seven years and it only happens around Galen." He crossed his arms over his chest, as if daring me to contradict him.

Yeah, well, I wasn't getting into that debate. Besides, we had bigger problems. "Where are the investigators?"

"Setting up in the visiting officers' quarters." Horace frowned. "They look mean."

Naturally. Okay, we had to get a handle on this. "Are they after anyone specifically?"

They might be forcing Shirley to put together a list of names.

Horace's eyelashes fluttered a mile a minute. "I don't know, but I'll bet they question the entire camp. I'll never hold up under questioning. I'm too beautiful for torture."

"Nobody's getting tortured," I said, at an absolute loss as to how to prevent it. "Here's what you do. Keep an eye on that tent." Horace could blend a lot better than I could. "When Shirley comes out, get her alone. Ask her what she knows. They're not going to do anything around here without going through Kosta first." An early warning from Shirley would be our one shot to know what the hell was up.

Horace wrung his hands. "Kosta can't stop them. They have power from the gods."

"True, but we can at least try to get the drop on them."

Kosta might be one to follow orders, but if they were going to hurt anyone in camp, I was betting the colonel would be able to hold them off with rules and procedures, to at least buy some time while he tried to wheedle some sanity out of HQ.

Meanwhile, we could get Galen and Leta to make their escape.

It would be a clean break, like ripping off a bandage.

Horace planted himself outside, near the main message board, where he had a straight shot at the visiting officers' tent.

"Let's keep what you find between you and me," I said, as he scanned the bulletin board, which was jam-packed with official notices from HQ detailing correct and committee-approved ways to sheath a sword, avoid hell vents, and chew gum while walking.

Too many people knew our little secret. There was Jeffe, who couldn't bluff to save his life. Holly. I wasn't so worried about her. Horace, who was starting to panic.

We were losing control and putting more people in danger.

I gave one final glance back at Horace before heading south toward a maze of low-slung tents that made up the officers' housing.

My hutch was dark when I made it back home. Rodger was snoring. Marius was on shift.

I reached for the door and about had a heart attack when Marc stepped out of the shadows.

"Petra." He grabbed my arm as my hand flew to my chest and I ended up slammed against him. "It's only me."

"Oh, God." I stepped back, shaking, relieved it was him and not the death squad. I crossed my arms over my chest, trying to recover. "I'm sorry for what you saw back in Recovery."

Heat flooded my cheeks. I'd never in a million years imagined Marc would walk in.

He stood ramrod straight, a muscle in his jaw worrying. "He's the one you fell for when you thought I was dead."

I had no idea how to explain it to Marc of all people. This was so wrong. I'd hurt him in a way I could never make right.

His eyes hardened. "I thought he was gone."

My throat felt thick. "So did I."

He reached for me, then pulled back, having come to a conclusion that neither one of us wanted to think about.

He cleared his throat. "So this is really it."

"Yes," I said, feeling the weight of the distance between us. I hated this emotional no-man's-land, but I had to live in it. The frustration, the guilt, we had to endure it and pull through it or else we'd never come out on the other side.

"I'm tired, Marc. I'm tired of all of this." I tried to explain, willed him to understand. "It's like pieces of me keep getting chipped out or torn away. I can't do this anymore."

But Marc wouldn't let it go. Couldn't. "What do you want, Petra? Do you want him?"

"I want to feel whole again." The sad thing was, I didn't think I'd ever get any of it back. "I'm sorry."

"Yeah. So am I," he said. Then he walked away.

chapter nine

The next afternoon, things got worse. I'd done my rounds, and I still hadn't heard from Galen. We were alive—so far—when Horace accosted me on my way home.

"Have you heard anything?" he asked, his wings beating up a dust storm.

"No." I stopped, bringing a hand to my eyes. "You?"

The sprite shook his head, setting off a cascade of glitter. "I couldn't get Shirley alone."

I'd never seen him this nervous.

"You weren't at mail call today," he said, as if it were a personal fault of mine.

I started walking again. "I never go to mail call." My father had been the only one on Earth who knew I was down here, and with him gone, well, let's just say I didn't get many care packages.

The sprite's forehead furrowed. "I picked this up for you," he said, holding out what looked to be a shoe box wrapped in brown paper. "They'd had it for a week," he added. That's when I noticed the Greek writing on the side.

Oh, no. "What's that?" An express delivery from the oracle?

Here's your knife, I hope it doesn't kill you this time.

I took a step back, then another. "No flipping way. You know what that is?"

He frowned. "It's your mail. It's heavy and I'm not going to carry it around for you all day."

On closer look, it didn't have a mailing label or postage marks and I really didn't want to touch it. If I laid so much as a finger on it, it would be mine.

The air between us seemed to hum, as if the thing were calling for me.

"Fine," I said, hefting it from him. It would probably follow me anyway, like it had all of the other times I'd been given the bronze dagger.

Darned if the package wasn't vibrating.

"See if I do you a favor next time," Horace muttered as he flew away.

Too many of these favors and I'd be done for. Okay, well, the least I could do was get this thing home.

It was less than a two-minute walk, but it might as well have been in another world. The box was heavy. I tore the end off the brown paper wrapping. The container inside was made of earthenware or some kind of stone. I couldn't tell. I slung it under my arm, making sure to keep a decent grip on it. No telling what the oracle or the Fates or whoever was pulling my strings would do if I broke their precious box. It's not like the prophecy had told me what to do with the thing.

It was mid-afternoon, and not a lot of people were out. Johnny Cash music filtered over from the enlisted tents. I'd bet anything it was the mechanics. Lazio had always said he wanted a boy named Sue. Maybe that's why he couldn't get a date.

I took the shortcut through the maze of officers' tents, all the way to the edge of the tar pits to my new place.

Rodger was visible through the mesh windows. He sat on his cot, bent over a notebook, no doubt writing one of his endless letters to his wife.

I didn't bother knocking. "Honey, I'm home!"

Rodger slammed the notebook closed and shoved it under his pillow. "Jesus!" His eyes were wild and his auburn hair was in serious need of a brush.

"What? You didn't smell me coming?" I ducked around an I BRAKE FOR WOOKIES shirt drying on the laundry line. "I thought werewolves were supposed to know these kinds of things."

Rodger crossed his arms over his barrel chest. "You think I want to smell any more than I have to around this place?"

Touché. "What's in the notebook?"

"Nothing." He gave an exaggerated shrug.

"You're blushing." Oh, this was just too good.

His whole face went even redder. "It's just a letter for Mary Ann."

Yes, well, that wasn't enough to get all hot and bothered . . . unless. "Is it a dirty letter?"

The tips of his ears flared bright red and he started to cough.

"Well done." I didn't know he had it in him.

I walked over to the door-turned-desk that Rodger and Marius had set up between their cots. He had a half-dozen delivery boxes stacked on top, along with other assorted junk. "It looks like you made mail call."

Rodger had brought back a crap-ton of sci-fi geek-dom from his time on leave, but now he'd gotten even more stuff.

He had boxes stacked shoulder high next to the front door.

There was Captain Kirk, Spock, Bones, red shirt guys, yellow shirt guys, aliens, the K-7 space station, a *Romulan-Bird-of-Prey* (I know because it said so on the box). "Must be a bitch not having shelves any-more."

"Just"—he clenched his fists—"be careful."

"Says the man who kept swamp creatures in his footlocker."

He snorted. "At least I resisted the urge to smuggle a few home."

"Is that true?" I asked.

He gave a half grin. "As far as you know."

I held up my mystery package. "Look what Horace just gave me."

Rodger glanced over his shoulder at the box, still mostly wrapped in brown paper. "Okay."

"It's freaking me out." Even if it was the knife, it's not like I knew what to do with it. Yet. Of course, I'm sure whatever it was would be dangerous and horrible.

Rodger cocked his head. "Why?"

That was the trick. I couldn't tell him. Rodger didn't know the real reason the bronze dagger had followed me around all those months before. And he didn't know anything about me seeing the dead. It was the way I was going to keep it, for his safety and mine.

So I settled on the obvious. "Who sends a stone box? And look at the scrollwork." Or writing, or whatever it was.

Rodger and I tore the rest of the paper off. "Ahh . . ." he said, studying it top to bottom. "Ancient Sumerian. And look." He pointed to a weird-looking owl/eagle creature. "It's cursed."

I bolted upright. "Really?"

"Nah. It could be Klingon for all I know."

"Don't do that," I said, taking the box from him.

"Why?" He grinned. "You should have seen the look on your face."

The box had a simple latch. It shouldn't be too hard to open. "Don't look," I said, forcing him to give me some space. An enchanted dagger is hard to explain.

"Go for it, Pandora."

I moved to Marius's side of the room. No sense letting an ancient Sumerian curse loose all over Rodger's shrine to the seventh fleet.

"Is he in here?" I asked, taking a seat on Marius's footlocker. Last I heard, the vampire was in the middle of renovating his lair. Word had it he was adding a game room.

"Who knows?" Rodger shrugged.

"Right." I ran a finger over the scrollwork and said a quick prayer that the alabaster box didn't eat me alive. The delicate gold latch did nothing to soothe my anxiety. Sometimes, the more harmless something looked, the worse it could bite.

"You want me to do it?" Rodger asked.

"No," I said quickly. I could do this. I knew what was inside.

I took a deep breath, held it, and opened the latch.

The top of the box flew open and flames shot out. "Holy hell!" I dropped it on the ground and both of us scrambled out of the way as it hissed and spun, shooting fire and sparks. It bounced off the iron stove and skidded in front of Rodger's cot.

Bang!

It exploded in a shower of hot glittering pieces.

I gripped Rodger's arm, my heart beating wildly, as we stared at a charred black cylinder amid the smoking rubble. I froze as a flame zipped across the spiral wick. There was no time to move, no time to run. Panic seized me and time slowed down.

It was a bomb. I'd unleashed a bomb on my friend. Rodger grabbed me, we clung together, and *bam!*

I slammed my eyes closed, waiting for the fire and the pain, and . . . nothing happened.

Swallowing hard, I looked down. A pink bear had popped out of the cylinder.

The air held the tang of sulfur and gunpowder.

I held fistfuls of Rodger's scrub shirt and blinked a couple of times. "What the fuck?"

"One more second and I would have needed new underwear," Rodger said, peeling me off his arm.

"You have any water?"

"No."

We waited for a second before venturing forward. I toed through the wreckage. The box had broken into little hearts. Anatomically correct ones, with mini aortic valves sticking out the top.

"Who the hell . . . ?" I squatted down to take a second, then a third look at the pink teddy bear. No way was I touching it. The smiling bear held a lacy baby shower invitation, complete with bottles and a stork, and written in dried blood.

Rodger crouched next to me. "Looks like it's a girl."

I didn't get it. I was so sure this would be the knife. "I don't know anyone who's having a baby."

Rodger plucked the card from the bear and flipped it open. "Aww . . . it's from Medusa."

My jaw slackened. "The gorgon?" Sure, I was giving her prenatal care, but, "I don't really know her." Only that she had a temper and lived on an island surrounded by a poisonous lake. "I'm her doctor, not her gal pal."

Rodger shrugged, handing me the card. "Maybe she doesn't have a lot of friends."

Had he met the woman? "Of course she doesn't. She's the serpent-goddess, executioner of men, scourge of Kisthene's plain . . ."

Bottles and skulls
stone heroes and more,
let's shower the baby
with gifts galore!
Please come to a baby shower for
Medusa, serpent-goddess, executioner of men,
scourge of Kisthene's plain,
on Sunday, March 5th, at noon.
Isle of Wrath and Pain,
Western edge of the world.
**If you encounter the Bottomless Pit of the Furies,*
*you've gone too far.**

Rodger plucked the RSVP card from the mess, grabbed a pen out of his pocket, and checked the "yes" box for me.

"What are you doing?"

"Getting you out of the house. I'll take this to mail call tomorrow."

He had to be nuts. "I'm not going to Medusa's baby shower. I don't even know how to get to the Isle of Wrath and Pain."

He held up a little yellow piece of paper. "It says here she's sending you transport."

I didn't like that one bit. "I don't want any winged monkeys."

"That's the Wizard of Oz. You know—the shit that's not real."

Fair enough. Still, "What is she sending?"

"Who knows?" He stuffed the RSVP card in his pocket. "I'd go with you, but no boys allowed."

"This isn't funny." Not that I thought Medusa would kill me. She needed me to deliver the baby. But come on—the dagger was still out there. I was surprised it hadn't turned up in my pocket yet. Or on my table in the middle of surgery.

I didn't have time for hearts and flowers and . . . babies.

Once the knife started following me, it was impossible to lose it. And anyone who saw me with a bronze dagger might start putting two and two together.

There might be goddesses at the shower. I really didn't want to have to endure eternal punishment over a party and a power and a knife I couldn't control.

Gods. I sat down on Marius's cot. What if I were talking to an investigator and the dagger showed up?

I would be done. Finished.

Rodger dug around in his footlocker and pulled out a warm can of Dr Pepper. I didn't know how he could stand to drink those things. "That would have been good to put out the fire."

"What fire?" He shrugged, popping the tab. "You know what you should get Medusa? You should get her one of those baby wipes warmers. Or a Diaper Genie!"

"I don't even want to know what those are." I sighed. Knowing my luck, she'd want a real genie. It didn't look like there was any way to get out of this thing. "I suppose onesies would be out of the question." Based on the last ultrasound, the little gal had quite a snake's tail.

How would you even diaper that?

Rodger sat up against the camp stove. "We used to have these finger puppets we'd use with the kids in the bathtub. First time I showed Gabe, he chomped the rabbit. Ate it in one gulp. We knew right then he was a go-getter."

I stuffed the invite into my pocket. "I wish you could go home."

He took a long drag of Dr Pepper. "Me too."

We sat in silence, listening to the tar bubbles in the swamp.

Sure, living with Rodger could drive any sane woman to drink occasionally, but he was fun. He was my best friend.

He was easy.

I eyed him as he scratched his belly and contemplated his soda can. "I missed you," I said.

"You should."

I shook my head. "I missed this."

That got his attention. "Things with Marc finally get to you?"

I sat, elbows on my knees. "He wasn't the one."

I stared at the postcards Rodger and I had tacked up on the wall. Los Angeles, Topanga, Malibu—all of the places he and Mary Ann were going to show me once we got out of here. God, I had more happy postwar fantasies with Rodger and Mary Ann than I did with my almost-fiancé. "Now Galen's back in the picture."

Rodger choked. "What?"

"He's back. I'm hiding him." Sort of. When he wasn't avoiding me.

My roommate stared at me. "When were you going to mention it?"

What was he? My father? "I just did."

"Oh, well, naturally," Rodger muttered.

I ignored him. I'd believed that Galen was the one man I could love with all my heart, but that wasn't going to work. I had no idea how I could ever trust myself to know anymore.

Not when I'd fallen so hard, and hurt so bad. I blew out a breath. "How do you know when it's right? You know: the One?"

He contemplated a second. "You don't."

Talk about a bullshit answer. "I'm serious." Rodger and Mary Ann had a fantastic marriage, one that kept him sane when everything else was going to hell. "Don't stand here and tell me it was all a happy mistake." Not when I needed a plan. "I want what you have. So give it to me straight. How did you know Mary Ann was the right one for you?"

The corner of his mouth turned up. "Did I ever tell you about her dimples?"

I was so not in the mood for a ramble down memory lane. "Rodger . . ."

He sat down on his cot and wadded up his pillow behind him. "Mary Ann has the cutest dimples. She can really light up a room. So at the end of every date, I'd ask her out again right away. And she'd smile and show off those dimples and she'd say, 'I suppose we could go another round.' "

Just shoot me now. "That's not even witty."

But he was already in another world. "It was perfect."

"Oh, barf."

He gave me a knowing grin. "You want it straight? Here it is. You may not be able to communicate worth shit, but you're ass backward in love with Galen. Stop overthinking it and be with him for whatever time you have."

My stomach hollowed. Maybe I didn't want what Rodger had—to love so deeply, but be kept apart.

"Petra?" Rodger leaned forward, elbows on his knees. "This isn't a microbiology test."

My head buzzed with a million issues and worries and fears until I blurted out the most important one. "I can't lose him again."

Rodger sat still for a moment. "It's better than cutting you both off."

"No it's not." I stood. I had to move, walk, do something. "Galen isn't even pretending that he can stay, that he can love me, that he's not going to walk away tomorrow or next week and get himself killed because he gave up his immortality for me."

He tilted his head. "And what are you willing to risk for him?"

"Shut up, Rodger." I crossed my arms over my chest and stared at the tar swamp. We were on two different roads. I never should have asked Rodger his opinion.

I stared at the swamp until I didn't even see it anymore. "You don't know how hard it is to have him right here."

"No, but I know you."

I did my best to ignore him.

He folded his letter and placed it back in its envelope. "Come on." He clapped me on the shoulder. "Let's grab some dinner."

"Good. Yes." Anything to get my mind on something else.

Before we left, we scooped up the box fragments. "What are we having tonight?"

"Meat loaf surprise."

"What's the surprise?" I dumped a handful of stoneware hearts in the trash.

"No meat."

We wandered over to the mess tent and grabbed a few trays. They were always wet. In the desert. I shook some of the drips off mine. I didn't know how the cafeteria staff managed it.

I did feel better—sort of—after unburdening myself to Rodger. I just wished things could be simple, or at least easier to take.

And it turned out Rodger was right about one

thing—I didn't detect much meat in the loaf. We moved down the line and I noticed he stuck to the buttered noodles.

The place was only half full. Rodger and I found a spot at a far table with Holly and Father McArio.

"How's Galen?" Father asked.

My tray rattled as I dropped it the last few inches and grabbed a chair. "You told him?" I asked Holly.

She shrugged, chewing her meat loaf. "I've told him worse than that. Besides, Rodger doesn't look too surprised."

I peppered my meat. Took another look at it and peppered some more.

"Galen is a big guy," Rodger said, shoveling in a forkful of buttered noodles. "He can handle himself."

Holly stiffened. "There they are."

I followed her gaze as a pair of overweight trolls walked in the door. They were dressed head to toe in red, with polished boots and the crest of the gods on each shoulder. Their uniforms would have been intimidating as heck, if these two didn't resemble overgrown cranberries.

Their military haircuts made their pointed ears look even bigger. And their jowls shook with each heavy step.

"We're scared of them?" Rodger snarfed. "I think I saw one of them at the airport working for the TSA."

I glanced past Father to the table of nurses huddled together, talking and glancing at the trolls, who had managed to snag the prime table by the drink station.

"Be very afraid," Father murmured. "They have the power to do terrible things. Once they find their pencils."

"Pencils?" I asked. I didn't want to imagine torture by pencil.

Father pushed his tray aside and leaned forward, elbows on the table. "Trolls always play by the rules. Evidently, HQ forgot to send number two lead pencils. Without their pencils, they can't fill out their paperwork. And without the correct forms filed in triplicate, they can't begin the interrogations."

Unbelievable. "How do you know these things?"

Father shrugged. "It's in the handbook."

Rodger brought his head in close. "I don't get it. We have a ton of number two pencils in supply at the hospital."

"Not anymore." Father winked. "Shirley and I hid them in the junkyard."

Well, color me impressed. "Isn't there something in the Commandments about stealing?"

"You mean rule number eight?" he asked with a shrug. "I think the Lord will understand."

"You're swiping stuff from investigators that could kill you," Holly said. I gave her the Look. "What?" She held up her hands. "I'm just pointing it out."

I pushed my chair back. "I've got to talk to Galen."

chapter ten

He wasn't in quarantine.

His tent was dark, the bed made. I grabbed a torch and stepped inside. Cripes. It didn't even look like anyone had been in here.

Leta's tent, on the other hand, glowed with lantern light. I jammed the torch back in the holder and went to her place. "Leta, it's me. Dr. Robichaud."

I pushed open the flaps. But her tent was empty too. The floor was strewn with pillows, blankets, even an empty water bottle. I snorted. You could tell she wasn't regular military. Then I saw the discarded hospital gown and an icy hand gripped my heart.

It was almost as if they'd left in a hurry.

He might be gone for good.

The thought lodged in my throat.

I hoped the investigators hadn't found them. Maybe they'd decided to take off, although that was bad news too. Galen might be okay to travel. Barely. But he wasn't at full strength. And Leta was still recovering. A long way from healed.

I shoved the tent flaps closed. He could have come to me. We would have hidden him better, worked out an escape plan.

He took too many risks. It was all about the mission. The endgame. No doubt he'd throw himself under the bus the next time too.

Laughter erupted from one of the supply tents down the way. I stood with my hands on my hips, staring at the cascade of stars, not seeing any of them.

Yes, I'd wanted him to leave camp. I did. But after how things had ended between us.

I rubbed at the back of my neck.

Raw hurt pricked through my veins. It felt worse, because I knew I had no right to feel betrayed.

When he left the first time, he'd had good reasons that had probably saved my life. This time, he was saving a creature who would have been enslaved, killed without him.

And there was nothing I could do to make it better.

I trudged across the blackened desert toward camp.

The rocky soil crunched under my boots. I should have grabbed a torch. Then again, if I fell flat on my ass it would almost be a nice distraction.

Maybe this was good. The investigators could leave peacefully if there were no Galen and Leta left to find, or—I shuddered—more likely they'd start looking for a scapegoat or two to make it look like they were doing their jobs.

My tent was dark. It seemed I was the only one

around who didn't have a life, someone to be with. I banged in the front door and flopped down on my cot.

I was fine with being alone. I was. It was just pathetic how it had come about.

Torchlight flickered from outside. I hoped Galen was okay. I had that hollow feeling in my stomach that I got when he was deployed.

"Petra." Galen's voice sounded from inside the tent.

I sat up like I'd been hit with an electric charge.

"Relax," he said, as if that would happen. I fumbled for the lantern above my bed. "Stop." His warm hand closed over mine. "We don't want anyone to see me in here."

"Right." Relief swamped me. He was alive. He was okay. I could practically feel his body towering over mine in the darkness. "You scared me half to death."

"I figured you'd be more alert. But instead you went to bed."

Yes, well, I wasn't special ops. Besides, "I wasn't going to bed. I was brooding."

"Want me to build you a lair?"

Har-dee-har. I set the lantern on low, the tiny flickering light bathing us in shadows. It caught the outline of his face and the curve of his lips.

Merde. I'd been so scared when I thought I'd never see him again. Now having him here, with me, it was almost too much. He looked good enough to eat.

Perhaps I should just turn the light back out.

Instead, I cranked up my courage and prayed my voice didn't shake. "What are you doing here? I thought you went back," I said, as if I'd been hoping it were true.

I didn't fool him for a second. "I needed to see you."

"Why?" I stood, crossing my arms over my chest, as if that would somehow protect me from the intimacy of having him here, in the dark.

He smelled like the open desert in the evening and I found myself wanting to bury my nose in the crook of his neck. But I'd given up that right. Or rather, he'd taken it from me.

He moved closer, until we were almost touching. "I knew you wouldn't come to me," he said, his voice tinged with regret.

"I tried," I said, and saw him smile a little.

Damn, he was so direct. Galen never hid from what he wanted. Maybe that's why I couldn't resist when he'd wanted me. "Look, I need to step back. I'm trying to keep my pants on," I said, trying for a little levity.

His mouth quirked at that. "And you're so confident I could get them off?"

I wasn't going to debate him on that one. I eased away from him and walked toward the cold potbellied stove, trying to put some distance between us. It didn't work. Galen's presence permeated this space and everything in it.

"What are we going to do about the investigators?" I asked.

He stood completely still, like a predator. "I thought it would take them more time."

"Just the opposite." The entire camp was in danger.

People's lives were at stake. These were my friends, my colleagues. I didn't have a home to go back to anymore. These people were all I had left.

His face hardened as he considered his options. "We can't leave. I talked with an associate who completed a similar mission last month. His dragon is gone."

"Freed?"

"Guess again."

"I understand why you can't take her back, but I don't know if it's any safer here."

He shook his head. "I don't know what to do with her. She's more dragon than human right now."

Oh, lovely. "Where is she?"

"Out flying."

"Damn it!"

"Calm down." He strode over to me. "The webbing on her wings is just growing back. She can only fly low. Besides, Marc is with her."

"You dragged Marc into this?" Wasn't it enough that he'd seen us naked together? Well, Galen was naked, but I was well on my way, and—

"He wasn't happy about it," Galen said stiffly.

Understatement of the year. "You asked my ex to babysit your dragon after he saw us . . ." I couldn't even say it.

Galen's jaw tightened. "It wasn't an easy conversation."

"I'll bet."

"Listen, Petra. This isn't how I'd choose for it to happen either. I'm just trying to be realistic here."

Oh, well, then. "I'm glad to see you have everything under control."

At least I was starting to piss him off too. "We can't keep this secret much longer."

"That's my point."

"Marc seems to have a way with her. He could help rehabilitate her."

"We can't hide her that long."

His face hardened as he made his decision. He seemed to stand even taller, if that was possible. "You're not going to like this," he began, as if I'd liked any of it so far, "but we need to tell the camp."

Did he just say what I thought he— "Are you nuts?"

If HQ learned we'd helped Galen and Leta, it would be fiery punishment all around.

His hands closed over my shoulders. "I'm not saying we come clean to the investigators. We'll talk to your friends and colleagues here in camp. Let them help hide us. We'd be hiding in plain sight. It's the only way."

I could see one big problem right off the bat. "What about Thaïs?"

Galen swallowed. I could tell he was warming to the idea. "All except for Thaïs. No one tells him anything anyway."

That was true, but my mind swam with everything that could go wrong. "It's too much of a risk."

Galen's hands slid down my arms. "We don't have a choice. We need their help. Besides, I trust them. Don't you?"

"Mostly." All except for Thaïs. "In case you haven't noticed, I have a hard time with trust."

He took my hands. "Then trust me."

I stared at my fingers, entwined with his. Galen always did know how to pull off the seemingly impossible. I didn't want to kick him out if Leta's condition was going to put them both in danger. And our small unit always did pull together in a crisis, especially in matters of life and death.

His lips brushed my forehead. "People care about us."

I savored it for a split second before pulling away. "There is no *us*." I ran a shaking hand through my hair. "I suppose they're going to find out anyway." Nothing stayed secret for long around here.

He was getting too close. This entire situation was threatening to veer right off the cliff. It was against my control-freak nature to include the entire camp, but I wasn't sure I had a choice at this point.

I couldn't believe I was actually considering this, much less ready to organize it. "If we do it, I get to handle how the news comes out," I told him. Damn. That sounded like agreement on my part.

Was I just crazy, or was it that Galen made me agree to do crazy things? Still, I had to have at least some concession to my mental health. "I'll call a meeting. Tomorrow night at the rocks." I stood facing him, hoping he'd listen, frightened out of my mind at what might happen between us if he didn't.

He stared at me for a long moment, as if he knew how weak I felt. "Then we're settled," he finally said, "until tomorrow night."

"Yes," I said, wondering what exactly I'd just promised.

chapter eleven

As anyone would have guessed, word spread fast.

It still made me nervous—to tell the entire camp about Galen and Leta. But Galen was right. We needed help if we were going to pull this thing off. And so far, we'd kept it under control. I'd informed key people: Shirley, Rodger, Father McArio. We'd put up signs around camp, announcing the rendezvous.

What I couldn't get was why people kept winking at me. I noticed it the next morning. By nightfall, I didn't know what to think.

Yes, I'd asked everyone to meet me at the rocks at midnight. It was a logical, out-of-the-way place. I didn't see what all of the snickering was about. Or why soldiers I'd hardly spoken to before—all men—were eyeing me like I was the last pork chop on the plate.

I'd just finished up my rounds in Recovery when Marius caught me. He lowered his chin, which made his sharp Roman nose look even more pronounced.

"Is it true?" he asked, as I signed out at the desk by the door.

I handed him the pen. "You're going to have to get a little more specific than that."

He hissed out a breath before drawing close. "Your group thing," he said, glancing behind him, "at the rocks."

Good. He'd been asleep all day and had managed to find out. "I'm glad you're going to make it," I said, opening the door for both of us.

It was chilly outside, but not terrible. Hopefully, we'd have good weather for the meeting tonight.

And that our revelation wouldn't end in disaster.

The vampire looked stunned. "I'm not going." He grabbed my arm and pulled me away from the torch-lit path, to the side of the building. "You're not going either."

"Hello, Marius. Grown woman, here." I extricated my sleeve from his grasp.

He didn't even notice. "This is completely out of character for you. I don't care what is going on in your personal life, that"—he flung an arm in the direction of the rocks—"is not the answer."

"Says you." There was nothing else I could do. Second guessing would only make me more tense. "If it's going to happen, I might as well take care of the whole camp at once." I headed back for the path, making him follow.

I steered Marius toward the officers' tents, waving to a group of clerks catching a smoke outside the supply tent.

The vampire was turning red around the ears.

I placed a hand on his arm. "Come tonight."

Marius about choked.

"You need to, Marius. It's important." Did he feel like that much of an outsider? I gave him a gentle squeeze. "I really want you to come."

The poor vampire had gone purple. "No!" he said, his voice pitching up an octave. His hands flailed, as if he could somehow pick the words out of the air. "I have had . . . concubines in Macedonia, a harem in Persia, countless orgies with beautiful mortals, but I am not going to take this coming from you. You are better than that. You are my friend. Even if you were the least bit attractive, I would absolutely, positively not get naked with you and—"

It hit me like a slap to the side of the head. "You think I want to have *sex* with you?"

"And the rest of the camp," he barked. "What has gotten into you?"

It was disgusting and unthinkable and, "Ew!"

For seven years, everybody had thought I was a prude. I'd had a total of two boyfriends for about five minutes each and now this? This was what happened when I stuck my neck out.

Now Marius thought I was coming on to him? Well, I had news for the wannabe sex stud vamp. "I don't want to sleep with you!"

"Good. Because I don't want to sleep with you!"

That's when we noticed people staring.

We started walking. Fast.

"Who told you this was an orgy?" I demanded, voice low.

He gave a strangled cry. "Ken, Frances, Emilio, Tonya, it's on the camp bulletin board, for Lilith's sake."

"I don't believe it." I turned around and charged the other way, with Marius on my heels.

"Oh, for Pete's sake," he snapped before turning on his lightning speed.

"Lover's quarrel?" A voice echoed from the path on the other side of the courtyard.

"Can it, Lazio!" I stopped next to the flagpole, hands on my hips.

I couldn't believe I had to deal with this. I mean, really—an orgy? I invite the entire camp to the rocks for a surprise and their minds immediately go to a giant no-holds-barred sexcapade?

I narrowed my eyes at the shadowed forms of Lazio and the rest of his buddies, guffawing at something or other.

Okay, maybe it wasn't as surprising as I'd originally thought.

Dust swirled and torch flames blew sideways as Marius shot up next to me, flyer in hand. "See?"

I took it to the nearest torch, careful not to set the parchment on fire. In looping script, it said:

> *Meet Petra at the rocks*
> *Midnight tonight*
> *For a special surprise*
> *Campwide fun! Everyone is invited.*

"This isn't so terrible," I said, defensive. It looked like Rodger had written it.

Naturally, someone had scrawled "Bring your own condoms!" along the bottom, but this was the same crowd who snickered the one time we had All You Can Eat Sausage Sunday.

I held the flyer up for Marius to see. "This is about a meeting at the rocks. Not sex. It's not like Rodger asked anyone to bring a pillow."

The vampire squinted at me. "You really need to get out more."

I folded the flyer and stuffed it into my pocket. "We have an announcement to make. You'll see." The meeting was in an hour anyway. I crossed my arms over my chest and sighed. "Maybe the possibility of sex will get more people there."

Marius stared at me.

"Just looking at the bright side," I pointed out.

Who knew the vampire could be such a prude.

"Hey!" Rodger waved from across the way. "Who's in the mood for an orgy?"

Marius and I scowled at him.

Rodger planted his hands on his hips. "I was only joking, but I take it back—both of you really do need to get laid."

Marius turned on his heel and left.

"See?" I said, pointing to Marius's retreating form. "You scared the vampire."

"We'll talk to him later," he said, handing me a torch. "Come on. Galen and Leta are already there with Father McArio."

It was going to be interesting to see how the camp reacted to hiding Galen and Leta. This wasn't your run-of-the-mill prank. We were up against bloodthirsty investigators, even if they were wound up in their own red tape.

Still, I had to believe we could pull this off.

The alternative was unthinkable.

Up ahead, I caught the faint glow of torches, and behind us, more. Good. Hopefully, we'd have a decent-sized crowd.

By the time we'd reached the last of the hulking mounds of junk, I smelled chocolate chip cookies. Father McArio had baked. Good man. Smart man.

He gave out fresh cookies every Sunday after mass, and let me just say, they were amazing. It was how he got the minor gods to attend.

Shirley stood at the crossroads as we exited the mine-field. "Welcome to the party. We're just getting set up."

The three of us headed for the rocks. "Thaïs isn't here, is he?" I asked. He was the one person who would rat us out.

"Nah," Shirley said. "He didn't want to have sex with you."

"Good."

We could hear the party at the rocks before we could even see the light of the bonfire.

"They're making s'mores." Rodger grinned.

That was fine. "As long as they're not getting naked."

Thank goodness they hadn't had enough time—or most likely enough booze. We walked up to a full-out party in progress. There were at least seventy people down there—talking, laughing, listening to Kid Rock's version of "Sweet Home Alabama."

It would have been like every lakeside party in high

school. Well, if we hadn't been in the fourth quadrant of limbo.

The rocks were in a slight valley, which was the only reason we hadn't seen the huge fire from a mile away.

"Where's Galen?" I scanned the crowd for him.

"Father's got him stashed until you make the announcement," Shirley said.

"Gotcha," I said, trying to locate the priest.

Red rocks jutted from the desert floor, which is how the place got its name. There was a sort of cave near the largest rocks. Lord knew what was going on in there. The rest of the rocks stood like a messy Stonehenge.

My gut twisted a bit. "They're burning the old officers' showers." I shouldn't have cared.

"They got part of your old lab too," Rodger said.

With a start, I realized he was right. Flames licked the boxlike structure that had acted as my lab bedroom, my haven, my port in the storm. Of all the . . . "That was *mine*."

Light played off Rodger's stoic features as we watched it burn. "You gave it up." He clapped me on the shoulder. "You moved on."

I did.

"Oh, hell," Rodger said, his voice flat.

A light shone off to the side of us. As it drew closer, we could see it was Father McArio. He had someone bundled in the crook of his arm. I couldn't tell who was under the dark cloak and hood.

"A priest and a monk walk into an orgy," I began, but stopped when I saw the look on the padre's face. He drew the hood off his companion. It was Leta. Her eyes were haunted, her expression feral. Dang. Galen wasn't kidding when he'd said she was on the edge. She shook as Father held her hand.

"She'd better not be about to shift," I said under my breath.

"I can't do it." She choked, her breath coming in pants. "The pressure. It's too much."

"Oh, this is bad," Rodger muttered.

"I've got you," Father McArio soothed, glancing at us, worried. "Where's Marc?"

"I don't know." Frankly, I'd been glad not to run into him today. "What's wrong with her?" He'd had her flying. He was treating her medical issues. She should be getting better, not worse.

The last thing we needed was to convince the camp to harbor an AWOL dragon, and then have her go crazy, shift, and eat half of them.

Marc came up behind Father. "What's the problem?" He gave me a pointed glance, then noticed Leta.

"I can't calm her down," Father told him. "She won't listen to me."

"I've got her," Marc said as she sank into him.

"What can I do to help?" I asked, watching him squeeze her shoulders from behind and murmur something in her ear. But Marc either didn't hear me or he didn't want to shift his attention from the other dragon.

"It's a shifter thing," Rodger said.

"Yes. That I get." It still didn't explain what the hell was going on. Marc began leading her away. I was tempted to go after them.

"Let them go," Father said. "He's doing his part.

You need to do yours. Come," he added, "let's get you to the party."

"We'll be there in a minute," I told him, unable to move from that spot. We sure as hell didn't need any surprises tonight. I glanced at Rodger. "We may have made a big mistake."

"I'd like to blow sunshine up your butt, but"—Rodger glanced at the departing priest, then back at me—"she needs a dominant right now or she's going to lose control."

Lovely. "So how close are we to being screwed?"

We watched Marc and Leta's lantern fade into the darkness. "In every pack, we have one person who maintains control. Physical control. Ours is our pack alpha. He says to fight and you fight. He orders you to stand down, you stand down."

"That's so dumb."

"Thanks a lot."

"Okay, sorry. But you have to admit, this is strange." I treated shifters all the time. And Marc hadn't led a single one of them down a darkened path before.

Rodger ran a hand through his wild auburn hair. "It's like this, Petra. You've got a loose cannon and it's a dragon. This is why shape shifters can be so scary. Because as an army, we can act as an overwhelming force. When the alpha says 'Go,' you go."

Yes, which is why I wouldn't last five seconds in a werewolf pack. "I haven't seen you need an alpha down here," I told him.

He snorted. "I'm not broken. You said it yourself. This woman has lived like an animal for the last six years. They had a collar on her. That collar was her control."

"And Galen took it off." He'd thought he was being kind.

"Oh, believe me, it needed to come off. Still, that collar acts like an artificial alpha. It restrains them, makes them do things they'd never do on their own."

"Like act as suicide bombers." I rubbed a hand over my face.

"The old army broke her down to her most primitive level. Now we took off the collar and there's nothing to hold back that primal side of her. She's strong, Petra, or she would have lost it long before now."

I got it. I really did. "She needs help."

"Yes. And she'll get that help. But first, she needs to get her head on straight. She needs an alpha."

"What? So Marc is becoming her alpha?" We had at least two other dragons in camp. There was one on maintenance, another who was an EMT. "What's involved in this alpha thing?" I asked, although I was afraid I had a pretty good idea. "What does he have to do to be dominant?"

Rodger shot me a look. "You broke up with him."

"Yes, I did, but I don't want to see him get eaten."

Rodger choked. "That's one way of putting it."

"Rodger," I demanded.

"It's not always unpleasant," he said quickly. "He needs to make her viscerally respond to him. As a dragon."

"I have no idea what that means." And I'd never thought of Marc that way—as a *dragon*.

"It's physical. It has to be." Rodger sighed. "You've heard of dominance battles, right? Shifters can beat the crap out of each other."

Somehow, I didn't think that's what Marc had in mind. "And if they're not fighting?"

Rodger winced.

Fighting or fucking. What a way to go.

At least he wasn't sitting home pining after me.

"So what do we do now?" I asked.

Rodger clamped me on the shoulder, steering me toward the crowd. "We hope he does it well."

chapter twelve

"Come on," Rodger said, leading the way down to the party. "We're here for a reason."

Ah, yes, we had to convince the camp to harbor two AWOL fugitives, one of which might shift into a fire-breathing dragon.

How in Hades had I let Galen talk me into this? I squared my shoulders and prepared to face the firing squad.

Have you ever known what it's like to have people cheer when you walk into a room? Neither did I, until we walked down that hill. I'd never been greeted so warmly in my life.

Enthusiastic grins, slaps on the back. The whole thing made me nervous as hell. I hoped they'd be just as happy when they knew the real reason we'd brought everyone together.

"Hey, Petra." I turned to find pale, shy Nurse Hume. He'd cut the sleeves off his scrubs. To look sexy? Yeek. I hoped not. It showed off his pasty, freckled arms.

"This is the best idea you've ever had," he said, walking quietly next to me.

"Well, that's great to hear." He'd seen me in surgery for the past six years. I'd developed an anesthetic for immortals. Yet the MASH 3063rd sex fest was my crowning achievement.

The supply clerks were already in their underwear. Not a pretty sight. Unless you liked your men built like spider monkeys. They'd taken it upon themselves to carry bedpans full of rubbers. "Condoms! Get your condoms!"

"So this is what I have to look forward to as a single woman in this camp," I mused. It was better than the alternative.

"Here." Bald Frank from the cafeteria had an entire cartload of mess hall trays. He handed me one—still wet. What was with these trays? "For your knees," he explained.

Oh, for the love of— "This is not an orgy!"

"Not yet." He winked. He leaned closer, smelling of oregano and orange drink mix. "What I don't get is what Father thinks he's going to do with the cookies. We need sticky things like chocolate sauce and whipped cream and peanut butter and—"

"Enough! Just . . . go that way," I said, pointing him in the direction of a gaggle of nurses.

I'd deal with it in a minute.

There was nothing else we could do except wait for the signal from Shirley that we were ready to start. She stood on one of the large rocks, holding a clipboard and taking attendance.

In the meantime, Father McArio had set up behind a

waist-high flat rock, with plates of cookies laid out in front of him.

"Petra." He was grave as he edged around the rock to see me. "What do we do if Leta shifts?"

"Pray." I wiped at the sweat on the back of my neck. If this didn't go right, we were screwed.

Marc was handling it. I hoped.

Father's eyes crinkled at the corners and he tried to make it right the only way he could at the moment. "I have oatmeal and double chocolate chip."

It was the first normal thing I'd seen. If you thought a priest handing out cookies in limbo was normal.

"Nice spread for a sex party," I said, taking a chocolate chip cookie.

"I didn't know what else to do. It's my first one." Father drew a handkerchief from his back pocket and wiped his forehead. "You really packed them in. Not that I'm a fire-and-brimstone type, but I think I'm going to be talking about Sodom and Gomorrah this Sunday."

"Be sure to tell them that it's not a vacation destination," I said, breaking off a piece of cookie. It wasn't even appealing. "I'm not sure this is such a good idea." We were already putting my friends and colleagues in danger by harboring two fugitives. "If we bring them into this, they're accomplices."

"If you don't, one of them could accidentally expose the situation," Father said. "Don't kid yourself. We'd still be in trouble. The gods don't split hairs like humans do."

Even with the entire camp being careful, all it would take was one screwup to land us all in eternal peril. It would be easier to strip and go along with the orgy than take that kind of chance.

I mean, these were my MASH colleagues, not the CIA.

The cookie crumbled under my fingers. "Who is the bigger idiot? The guy handing out orgy knee trays or me for thinking that these were the people I'd want on my side when all hell breaks loose?"

Father placed a hand on my shoulder. "Trust them."

"Thanks." But he kind of had to say that. I checked my watch. "We're coming up on midnight." I had to trust that we could pull this off.

Too bad I sucked at trust.

"There it is," Father said, as Shirley gave us the thumbs-up signal. He brought his fingers to his lips, letting out a whistle loud enough to rattle the dead.

"Agh!" Several feet away, Rodger winced, clutching his ears. "Is that left over from the Inquisition?"

Father looked a little embarrassed. "Choir camp."

Either way, it had done the trick. All eyes turned to us. Showtime.

My stomach churned as I found a flatish rock and climbed until I was standing above the crowd.

Was it me, or were there a ton more people here than I'd thought? There was no way we could possibly trust all of them. Somebody was going to slip up and it would be all our necks. My heart hammered and I could have sworn I saw the shadow of smoke coming from the top of the trail.

Hold her together, Marc.

A trickle of sweat ran down my back.

We really did have almost everybody here. Except

for those on call at the hospital, and Thaïs—who didn't want to see me naked. At least there were some things right in the world.

"Take it off!" a voice called from below.

Lazio. If I could have worked up the attitude, I would have told him to shut it.

I cleared my throat.

"Kill the radio," I hollered, my voice grainy.

It was amazing how well sound carried in that valley. It's like we had some kind of natural acoustics going on. Soon, Kid Rock was silenced and my colleagues were starting to take off their clothes.

Oh, hell no.

"Stop it!" I yelled.

They kept going.

Pants dropping. Shirts opening. Bras falling to the ground. "Stop it! This is not a sex party!" Did anyone even hear me? "No. Sex!"

"Why not?" someone hollered.

"You," I said, pointing to Doug the mechanic. "And you." I singled out Fran from supply. What did they say about mob actions? Call out individual people, let them know they were responsible for their own . . . "Oh, now that's just wrong, Cletus."

I found myself unable to look at half of them. "Can you just . . . cover yourselves?" I focused on the stars twinkling in the night sky. I was all for sex and blowing off steam, but, "I have a life-and-death issue to discuss and I'd rather not do it while eyeing your junk."

That got a laugh. I'm glad some people thought this was funny. Some of them were still undressing. Jesus Christ.

Fine. Out with it. "The entire camp is in danger. Right now." That shut some of them up. "I may not know much," like why the hell I put up with these people, "but I do know that in times of crisis, this camp comes together."

I cringed. Bad choice of words.

Damn them. Only about half of my colleagues were paying attention. I could feel my grip on the crowd slipping—if I'd even had one to begin with.

Jesus Christ, this is important!

These were intelligent, focused, war-seasoned people. If I could just get their attention.

Thank heaven Galen picked that moment to walk out of the cave at the base of the rocks. If he was feeling any of the worry and frustration that was going through my mind, he didn't show it. Well, he'd better do something quick because this was his idea.

A collective gasp went up from the people around him. He had that elite military bearing that even made them start standing a little straighter. He grinned as they stared. "Don't everyone greet me at once."

The crowd surged and Galen was treated to more hugs, back slaps, and jostling than I would have wanted from my overexposed colleagues. He caught my eye and flashed a too cocky smile.

What? Did he think we were in the clear with this? I didn't like it.

Galen walked straight for me. It took him a while, but that was okay. At least he was getting somewhere with the crowd, and I hoped to Hades he had a plan.

He climbed onto my rock. "You're doing good, Petra."

"Easy for you to say." I didn't want it on my head if the gods came down on my friends.

Galen stood tall beside me, enjoying the shouts from my colleagues. Of course he could instantly command both the attention and the loyalty of the entire camp. And look good doing it.

I didn't know whether I wanted to be happy or if I'd just rather push him off the rock.

He nudged me with his elbow. "We should have come clean right after I arrived in camp."

Was he kidding? "We weren't that desperate."

"Right," he said, surveying the crowd. "Well, I'm glad things are back to normal."

"Speak for yourself."

"For gods' sake, put some clothes on!" he hollered, as my colleagues continued to shout greetings.

The noise died down, and wouldn't you know it? They listened to him. The jerk. Add that to his resume: *Galen of Delphi can stop man-eating scorpions, soul-sucking Shrouds, and orgies.*

Galen cleared his throat. "We called you here to-night because we have a problem." He took a measured breath. "I'm thinking about harboring a fugitive."

"What did Petra do now?" someone shouted from the crowd.

Galen crossed his arms over his massive chest. "Can it, Lazio." But the crowd had already quieted. They were watching Galen with a level of focus they usually reserved for our commanding officer. Still, these were the same people that excelled at pranks and off-key karaoke.

I was stuck with that, and them. I loved them, but they were idiots. We were so screwed.

Galen's expression grew stony. "I was on a mission in the sixth quadrant. Hostile territory," he told them. "As you've seen, the other side is using dragons as weapons. I was under orders to acquire one."

A murmur spread across the crowd.

"I fulfilled my mission." Galen answered the unspoken question. "But the dragon I rescued is special. She's also injured, which is why I brought her here." He neglected to mention his own brush with death, or Leta's precarious grip on humanity. "If I turn her in, our side will interrogate and kill her."

"That's why the investigators are here!" someone else shouted.

Galen gave a curt nod. "I've gone off the grid while I figure out who's a friend and who's not. But it looks like someone at HQ suspects. They want her bad. But if I could just buy some time. Have a place to hide. If I can get through to her and rehabilitate her, we might have the key to ending the dragon bombers for good. Then I can deliver a solution to our side." Rather than an out-of-control weapon.

"Just tell our side not to kill her!" Fran the supply clerk shouted.

Galen shook his head. "Have you ever tried to reason with the gods?"

Obviously not. I had to appeal to their better selves, their innate sense of right and wrong. Deep down, and even half naked, they were good people. "The gods, even on our side, could kill first and ask questions later," I reminded them. "We have a chance here to do something different. To show some mercy." Isn't that why we'd gotten into medicine in the first place?

The crowd had gone silent, the tension palpable.

Baldie from the cafeteria crossed his arms over his chest. "You're asking us to commit treason."

He was right. I felt myself flush. I hadn't liked it one bit when Galen had dropped this in my lap back in the OR.

"I'm asking you to examine where your loyalties lie," Galen said simply. "Are you in it for what the gods tell you to do? Or do you want more than that? You save lives. And you're good at it. Now let's save these shifters before they end up as cannon fodder. Let's protect the dragon we have here in camp, so she's not murdered in the name of army security."

"Think about it," I said, "If we listened to orders, we wouldn't even be here. We wouldn't have the rocks or the minefield."

"A little fun is different than treason," a nurse grumbled.

"Give me one week," Galen said. It was more of an order than a request.

I had to admit, Galen had done wonders in the short time he'd been in camp before. He looked to Hume, whom he'd helped find his spirit. Marius had gained a new lair and the privacy he needed to keep himself sane. Even Jeffe had come out of his shell. Although we could do without him flaunting his new manicure.

Galen's voice carried above the crowd. "Whoever is with me, say so now." His tone demanded an answer, either way.

I found it impossible to take a deep breath as I

watched the faces in the crowd. They wanted to, I could tell they were torn. Damn it. I was scared too. I was the worst person in the world to try and talk anybody into this. But when I thought about it, I realized I'd already made my decision.

I'd sacrificed my safety the minute I'd agreed to treat Galen and Leta. A lot of us had. Leta was important, not only as a living, breathing being but as the key to the suicide bombers.

"I've seen investigators before," one of the guys from the motor pool called. "They will nail you to the wall. Literally."

True enough.

The crowd murmured its assent.

"I've got kids to worry about," another called.

Father climbed up next to me. "Everything carries risk. This too. We can't let them hurt us. We can't stand by while they hunt our friends. We have to find a nonviolent way to come together and fight this."

"Like you did?" someone in the crowd called. There was a smattering of applause.

Father and I exchanged a look. What did I say? Nothing was a secret.

"The investigators may be terrifying, but the number two pencils prove they have a great weakness," Father announced. "Like David facing Goliath, we can strike at that weakness and bring down the giant. We must hit them where it counts . . . Protocol."

"But Father!" Shirley yelled from the back. "They're getting new pencils in tomorrow. What do we do then?"

"Nail their hut door shut," Nurse Hume called.

"Too obvious," I countered. We had to make these tricks seem innocent. "This is not our usual 'set the guest showers on fire' mode of working. We have to innovate. Change."

We had to elevate practical jokes and useless stupidity to a whole new level.

Penny Henriksen in operations spoke up. "I think I accidentally left a box of pens in my pocket. I hope their uniforms don't go through laundry with mine. Regulation dictates they can't be seen in public without standard uniforms."

"I'm worried their forms are going to get lost," said Sheila Parsley, from supply.

"I hate it when the VIP shower gets a flying leech infestation," one of the maintenance workers announced. Thank the stars he'd put his pants back on.

"We may be running critically low on leech repellent," I added. "Hey, supply! What's the estimate on when we can get some in?"

"Eight years!" he called.

They were starting to laugh, I realized on an exhale. They were actually getting excited as they talked about the possibilities.

I was too.

Galen had been right—this camp did stick together. But we'd never pulled off anything this big before.

Matt Shively, a linebreaker of a man from supply, found his own small rock to stand on. "We can set up an extra tent. Out of the way. Keep it off the registry."

The clerks below him started yelling out suggestions. "Yeah, yeah. And a uniform. Furniture . . ."

"I'll do ID," Lazio called.

"I'll do *legal* ID," Shirley countered, then caught herself. "Well, close enough."

Lazio stood in the middle of the mechanics. "We can do it. We can own these assholes."

The crowd began clapping.

We could. I glanced at Galen, then said as loudly as my voice would let me, "We can take this camp's need to perform stupid and outrageous pranks and use it for the good of mankind."

People were high-fiving and cheering now.

"Do we want to do some kind of central command?" I called down to Lazio, not sure at all where this was headed.

He winked. "The less you know, the better."

Oh, yeah, that was really great for a control freak like me. I glanced at Galen. "This could go so wrong so fast."

"Have a little faith," he said, looking a little too confident for my taste.

This was going to be like the minefield, plus the sea monster breeding disaster with a heaping pile of chaos thrown on top. And to make it worse, it wasn't like we were sneaking in a kitten and feeding it under the bed. No. We had to hide a fricking dragon.

Something had to give.

Still, if we could hold it together long enough for Marc to stabilize Leta and for Galen to find a port in the storm for both of them, we just might pull this one off.

chapter thirteen

I managed to keep my head on straight until the meeting degenerated into chitchat, pats on the back, and lengthy discussions of how great it was to have Galen back, if only for a little while.

I slipped out and headed up the path, toward the minefield.

"Yo!" Rodger called from behind me. I kept walking and he jogged to catch up, falling into a long-legged stride beside me. His torch bobbed with every step.

Why did I keep forgetting to bring a torch?

"You didn't say good-bye," Rodger huffed next to me.

I was done being polite. "I'm not your girlfriend."

"No, but you're Galen's—"

"Rodger!"

"Never mind," he said, as if I were the one being unreasonable. "I know when to shut up."

No he didn't.

I could see my nosy friend out of the corner of my eye. Watching me.

He sighed. "Why do you always have to make things so hard?"

Me? "That's rich." Things would be perfectly easy if people would just leave me alone. "I'm not the one waltzing into camp with a dangerous fugitive. I'm not the one who thought it was a good idea to come clean to everyone from deputy supply to mess hall table washer." Yes, I'd agreed to it. But now, I felt so *exposed*.

Rodger balked. "It could work."

We took a left, through the darkened maze of the minefield. I stared straight ahead, keeping my eyes on the path. Nighttime shadows seemed to come alive in the desert.

"Okay," Rodger mused. "Yes. I admit it. Somebody in camp will screw up eventually. But we only need to pull this off for a week, and then he'll be gone."

Yes, he would.

Rodger kept at it. "I think it's good that people know what's going on. Teaming up like this will keep the investigators off our backs longer."

"Maybe," I said. It was as much as he was going to get out of me at the moment.

Of course Galen could draw people together, and, sure, he was willing to blindly trust in the universe, but I knew firsthand what it was like to be screwed over.

I puffed out a breath of air, and saw it form a cloud in front of me. "I just want Galen to find a safe approach, and be able to handle Leta so they can both leave."

Rodger held the torch high while I squeezed between two wrecked Jeeps. "You need to give the guy a break."

"I never should have told you anything," I said, avoiding broken windshield glass.

Rodger shoved through after me. "Why does it have to be all or nothing with you?"

I wanted to tip him straight into a wrecked cannon cart. "Because that's the way love works." Even Mister "I married the right girl and now I run through daisy patches" had to see that. I stared up at the red moon. I was right. I knew I was right.

Maybe that was my problem with Marc. I couldn't love him deeply enough. And when that happens, you have to let go.

Of course, I had to let Galen go as well. So maybe my theory was all bullshit.

"Okay," Rodger said, as if that settled it.

"What do you mean?" I asked, suspicious all of a sudden.

He nudged me along. "You've made your decision."

"Ha." I was nothing if not decisive.

"If you want to be miserable, that's up to you."

Suddenly, it wasn't as much fun to win.

I wrapped my arms around me, feeling the chill of the night. To hell with it. I didn't need Rodger's approval. Or Galen's. Or anyone else's.

I was used to being alone. I'd proven time and time again that I could count on myself. It would just have to be enough.

The next day, I sat brushing my hair after a shower. Rodger huddled on his bed, reading letters from his kids. And Marc was outside, pounding on our door.

"Petra!" He was going to put a hole through the mesh screen if he wasn't careful. He had dark circles under his eyes, and a wild look about him. His uniform was ripped at the neck. "Come with me. Now. I've got a problem with Leta."

Worse than before? "What happened?" I opened the door, but he didn't come in. He smelled like he'd been sleeping in the minefield.

He raked a hand through his hair. It spilled out in wild spikes. "I've been up all night. She's fighting me." His eyes caught mine. "This could get ugly."

Of all the . . . "How am I supposed to help with a dragon?"

His jaw flexed. "I may need medical assistance." He turned and began walking as if he'd expected me to follow.

Oh, great. We were about to get violent. At least Marc planned ahead.

"Damn," Rodger said as I grabbed my medical kit. "I got your shift."

"Thanks, buddy." I banged out the door after Marc.

I had to jog to catch up with him as he wove in and out of the maze of officers' tents. Even then, it was tough to keep up. "What happened last night?" I asked.

His jaw was bruised, his body drawn tight. It looked as if he hadn't slept in a week. "I took her out past the helipad. She knows she needs me, but still she fought me every step of the way."

I focused on the dusty path that wound through the low-slung tents. "Did you battle it out, or did you . . . ?"

I suddenly didn't want to know the answer. I thought I could be mature about this, but no, I was jealous as hell. It was completely selfish and illogical because I didn't have a right to him anymore. Still, I couldn't say it. I couldn't ask him if he'd fucked her.

"No," he said, stark aggression hardening his features. "She nearly took my head off. She's not accepting me as her alpha. She's on the edge of the cliff and I've got to get her to back down."

Good luck with that. "What are you going to do?"

"I'm going to teach her control," he gritted out.

Shit. The stark reality of it sank in. He was a dragon. She was a dragon. This was going to get nasty.

We needed more help. "What about Galen?" I hated to bring him into this after everything that had happened, but—

"He's already on the way."

"Good." I shifted my medical kit from one sweaty hand to the other. I was glad Marc could see beyond what had happened with Galen.

The three of us together at least had a fighting chance. I hoped.

For better or worse, Marc and I tended to approach things the same way. It made us good partners. Bad lovers.

But I wasn't going to dwell on that right now.

Not with Marc practically snarling next to me.

Up ahead, Galen stood in the shadows between the OR and Kosta's office. He looked completely edible in a rust-red helicopter flight suit. Nice cover.

The pilot scenario might have even helped him

blend in, if it weren't for the raw masculinity that made me take a second look. And a third.

Galen stood, shoulders back, his gaze lingering on me. "You ready?" He reached into the shadow of the tent next to him and pulled out a weapons belt, complete with a long sword.

"Way to be inconspicuous," I said as he buckled it on.

He drew the thick leather straps tight. "The inspectors are in the triage clinic, being tested for dragon pox."

That was weird. "We haven't had a case of that since . . ." Then it hit me. "Right."

My colleagues didn't waste any time.

We made our way through the shadows and out back. The sun beat down, warming the top of my head as we headed west, past quarantine and up toward the large cliff face that served as our helicopter station.

On top of the half-mountain of dirt and rocks, we had four choppers, five landing pads, and an emergency triage unit. We might have a few mechanics up there, but no one to report us.

The awareness of Galen, right next to me, thudded dully in my gut.

Yes, it was hard to be close to him, but I had to bury the emotion and focus on the job. I'd done it more times than I could count as a professional. Even if this was personal, we had serious work to do.

If Leta lost control, we could get a lot of people hurt—or worse. And if we couldn't rehab her before

Galen was forced to take her back, or before the inspectors learned what was happening in camp . . . I didn't even want to think about it.

My colleagues—my friends—had trusted us to make this right. They'd given Galen and Leta a place to live, given us a place and the freedom to work. I refused to blow this just because I had a hard time being around Galen.

His hand rested on the hilt of his sword. He was on high alert. Every movement was focused, smooth, as he guarded against what lay ahead.

Marc was watching him too. His hand went to the scar on his neck, the one he'd gotten when he'd been attacked by new army forces and nearly slaughtered.

One of our own soldiers had been ordered to slit his throat, but the man pulled his blade at the last minute, for which I'd be eternally grateful.

Marc watched Galen through narrowed eyes. "I finally remember how I know you."

Galen gave a stiff nod at his rival, and at the scar slicing across his jugular. "I'm just glad I got there in time to stop it."

It took me a second to put it together. "Jesus. Was it you, Galen?" He'd never said anything about it before, and yet, I could see the truth settle between them.

Galen was the one who'd saved Marc all those years ago. Without planning it, without ever knowing, he'd made it possible for Marc to come back to me.

Because he was a good man.

And then he'd watched as Marc claimed me.

He hadn't said a word. Maybe he hadn't recognized Marc at first either.

Galen looked distinctly uncomfortable as he avoided my line of questioning, choosing to focus on Marc instead. The corner of his mouth tipped up. "You can owe me one."

Marc's sharp glare caught me, before shifting to Galen. "I owe you nothing."

Marc stopped in front of an opening in the rock face, a cave from the look of it. Beyond it, a flat, red wasteland stretched out into an endless desert.

He was still glaring at Galen. "Watch yourself," he said to me as we made our way inside.

The cavern was huge, much bigger than I'd imagined from the outside. It stood at least four stories tall. Quartz crystals pierced the ceiling and littered the floor. The wide entrance narrowed into a long, darkened chamber. Leta stood in the dusky back, shaking despite the heat of the desert.

Her eyes were hollowed and her breath came quick as Marc approached her. She dipped her head, and a curtain of hair fell over her face. "Leave me alone."

His steps were steady. There was no mistaking the steel in his voice. "I'm here to help you, Leta."

"I'm fine," she snapped. "I'm in control," she practically shouted.

Galen drew close enough to murmur in my ear. "I've got you."

"I hope," I murmured. This didn't look good.

He slid a protective hand down my back. I felt it every inch of the way.

Lightning quick, Leta tried to bolt around Marc. She cried out as he caught her by the wrist. "I don't need you as master over me!" She clawed at his eyes with her one free hand as he dragged her close. He pinned her to the wall and she let out a long and anguished roar. "I've had a master long enough!"

Holy hell. She *roared*.

Marc restrained her against the wall, his arms shaking. He had a grip on both of her wrists now. His body lay thigh to thigh, chest to chest against hers. "This is the way it has to be," he growled. "You're a danger to everyone, including—oof—yourself."

"Galen," I started, my pulse thudding in my ears.

His grip on me tightened.

The cave suddenly seemed very small.

If Leta had started spitting fire, I wouldn't have been surprised.

"You don't own me!" she shrieked. "You can't control me! I've been controlled half of my life. Tied down. Manipulated. Shackled. I finally have freedom and I'll be damned if I'll be tied again." She head-butted him, snapping his neck back.

His grip tightened. He shoved her up against the wall once, twice. "You've already taken a part of me."

The heart string. I'd seen it in the OR.

She went after him with teeth and claws. He pulled sideways, but he had her roped in too close and her teeth sliced his shoulder.

She whipped her head back, hair tangling in her eyes. "I didn't ask for that! I didn't ask you to save my life. Let's end it. Right now." Her teeth were bloody, her eyes wild. "Let's see who wants to live and who wants to die."

Seven hells. She wasn't just a wild dragon, she was completely unhinged.

She was an old army weapon, ready to be unleashed. On us.

Marc stiffened and shook as he held her at arm's length. "You need to get a fucking grip."

"You haven't been a dragon in years." She snarled. "I can smell it on you. Human." She spat it as if it were a curse.

"Enough!" Marc lowered his head, the air around him shimmering as his body expanded—shoulders, chest, haunches. Silver scales raced down his back and steam hissed from his snout.

Galen drew his sword and yanked me to his side. "Move. Now." Together we backed up toward the mouth of the cave.

Marc had shifted into an immense silver dragon. He bellowed, the sound pounding off the cave walls.

Fire shot from his snout. Shit on a biscuit. "My ex is a fucking dragon."

I'd always known he was a dragon. I'd ridden on his back. But I'd never seen this side of him before.

Leta bent over, screaming. The muscles in her back expanded, muscle and sinew and bone refitting. Her skin formed scales, her hands and feet morphed into six-clawed talons that could rip a person apart. Her neck lengthened and her body expanded until she grew to the size of a horse, then larger still. Hard plates formed and re-formed along her underbelly, racing to keep up with her expanding form.

The ground vibrated as she rose up to her full height.

"Holy fuck," Galen said under his breath.

Leta snarled while I stood rooted to the spot, looking up at a huge, bronze dragon.

Leta bared her teeth. Marc hissed and launched himself straight at her. Holy fuck was right. Leta slid sideways, directly at us as we scrambled to get the hell out of the way of two angry dragons.

Galen and I dashed outside. The full sun made me see spots as we planted ourselves against the cliff face. I gasped for breath, shading my eyes to see as Leta rolled sideways out onto the hot desert plain.

Marc charged after her as she regained her footing, the sun glinting off her scales.

I could hardly believe it. I pounded the rock face with my hand. It hurt like a bitch, but I needed to feel something, know something besides the prophecy echoing through my head: *The healer shall receive a bronze weapon.*

I'd never seen a bronze dragon—complete with a tail, fangs, and honest-to-god bronze spikes running down her back. "Why? Why couldn't it just be the dagger?"

Galen closed his hand over mine and yanked it back, my blood slickening our skin. "You said you didn't want it."

"I lied."

This was it. Fate was giving me the finger.

An array of needlelike whiskers framed her long, bottle-shaped face. Massive wings unfurled at her back. *With it, the healer shall arrest the gods.*

At least I could control the bronze dagger, keep it hidden in my pocket. It was a weapon I could use.

There was no way I'd ever get a handle on Leta.

The dragon chomped at the air, black smoke trailing from her nostrils.

"How the hell am I supposed to control that?" Marc couldn't even get her to work with him and he *was* a dragon.

Leta growled low in her throat and shot a massive fireball into the air. She beat her wings, struggling to go airborne.

Oh, no, no, no. She couldn't leave. She couldn't be seen.

"Where the hell is she going?" I scrambled sideways to avoid the swipe of a tail.

Galen covered me, sword in hand. I wasn't sure what he planned to do with it. It's not like he was going to stab her. It would just piss her off.

She let out a bloodcurdling roar and banked straight toward camp.

Marc slammed into her, sending them both flying sideways.

Galen flanked them, dashing around the side of the battle and putting himself on the hill between the dragon and the camp.

"Galen!" It was ridiculous. I started to run after him, then took a bunch of quick steps back. With every reason on God's green Earth to do so. It was insane. He was human. He couldn't do anything.

Marc barrel-rolled Leta and I watched in horror as her teeth sank into his side. She shoved off him. He stumbled back and she charged straight for Galen.

He drew a heavy chain from his belt. It expanded in his hands and it had better hold eighteen other kinds of magic too because he was going to need a hell of a lot more than a dragon collar to stop her.

chapter fourteen

Blood pounded in my ears and every instinct I had screamed for Galen to get out of the way.

But he couldn't. She was heading for camp. We had to stop her or the first thing she'd hit would be the recovery tent.

We couldn't reason with her.

We couldn't shoot her.

No, not unless it was a last resort.

He had to collar her.

The chain connected to a black, spiked loop.

If she got past him, it was all over.

Leta saw the collar and completely lost her mind. She reared her head and shot a fireball directly at Galen.

He dodged sideways. I screamed. He somehow missed the fiery blast, his uniform singed. "Alala!" He yelled the Athenian battle cry as he took a running leap at her.

She whipped out her claws and sliced at him.

Holy shit. "Galen!"

He kept going. He grabbed hold of her massive neck. She twisted, trying to bite him, but he was too close to her head. Her spikes tore into his chest and neck. She bucked like a wild horse and flung him off.

Galen rolled sideways. He was bleeding, his flight suit torn.

I'd never felt so helpless in my life. He was nearly killed by the first bronze weapon. What was I saying? He did die. Now he was about to be annihilated by this one. He wouldn't survive another direct attack.

He was trapped between her and the side of the hill, with nowhere to run as she raised her spiked tail to crush him.

"Here!" I cried, throat parched, voice raw as I rushed the dragon.

Marc tackled me, his silver body trapping me against the ground, as the dragon launched fire at us. The heat of it tore into me, a sickening burst of superheated death.

Marc pulled away and I crawled a few paces before stumbling to my feet. I'd seen burn victims. I knew what would happen. I checked my arms, my legs, my hands. "I'm clean," I said, shaky, my voice tilting wildly. What the hell?

Or was I so badly burned that I was delirious?

Marc launched himself onto Leta, rolling her back down the hill, nearly taking me with them.

My knees were rubber as I rushed to Galen.

"Go. Now," he said, dragging me with him. I ran my hands across his chest, up his arms, ecstatic to have him all in one piece. He checked me over as well, which was annoying because I was somehow fine, but he wasn't.

He'd taken a hit to the shoulder, possibly the chest. I didn't know how bad.

I gasped for breath as Galen and I stumbled back to the cave, narrowly avoiding Marc as he rolled Leta onto her back.

Claws ripped. Jaws snapped. Marc caught her around the neck and she roared with fury. She shoved him off and he careened straight at us.

We dodged together, Galen's hand in mine.

"This way!" Galen ordered, as Marc's thrashing, spiked tail smashed into the ground not two feet in front of me. Dust and debris rained down.

My eyes watered and I choked as I clutched Galen's hand, running for all I was worth. He shoved me flush against the cliff face and covered my body with his.

"We're going to die," I said against his neck. They were going to stomp us, and what was worse, they wouldn't even notice.

"Not today," he said, turning to watch the two dragons, locked together, rolling over and over in the sand. At least they were moving away from camp. For the moment.

Marc let out a bellow and forced Leta onto her back. She snapped wildly as he closed his jaws over her neck. She struggled, keening as he locked his mouth over her underscales, drawing blood.

I gasped. "What is he going to do? Kill her?" Marc wasn't a murderer, but who knew what he'd do in the throes of dragon blood lust.

"No." Galen's grip on me tightened. "Watch."

Leta's body loosened and the fight drained out of her. She groaned helplessly, bellowing out every so often, as Marc held her steady. Then gently, slowly, he let her go.

They lay still for a moment, before she touched her snout to his and let out a low huff.

He huffed in return, and then gave a half snarl, half purr as she nuzzled his face.

"Oh," I said, red-faced. They weren't fighting at all.

Galen pulled back. "Let's give them their privacy."

I turned my attention to his shoulder, next to his torn collar. "You're hurt."

"It's nothing," he said, his voice throaty, as I stroked my fingers down the uninjured part of his neck.

My heart pounded. "That's your adrenaline talking." He was lucky to be alive.

We made our way just inside the cave, away from the dragons and the battlefield.

I went straight for my medical kit. "What kind of a doctor would I be if I let you bleed to death?"

I tried to make light of it, but the truth was, I didn't know what I'd do if something happened to him. I needed this moment to see for myself that he was all right.

He'd planted his back in a nook of rock just inside the entrance. He was breathing heavily as I found the zipper of his flight suit under the notch of his collar. I lowered it, exposing a gash to his chest, the torn flesh on his upper arm.

"It's not bad," he murmured.

"Always the hero," I said, preparing medicated gauze to clean him.

He let me. The muscles in his throat worked as I

touched him, cared for him. It was all I could do at that moment.

Luckily, the wounds appeared shallow. The thick flight suit had absorbed the worst of the trauma.

He'd risked his life for me. Again. And he'd driven Leta away from our friends.

And if he left tomorrow?

At that moment, it didn't matter that he was leaving, that this war would never end. He was here with me. Alive. Protecting me.

I curled my fingers around the back of his neck and kissed him.

His breath whooshed in surprise before he took me in a searing kiss that made me forget everything but the heat of his lips and the feel of him against me.

We were alive. We'd made it and I was damned if I was going to let this moment pass.

Heat poured through me as I met him full force with lips and teeth and tongue. It was impossible and insane and I needed it more than I needed my next breath.

He dragged me against him and I felt every hard inch of him, primed and ready for me, just like in my fantasies. Only this time, he was real and he needed me just as much as I needed him.

We surged together, grinding, pushing, pulling as if this were all we had. One kiss. And if we stopped, we might never have it again.

His hand shoved down my pants and his fingers found my pulsing hot core. God, I was so wet for him. Needles of pleasure shot up my spine as he slid his callused fingers through my delicate folds. The friction was unbelievable.

We both gasped as he slipped a finger inside me.

I needed him. I needed more. I needed . . .

I unzipped his flight suit in one fluid motion and opened it up like the best present I'd ever gotten. His chest was sculpted, his abs a work of art. I ran my hand lower. His cock strained, hard, hot, and throbbing. He hissed out a breath as I took it in hand.

God, I'd missed this. I knew just how he liked it. I held him tight, ran my hand down the underside. I used the other to grasp his balls. His cock lurched and he groaned, lifting me, pinning me back against the sandy rock as he shoved his cock into me.

Sweet Jesus. I gasped as he filled me completely. He wrapped a fisted hand behind my shoulders, hissing as he worked me hard. I wrapped my legs around his hips, his other hand clutching my ass as he rode me.

There was no holding back. No flowers or songs or poetry. He took me with pure, unleashed need. He pinned me against the wall with his rock-hard cock.

Pure shining lust surged through me. God, what I would give to own this. To have him be mine.

Our breathing was shallow. Our gasps echoing off the walls of the chamber.

Pleasure swamped me. He was here. Now. "Mine." I nipped him on the shoulder, on the ear, ground my mouth in that sweet spot under his chin as he pumped furiously.

The pleasure built. My entire body sang with the need to have him. To fuck him. To take him all in and to be with this man the most elemental way possible.

"I want you to come," I hissed. "Come inside me."

His breath caught. I was so close. "Come," I urged,

gasping, shaking as I exploded around him. I felt him grow even harder inside me, he groaned my name and his powerful body shuddered as he shot his hot seed inside me.

chapter fifteen

We stayed in the desert cave for the rest of the afternoon, which gave Galen time to make love to me twice more. I should have said no, or at least reined him in and not let him go down on me for that blissful lust-soaked hour, because truly—nothing had changed.

Leta had an excuse for her wild animal side.

Me? Not so much.

It wasn't that I didn't love Galen. I did. But we were both at the mercy of the gods. He was going back to war and he was going to break my heart.

Now was the time for damage control. Or at least some sanity.

If I could only find it.

Presently, I was laid out on top of him, too content to move. But damn it, when did I ever do anything for myself?

I only wanted a few more minutes. Then I'd be a sane person and never touch him again.

His large hand caressed my back in lazy circles.

"What are you doing tomorrow?" His chest rumbled under my cheek.

I tried to think. I'd asked off for something. My breath caught. "Oh, frick. I have Medusa's baby shower." Guilt pricked at me when I realized I hadn't even thought of a gift. In all fairness, I'd had a few things on my mind.

His hand stilled. "Where?"

"Her place." What did the invite say? "The Isle of Wrath and Pain." Come to think of it, a gift was the least of my problems.

He stiffened underneath me. "I'll take you."

I rose up on my forearm, bracing it on his massive chest. His jaw was set, his expression inviting absolutely no debate. Not that I didn't appreciate the gesture, but, "Don't you have enough on your plate?"

His brow knitted. "You're my girlfriend. There's no way in hell I'd let you go out there by yourself."

I sat up. His gaze caught my breasts and I quickly covered them with my hands. "I'm not your girlfriend. I'm not your anything," I clarified, realizing how terrible it sounded since we'd just spent half the day making love.

His eyes narrowed. Oh, I'd pissed him off. Good.

"I love you," he said, as if it were a contact sport.

Of all the . . . "I love you too," I said, standing, "but that doesn't mean we're in a relationship."

"Then what the hell does it mean?" He rose to his feet as I tried desperately to find my pants.

You're screwing this up, a part of me screamed. The other part of me realized that it did no good to live in a fantasyland, especially where Galen was concerned.

"You said it yourself," I reminded him, navigating the uneven rock floor of the cave, locating my scrubs, dragging them on. "Your job is with your unit. There is no way you're not going back eventually." Then on to the next assignment, and the next.

I spotted my underwear on the ground by his flight suit and grabbed it, stuffing it in my pocket. "Admit it. You're going to ditch me—us—the minute you think any of those security checks or background checks or whatever you go through is going to expose me."

He glared at me. He was naked, frustrated, and unable to say a word. Because I was right.

We needed to stop the debate. Right now. It wouldn't do either of us any good to want what we could never have.

"Think of it this way." He advanced on me and I found myself backing up a step. Two. Until I felt the warm rock wall against my back. "We're almost through the prophecies. You have your bronze weapon."

"Yes. It's been lovely."

He ignored my sarcasm.

He pinched his fingers together. "We are this close and you want to cut and run."

"Close?" I wanted to laugh. Or perhaps cry. It didn't matter. "We don't know what the prophecies are going to be. It could take the oracle a day, a week, or a god-damned decade to come up with the next one."

He held his hands out. "And what are you doing in the meantime?" Like I was supposed to jump him.

Well, in case he hadn't noticed, "In the meantime, I've got an ER full of burn victims and a kamikaze dragon on my hands."

"You think I don't know that?"

"Then don't talk like it's a fucking walk in the park."

"Hey, I know this doesn't look good. Every day is hard. I get that. But you know what? You and me? We're all we've got." He drew close enough to kiss. "One of these days, you're going to have to learn to trust that."

I twisted away from him, toward my shoes, my sanity. "You make it sound so easy." Well, it wasn't. And we were not in control. "It could take the next fifty years to complete these prophecies." If we even survived that long. "And at what cost?"

He was pissed. I could see I was frustrating the hell out of him. Tough. I couldn't make things easy just because he wanted them that way.

"What if you're wrong?" he demanded.

I gave him my best level stare. "What if you are?" I sighed, dug a hand through my messy hair. I had to get out of here. "I'm going to Medusa's on my own tomorrow."

He frowned. "No you're not."

It wasn't his choice. It was mine. "You're not invited. She's sending transportation for one." Me. "I don't need you."

He wasn't buying it. Shit.

His face was deadly. His voice rough. "Because right here. Just now didn't mean anything."

"It can't," I said simply.

He cringed like I'd delivered a physical blow. "We need each other, Petra, we always have. I never wanted to fight this war. I did it because it was my duty. But this? What we're fighting for—what we have between us—this is worth dying a hundred times over." He towered over me, as if he expected me to say something. To make it right. But I didn't know how. "How long are you going to punish me?" His frustration, his anger, his sadness radiated from him.

"It's not about that."

His expression went cold. "Then I don't know what else to say to you."

We dressed in silence. His movements were jerky. Mine resigned, accepting.

I wasn't going to kill myself trying to have what was impossible. It was the most sane decision I'd made all day.

So why didn't I feel even the remotest slice of peace?

When we left the cave, we saw Marc and Leta a short distance away. The two dragons had resumed their human form and sat out on a rock, naked, in deep conversation. They had obviously found some kind of common ground.

Maybe she'd try not to go bat crazy and attack him all the time. And he'd try to help her control her dragon impulses.

If only it were that easy.

Galen raised a hand, and Marc nodded.

My ex had it handled. For now, at least.

And so, we moved on.

Galen walked me back to my tent and stopped at the door.

"When I left you, I did it because I had to, not because I stopped loving you."

"Fine," I said, voice wavering. "Perfect."

He didn't even look back as he walked away.

I changed clothes because let's face it—I could use some new underwear. Then I headed over to see if I could lend an extra set of hands. Rodger was working a double for me. The least I could do was lighten some of the load.

Recovery was still jammed. Over half of our patients were burn victims, and those kinds of cases took time, even for immortals. Most of them would never fully recover. And if they did, they'd carry the scars for the rest of their lives, however long or short that might be.

It was so wrong, such a waste.

Peace would come too late for these soldiers, if it ever came at all. There would be no happy endings. No joyful homecomings.

At least I was giving the rest of the staff a break.

"My name is Dr. Robichaud," I said to the soldier in bed 15B. Private Kenny Jones. Suffering from third-degree burns to more than twenty percent of his body, as well as inhalation injuries. He was pale, his fingers twitchy. His chart said he was from Pensacola.

"Hey, I'm from New Orleans," I told him. "We're practically neighbors." He let out a choke that could have been a laugh or an acknowledgment. "Don't talk," I said quickly. We'd intubated him to drain fluid off his lungs. I smiled, as if I were sharing a joke rather than listening to him choke on his own fluids. "You just get to listen to me."

Private Jones was lucky. He was a wereleopard and

shifters—feline shifters in particular—didn't usually make it this far with half their lungs burned out. He closed his eyes, nodding, listening as I made small talk about home while I worked to send him back into battle.

This man's life as he knew it—at home in the deep south, surrounded by his family and his tribe—that was over. War had taken it from him and he'd never be the same. We could play "normal" all we wanted. But some scars never heal.

And no amount of zippedy-do-dah "look to the future" bullshit was going to change that.

I glanced up from my patient, down the rows of beds crowding either side of the long recovery tent. These soldiers deserved some privacy, or at least a quiet place to suffer. But we were at capacity. I didn't know what we'd do if we got another influx of wounded.

Rodger nudged in next to me when I was back at the sink washing up. "How'd it go with Leta?"

The ward had grown quiet for the night, the patients settling in as best they could. I kept my voice down and gave Rodger the short version on how Marc had dominated Leta, and how they seemed to be connecting.

"Good." He blew out his breath, like we'd dodged a bullet. Which we had. "Now how did it go with Galen?"

I dropped the soap.

Rodger fished it out of the bottom of the sink. "You're right. You don't have any business going near him." He scrubbed the bar over his brawny arms. "It would only end with you whimpering and me trying to pick up the pieces."

Actually, it had ended in a screaming orgasm, but I wasn't about to tell him that. I rinsed and grabbed for a towel.

Rodger shook his head. "I mean, you obviously love the guy. Why torture yourself?" He glanced at me. "See? You have that look again. It was bad enough the first time," he muttered under his breath.

"I'm fine," I said, tossing him the towel.

He glanced at me. "All I'm saying is you need a clear head right now."

Then he needed to stop talking about sex.

He tossed the towel in the laundry barrel. "Otherwise, we really are fucked."

Case in point.

"I'm not going to be around anyway," I said, changing the subject. "Medusa's shower is tomorrow." That would at least give me a day to clear my head.

"Right," Rodger said, smiling for the first time. He had retrieved part of the invite and set it up on his desk. The stone hearts amused him. "Did she ever say what kind of 'transport' she was sending?"

"No." Nerves clawed at me. "I'm just supposed to wait by the tar pit tomorrow." Maybe this journey would kill me. It would at least put me out of my misery.

We walked up to the front to pick up our new charts. "What are you going to give her?" he asked.

"I have no idea." What did a gorgon expect when she was expecting? "It's not like she's registered at Babies 'R' Us."

"You should have been shopping before now."

"Where? At the PX?" At that rate, I'd be buying her shower shoes and stale Fruit Stripe gum.

"Maybe you can make her something."

He had to be kidding. "Have you seen me make anything in the last seven years?"

Rodger snorted. "I haven't even seen you make your bed."

"Maybe I'll get called away on an emergency," I said, leaning against the nurses' station, glancing out at our patient load. It's not as if they didn't need me here.

Rodger dug through the charts. "You can't skip. You RSVP'd."

"No, you did."

Holly barged past me. "Out of my way." She took the charts from Rodger. "Stop it. These are done. We're all caught up, if you can believe that."

I strained my eyes to see down into the pools of darkness settling over the unit. "Who's on night?"

She glanced down the row of beds. "Thaïs and Marius."

"Dang." I knew it was late, but, "Marius is on already?"

"Has been for hours," Holly replied. "You really do need to get out more."

I could say the same about her. Rodger and I signed out, and headed for home.

A harsh wind blew in from the desert, buffeting the flames of the torches. "I really should make my excuses for tomorrow." No good could come of a trip out to the Isle of Wrath and Pain.

Rodger dug his hands into his pockets. "You will not. It's one day out of your life. I'll even help you find a present."

I breathed in the tang of torch fuel and desert dust. "I am not getting her anything Star Wars."

"Girls like Star Wars."

"Rodger," I snapped. But really, what was the use? I didn't have anything to give her. The entirety of my worldly possessions consisted of uniforms, books, and my shower kit. And she wasn't getting any of my books. Not that she'd appreciate them anyway.

Back at the tent, I rolled down the shades while Rodger lit the lanterns. The wind off the desert was chilling me to the core. I pulled on my New Orleans Zephyrs jacket while Rodger dragged a crate from under his bed.

He unhinged the lid. "Take a look at this."

Inside was a good portion of his rock collection. While I tried to work some circulation into my cold fingers, he started pulling out various trays, lined with felt.

I appreciated the thought, but, "I can't get her a rock."

"Oh ye of little faith," Rodger tsked. He drew out a white velvet bundle and proceeded to unwrap a gorgeous pink crystal cluster. He held it out to me and I watched as the lantern light caught the facets of the crystal. "It's cobaltoan calcite. Used to stimulate love and beauty."

I snarfed. "In that case, we need a truckload."

Rodger shrugged. "It's symbolic. And it's yours if you want it."

It was sweet, but, "I don't know. Do you have any crystal skulls?"

He handed the pink calcite to me. It felt heavier than

expected. I had to admit it was pretty. And unique. "You don't think she'll think this is too girly?"

"She's having a girl," Rodger said, as if pink and girls went together like . . . oh, I guess they did. He turned back to his collection and began putting the trays away. "Shopping's over. Five minutes is my limit."

Men. They never changed, no matter the species.

I hefted the rock. It really was pretty. "Thanks, buddy."

He tossed me the velvet cloth and I rewrapped it. If I had time, I'd grab some pink medical tape and make a bow.

"Maybe you should come with me," I mused.

"No way." Rodger flopped down on his cot. "I don't do showers. Besides, tomorrow's my day off. I plan to waste it in front of the TV."

I placed the rock on my dresser and began shucking off my boots. "Don't you ever get tired of it?" Our television only got one station—PNN. And there was only so much of it I could take.

Rodger stretched out on his back. "Nah. Especially not with the new prophecy coming in."

I dropped my boot.

"See what you miss when you're out playing with dragons?" He rose up on his elbows. "Yeah. Evidently, the healer got a bronze weapon."

I cleared my throat.

Of course I did. The oracles sure didn't waste any time.

"They're back to their soothsaying," he said, bunching up his pillow and lying back down. "The media is going nuts."

"Glad I'm going to miss it," I said, heart pounding, lying through my teeth. Whatever the oracles predicted could impact me immediately. I needed warning. I needed to know as soon as it happened, exactly what I was going to face.

If only the oracles worked that way.

The next morning, I stood out waiting by the tar swamp, still unsure as to exactly what kind of transportation one took to a gorgon baby shower.

Please let it be a jeep. Or as long as I was wishing: a tank.

There was no telling how far it was to the Island of Wrath and Pain, but I had a pretty good idea it wasn't a hop, skip, and a jump around the corner. I hadn't seen a puddle of water, much less a lake, since I'd left home all those years ago.

At least I'd get to see Medusa. She'd canceled on her last prenatal appointment. The poor mom-to-be was scared to death of dragon pox. I tried to explain to her that being half rattlesnake, she couldn't get the disease (even if the camp had been truly infested—which it wasn't), but it was no use. Once the gorgon got something in her head, well, it was set in stone.

My fingers tightened on the handle of my medical kit. My other hand held the wrapped-up rock.

I was still trying to figure out how I'd gotten myself into this.

"You see anything?" Rodger yelled from the window of our hutch.

"No," I said, my voice carrying over the tar pits. If

he wanted to talk to me, he could walk over here like a normal person.

And then, I saw something in the distance. It looked almost like a horse. Dang, what I wouldn't give to see Marc's friend Oghul at this moment. He was a berserker, and a little rough around the edges, but his enchanted horse was a wicked fast ride.

Whatever it was, it was kicking up an enormous dust cloud.

As it got closer, I saw the animal had shaggy fur. There was no man, or berserker, on it at all. Rather, it had two heads. No, three!

Dread clenched low in my stomach.

This creature could be coming for something else. But no, it was hurtling directly for me.

"What the hell is that?" Rodger hollered.

It was the size of our tent, with the shaggy, muscled body of a lion. It roared as it charged straight for the place where I stood.

Cripes. The thing really did have three heads. The largest was that of a lion. It snarled as the creature skidded to a stop inches from where I stood. I choked on the dust and the heat and the acidic gamy stench of the beast.

The lion's head huffed, bathing my face with its humid breath. The second head looked like a big, ugly, hairy half-possessed goat. It champed its teeth, and I dodged to avoid twisted horns as long as my arm.

The third head, that of a cobra, was attached to the beast's tail. It coiled over the body as the hind legs thumped to the ground. The soil beneath my feet vibrated with the impact as the serpent hissed and showed its fangs.

"Fuck no." I dropped my bag and backed away slowly.

I breathed heavily, trying not to show fear. If it attacked . . . hell, I didn't know what I'd do.

Maybe I could bash it over the head with my crystal. While the other two heads ate me.

It was a chimera—part lion, part goat, part serpent. They were known for their bad tempers and their willingness to devour nearly anything made of meat.

And oh, look, it had a little saddle on the back of its massive body.

I backed up toward Rodger and my tent, afraid to take my eyes off the thing. "Rodger?"

No response.

Goddamnit. Where was he?

"Rodger . . ." Every instinct I had screamed for me to run. But I didn't dare. Fleeing equaled prey.

But each step I took backward, the beast followed me, mouths snarling, fangs drooling. It wasn't letting me go. At this rate, it was going to follow me straight into camp.

"Rodger!" I yelled at the top of my lungs.

Footsteps crunched on the sand behind me, steady and sure. Definitely not Rodger.

"Calm down." Galen drew up next to me, as controlled as I'd ever seen him. "They can smell fear."

"Oh, yeah," I said, my voice not as steady as I liked. "And what does that smell like?"

He stood between me and the beast. "Tasty."

"All the demigods in limbo and I had to pick the comedian."

Galen wore a crisp, new flight suit and his sword belt. The snake dripped venom that hissed in the sand at his feet. "I'll say one thing for you. You picked a hell of a ride."

He took one step toward it, then another, his hand on the hilt of his blade. "Stop it," I hissed. He was going to get himself killed.

He ignored me.

I stood rooted to the spot. The creature had stopped advancing. "Maybe it'll leave."

Galen didn't take his eyes off the beast for a second. "No. It's here for you."

The chimera pawed the ground, restless.

"It's going to take you to its owner, no matter what," Galen said. "Don't make it drag you by your toenails."

Damn Medusa. Damn her and her baby shower and anybody else on the western edge of the world who thought it was a good idea to hold a party on the Isle of Wrath and Pain.

"Come on." Galen reached back for me.

I hesitated. "Is it tame?"

"No," he said, "but it will let us ride."

"I'm going to kill her," I said, trying to get my mind around it. I found my medical kit. I tucked the crystal inside before following him.

"Trust me," Galen said, "that's hard to do." He reached up and gripped the reins dangling from the lion's neck.

The chimera leaned down and snorted, its hot breath tickling my leg.

I froze.

Belatedly, I realized it was lowering itself down to let me mount.

Galen cracked a grin. "You still want me to stay here?"

And miss all the fun? "Get on."

chapter sixteen

Even with the chimera leaning down, it was a chore to get me close to the saddle. Galen, on the other hand, straddled its massive lionlike shoulders like he was born to it. He stashed my medical bag and my gift, before I let him pull me up. Sort of.

He had me by both arms while I tried to fling a leg over the back of the thing. Only every time I tried, the snake on the end of its tail coiled up and hissed, showing a red forked tongue and razor-sharp fangs.

"There. You see that?" I asked, backing down.

Galen was unimpressed. "Don't let it know you're scared."

"Too late." I wondered if Kosta would have cleared my day trip if he'd known I'd be riding through limbo on a mythical beast who wanted to eat me.

The lion's head belched fire.

Oh, that was just perfect.

"Come on," Galen prodded. "It's just like riding a bike."

"Have you ever ridden a bike?"

"No."

I shook my hands out, trying to get some circulation going.

This was in no way like my ten-speed back home. And what if I could actually manage to climb onto a chimera? I didn't know the way to Medusa's—or the way back. And I'd better be home by tonight because I had a shift bright and early tomorrow—working with my roommate, so this time Rodger couldn't cover for me.

Merde. This was such a bad idea.

"I'm not afraid," I lied. I pressed my body into the rough fur on its back, muscles burning as I shoved a leg up into the air. *Now or never.* "I've always wanted to ride a three-headed monster."

Thank the universe Galen was as strong as he looked. Between the two of us, we managed to thrust me into the sad little saddle. I noticed, with some satisfaction, that he was breathing as hard as I was.

His gaze flicked to the space behind me. "Down," he ordered as the snake head hissed in my ear.

I didn't even want to look to see how close it was. But I could feel the lower half of it, winding against my leg.

"Are you ready?" he asked, reins in hand. He'd positioned himself in front of my saddle, riding bareback.

"I'm sure not getting off." At this rate, I was tempted to attend Medusa's shower on the back of the animal, rather than try to climb up again.

I ventured one last glance back at my tent before bracing myself against Galen's hard, muscled back.

"Go!" He leaned forward, pulling me with him as the beast let out a mighty roar and took off like a shot.

Christ Almighty—my teeth vibrated and my bones clattered together as we lurched across the desert. It was like driving eighty-five down a road full of potholes and speed bumps.

Wind tore at my hair. Sand pelted my eyes and my face. I could barely see the blur of the desert as it streaked by.

Galen crouched low, holding the reins steady, steering with his legs as he took the chimera left past what could have been a hell vent, or a caravan, or, cripes, I didn't know.

The beast's heads lolled, tongues out like dogs on a car ride.

I buried my face against Galen's warm back, as I felt the chimera accelerate to an even more mind-numbing speed. I squinted, not daring to open my eyes fully against the stinging dust. The desert was a whirl of red-on-brick-on-red.

The chimera's muscles worked between my legs, in a full run. I didn't know how fast we were going. Didn't care. As long as Galen made sure we got off this thing in one piece.

And I did trust Galen.

The kicker was, I wasn't even risking myself for a prophecy this time. No, I was doing it out of sheer obligation. That and the fact that I needed to see my patient. This was pioneer medicine—limbo style.

Medusa was technically full term—only two weeks from her due date. If I'd had her in my clinic back home, she'd be making weekly visits to my office. As it stood, I hadn't seen her in a month.

The beast jarred, and I gripped Galen with everything

I had. Its smooth gait went rocky and I slapped hard against the saddle as we slowed to a reckless hundred or so miles per hour.

We were beyond the limbo desert, in a volcanic wasteland. I tasted fire and soot and sulfur. The beast padded over fields of rock and black ash, leaping over tendrils of red lava that oozed from the ground.

Cinders pelted me as we took a particularly hard leap. What the hell?

We dodged the spiny horns of the goat as it threw its head back and bleated out a small fireball. And there, ahead of us, I saw it—a massive stone house on a hill.

Dang. I squinted. The thing looked more like a rotting temple. It sat in the middle of a large lake. Galen shifted and I struggled to catch an unobstructed view around him, watching as the mist rose off the water.

We rocked from side to side as the beast padded toward the lake. It made no move to let us dismount and I wasn't about to piss it off, so I hung on. Still, it had to know the water was poison.

The chimera stopped at the water's edge. The shore was crusted with sulfur. Bones lay tangled in the sand. The creature bent its lion's head to sniff at the bubbling water and I almost felt sorry for it.

I'd feel even sorrier for us if it keeled over and dumped us in.

"Steady," Galen said under his breath, sounding more confident than I felt as the creature took one step back, then another.

"You don't think it's going to—" I ended on a shriek as the beast drove forward.

I almost jumped off, would have if Galen hadn't held tight to the hands I had wrapped around him.

We hurtled over the massive lake of fire, on the back of a suicidal beast, and came down teeth-rattling hard on the other side.

My head pounded, my vision swam. I swallowed, trying to make my throat work, and when I recovered enough, I saw all three heads watching us.

"That's our sign," Galen said, sliding off the beast. I was less graceful as I half dismounted, half fell into his arms.

I held him tight, my knees useless, grateful to be here and alive and in one piece. I braced my hands against his chest and noticed he was wearing armor.

"Are you okay?" he asked, when I didn't show any signs of moving.

I looked back to see the lion's head snarling at me. "Oh, sure. I'm fine. Peachy."

As long as he got me the hell out of here.

The chimera hissed, growled, and—for lack of a better word—bleated at us as Galen led me to a staircase cut into the rock.

The cliff face towered above us. It was impossible to know how many steps it held, but I didn't care. It was becoming increasingly evident that chimeras didn't take the stairs and that was fine by me.

Galen and I tackled them together, side by side. By the time we were halfway up, I was wheezing and convinced my legs would fall off. Galen was, at least, sweating.

It was humid here, most likely from the lake. Still, I

hadn't felt humidity since I'd left New Orleans. It hadn't been something I'd missed.

At the top, I gasped for breath as I followed Galen down a winding trail littered with fallen columns and statues of fallen soldiers. Only on second look, I could tell that they hadn't always been statues. Damn. I stopped in front of a young man dressed as a gladiator. He held a long, oblong shield and an infantry sword. His eyes were frozen in terror.

I inspected his face. Part of his chin had chipped away, as well as an ear. That didn't bother me near as much as the weathering on his neck. I could treat flesh-to-stone injuries if they were fresh. He'd been turned too long for me to do any good.

My fingers lingered on his rain-stained cheek. "Why?" I said to myself, to him, to the whole bloody universe.

Galen stood close behind me. I could feel him. "He was the enemy."

"I'm trying really hard to understand that." I wiped the sweat from my chin, leaving the soldier.

We passed at least a dozen more like him on the steamy, twisted path that led to Medusa's lair. I stepped over blackened gouges in the earth, places where the trail itself had been ripped away.

So much death. So much anger.

And for what?

We reached the courtyard and found it scattered with even more crumbling bodies of the dead. Spindly silver artemisias sprouted from the cracks and in between fallen columns, their branches reaching toward the pink and gray sky.

The winds blew harsh up here, buffeting an arrangement of pink balloons, tied to a long-abandoned sword cleaved into the stone porch.

"Hello, hello!" a voice echoed from inside.

Galen drew his sword as a skinny little man in a toga two sizes too big scurried out of the house and down the battle-stained stairs. "Please," he squeaked, when he got a look at Galen. "Doctor." He nodded to me. "Er . . . friend." He bowed with trepidation toward Galen. "If you will come inside. No battles today." He wagged a finger with forced cheerfulness.

Galen sheathed his sword as the jumpy servant led us down a long hallway of pink and green marble. Our footsteps echoed as we passed more stony dead. Only these heroes were missing heads, limbs, and other vital body parts.

I gripped my medical bag and kept moving. There was nothing I could do for them.

"Here you are." He led us through a pair of large bronze doors and into a sunny room that could have belonged in any upscale villa. The marble floor gleamed. The walls were hung with paintings and tapestries, and a strange gorgon slithered beside the gift table.

She was thinner than Medusa, with a mass of red snakes tangling at her shoulders.

"Stheno?" I guessed, taking the safe bet. Stheno was the oldest and most powerful of the three sisters.

Her lips turned up at the corners as she slithered to me. "You must be the doctor," she said. I handed Galen my medical case and allowed Stheno to grip my hands in hers. Her touch was papery and cold. I tried not to react as her wan smile turned to a hiss at the poor servant.

"The human should have introduced us," she snarled. "It's impossible to attract good live help these days."

"Maybe if you give him time," I said, not quite sure what else to say.

She growled under her breath. "He's a temp," she said, ignoring Galen as she led me to an arched doorway. I glanced back to see him depositing my wrapped crystal on the gift table.

"Back in the day," Stheno said, dragging me along, "entire families served. Now everyone worries. Will my child fall into the poison lake? Will they be devoured by the flesh-eating crabs on the shore? Will I be struck in a lighting storm?" She leaned chummy close. "Used to be you had so many children that if one went missing, you chalked it up to fate."

Sure. Right. "So you live here with Medusa?" I asked, changing the subject as she led us through a portrait hall. It was a veritable who's who of sea monsters and the damned.

"I help out in the spring and summer, when the gorgon killers get their big ideas." She snorted.

I knew I was treading on dangerous territory, but, "If you ever decide on mercy, I can treat their injuries."

"Not when we knock the heads off."

I stood dumb for a moment.

"Come," she said, turning me into a room with a very pregnant Medusa. She lay on a couch of pink velvet, her stomach much more distended than when I'd seen her last.

She was flanked by a third gorgon, who must be her

other sister. The rest of the intimate room was crowded with a gaggle of fearsome women with sharp teeth and claws. They sat uncomfortably in a semicircle of metal folding chairs. Roundly, I was introduced to Ekhidna (the Viper), Skylla (the Crab), Ladon (the Dragon), and Graia (the Gray).

I'd never keep all their names straight. So I just smiled and accepted a cup of punch.

The viper lurched, her entire body seemed to coil as she sat ramrod straight. "What is this?" she hissed.

I followed her gaze and found Galen in the doorway, looking delicious as usual.

"He's mine," I said, without hesitation.

"Too bad," muttered the gray woman.

Medusa's younger sister caressed her punch cup. "Of course if she dies, he's mine," she mused, to the titters of her cousins.

Medusa knocked the punch out of her sister's hand, spilling it like blood, the cup skittering across the marble floor. "Do not kill her," she thundered. "She's my OB."

The sister scowled, then brightened. "Perhaps after the baby?"

I found a chair far, far away, next to the crab monster, who sat like a large lump of clay. I liked her for that.

"Now that we're all here, let's play a game." Stheno glided over to a table laden with small prizes. "Ekhidna gave me the idea for this one."

The viper woman grinned as Stheno held aloft an apothecary jar. "Guess how many teeth are in the jar!"

Oh, my Lord. They were human teeth!

"I got them from the one who knocked you up!" Stheno tittered.

Medusa gasped. "You took Helio's teeth?"

"Ha!" The crab lady nudged me, her fish breath singed the air. "I knew it was her bodyguard."

"Relax," Stheno said, "I didn't take his teeth." She rattled the jar. "I just found these around the house."

I swallowed hard, determined to make it through this, confident that Galen lingered nearby.

The winner of guess-the-teeth was gifted with a lovely necklace made of spiders.

"They're alive!" The gray woman clapped her hands as Stheno fitted her with the prize.

"I hope," Stheno replied, trying to get the clasp to work. "You didn't close the box too tight, did you?" she asked Medusa's other sister.

She hadn't. I saw one of the legs twitch.

This was one shower where I was determined to lose big.

I didn't have to try hard. The next game was guess-the-food, where three smidges of baby food were presented on a tray and we had to decide what was what. I guessed peas, carrots, and beets. I should have known Medusa would go organic with ground eel, lamb's brain, and ox blood.

It's not like I could have used the prize: papyrus note cards with poison ink.

The sun was setting outside the window. I had to get out of here. Not only for my own preservation but for the fact that I had to work tomorrow and it was a long chimera ride home.

Only I had to give Medusa her checkup. She looked

like she was feeling good, and she'd certainly been hitting the snack table hard. They were both good signs, but certainly not in any way a replacement for proper prenatal care.

"Gift time!" Stheno announced as Galen wheeled in a cart of presents.

"Where have you been?" I mouthed to him.

While the sisters ogled his ass, he made his way behind me, placing a hand on my shoulder. His breath felt warm against my ear. "The Fates are here."

I stiffened. I figured they might be real, just like all of the other mythical creatures I'd encountered down here. Still, I never thought I'd be meeting the Fates.

We looked to the doorway and there stood an old woman, with two more behind her.

"Aunt Klotho." Medusa tried to turn around, her stomach impeding her.

My fingers tightened on my chair. "Aunt?"

"Friends of Medusa's mother," he said, matter-of-fact. "Can you believe it?"

Yes. No. He'd had a few minutes to get used to it. Me? I was staring for all I was worth.

Klotho was the spinner of the thread of life, if you believed in that sort of thing. I didn't. Still, I could feel her power touch the room as she stepped over the threshold.

Klotho was followed by Lakhesis, who measured the thread of life, and Atropos, who cut it.

And, no, I wasn't that smart to tell the difference on sight. But Klotho held a spinner, Lakhesis walked with a staff, and Atropos carried a pair of very sharp scissors.

They assembled behind me, cackling when I offered them my chair.

"We are old, but we are strong." Atropos nudged me with her scissors. "It does no good to buy us off."

It hadn't been what I'd been doing, but I didn't argue. Even if I didn't quite believe in the Fates, I wasn't about to tempt them.

I could feel their weight behind me as Medusa opened her first gift. It was from her older sister. I'd never seen Medusa squeal, and I never wanted to see it again.

"It's the death shroud of Theseus!" She clutched it to her chest. "Does this mean you finally killed him?"

"He attacked us!" Stheno protested.

Silly man.

Galen kept his hand on the hilt of his sword as Medusa reached for a trembling box. A flat, black nose sniffed from one of the airholes.

"It's from us!" one of the monstrous sisters announced.

I braced myself as Medusa unwrapped a brown bat the size of a dog. "An Olitiau!"

As her doctor, I should protest the hairy, fang-toothed creature. It was the worst baby gift ever. That thing looked like it could eat the baby.

Crab lady nudged me. "Every little girl needs a pet."

"And this"—Medusa's baby sister lifted a crown out of a gift bag—"I made myself."

It was a knobby white headdress of sorts. One thing was certain, the youngest gorgon was not very good at crafts.

Medusa placed it on her head uncertainly.

Her sister clapped her hands together. "It's the bones of your enemies!"

The women let out a collective, "Ahhh . . ."

"You." Medusa nudged her. "This must have taken ages to make."

"I've been collecting them for years," she admitted, twirling a red snake around her finger. "The little name-plates on the back of each bone mark whom it's from."

A teary-eyed Medusa reached for my gift. Nerves tickled my stomach. I hadn't shopped for anything truly memorable. Although I was really glad I hadn't been able to get anything from Babies "R" Us.

Medusa unwrapped my gift and studied it for a moment. "A crystal," she said, unimpressed until a thought came to her and lit her up from the inside. "It's baby-sized! She can use it to smash the skulls of her enemies!"

The other ladies voiced their approval while I fought the urge to slide boneless onto the marble floor.

Now if only I could get her away for a quick exam, I'd be able to get out of here.

"Wait," Atropos said behind me, as if she knew what I'd been thinking. "We have a gift."

Everyone turned to the Moirae sisters.

Klotho gave a beneficent smile. "We are so proud of you. And we know you will make a wonderful mother. You will be fierce and loyal. Loving and strong. Ask what you would like for your daughter, and we will give it."

The room hushed.

"Ask for revenge," Stheno urged.

"Or the destruction of your daughter's enemies," said the gray woman.

"She doesn't have any enemies," I protested. Medusa's daughter hadn't even been born yet.

"Right," Medusa said. "Maybe I can ask for some enemies for her."

No. Wrong. Geez, these people! I had to get out of here before I clocked them over the head. "Let her make a difference in the world."

They looked at me like I was sporting five heads and a unicycle.

Oh, come on. "Let her be someone who impacts the world for good." It's what I had always wanted to do. And now, I might never get my wish. But this kid could. "Let her be the one who changes lives for the better."

Medusa frowned. "And this will make her happy?"

I sighed, losing some of my steam. "It's the only thing I've ever wanted," I told her.

She gave a sly grin, turning to the Fates. "I want my daughter to make a difference. Change lives. I want her to be epic!"

The Fates nodded, while Medusa's relatives grumbled.

I only hoped Klotho and company would work for the good. Medusa had left that part out. I doubted she'd include it even if I reminded her.

But it was refreshment time and everyone was hungry. While the guests crowded around a table laden with olives, cheeses, and cake, I managed a word with Medusa.

She wore her crown of bones and clutched her belly with grim determination. "I feel like a kraken," she grumbled. "I want this baby out of me now."

"Your daughter will come when she's ready," I assured her.

"I'm not sleeping. I can barely eat. Nothing else will fit inside me." She caught Atropos by the sleeve of her long dress. "You. You control fate. Get this baby out of me."

"Don't even think about it," I warned, noticing Galen in conversation with Klotho and Lakhesis. He'd better be charming the Fates. "Come," I said to Medusa, "is there somewhere private we can go? I'll give you an exam and let you know how close you are."

Medusa showed me to a nursery, decorated in pink and sea-foam green. A lovely mobile of dried bones crackled above a crib straight out of the Pottery Barn Kids catalogue. How did she even get that down here?

Pink teddy bears brightened the matching white changing table, along with bubbling vases of heaven knew what.

"How are you feeling?" I asked as she slithered past the bookshelves lining the walls, running her hand over titles like *Grimm's Fairy Tales* and *The Gashlycrumb Tinies*.

"Tired, bloated." She sat on the daybed by the window and I opened my medical kit.

Her blood pressure looked good. Weight was up (although she refused to look at my portable scale). Her measurements were on track as well.

"My mother will not even attend my shower," she said, as I listened to her heartbeat.

"She'll come around." I hoped so, for both their sakes.

"She'd better," Medusa hissed.

There was a sharp rap at the door. "Just a minute," I

said, as she shrugged back into her party dress. "Do you need a refill on your prenatals?" I asked. It's not like she could get to the MASH 3063rd pharmacy if she refused to set foot in camp.

When she didn't reply, I handed her a bottle.

"Horse pills," she grumbled, accepting them.

"Petra." Galen gave a double knock.

"I am dressed," Medusa said, stuffing the vitamins into the pocket of her gown as Galen entered the room.

His face was drawn, his body taut. "The second prophecy is in."

"That fast?" I asked, wide-eyed. So Leta *was* our bronze weapon. A fricking dragon.

"I saw it myself," Galen said, joining us. "The servants have a television set up in the butler's pantry."

Medusa rolled her eyes. "Temps!"

"So what did they say?" I pressed.

Grim, he looked at Medusa's belly, then back to me. " 'The child of the damned shall damn us all.' "

chapter seventeen

Medusa clasped her hands to her chest. "My child is going to be someone!"

Never mind the child of the damned was going to damn us all.

Oh, my God. This was my fault. I told Medusa to wish for a special child. I'd influenced the prophecies in the worst way possible.

I stepped back, tried to think. "The child of the damned . . . It might not be her," I said, pointing to my patient, desperate for that to be true.

Medusa could be a handful from time to time. Okay, all the time. But I couldn't see her child bringing about the destruction of . . . everything.

Galen hooked his thumbs under his weapons belt. He wasn't buying it for a second. "The oracles are wearing snakeskins," he said in that you've-got-to-see-this-coming kind of way.

"Coincidence?" I answered, ready and willing to be as difficult as possible.

For God's sake, I was her doctor.

Medusa coiled to her full height, her tail rattling. "Are you saying I'm not evil enough?"

"What?" No. This wasn't a challenge. It was a sick mistake. My mistake and I didn't know how I was going to fix it.

I didn't want to deliver the child who would damn us all.

"This is not why I got into medicine," I said, as if that made a difference.

The snakes in her hair writhed in fury. "I am Medusa," she rumbled, her voice echoing off the walls, "serpent-goddess, executioner of men, scourge of Kisthene's plain."

Shit. Her eyes were glowing.

"Look away," Galen warned.

Medusa hissed and the air itself thickened. "You will not say my child is unworthy!"

I brought my hands up to cover my eyes, ready to squeeze them shut if she lost control.

"We just heard!" The door banged back on its hinges as Stheno and an entire gaggle of women slithered into the room.

Medusa's snarl notched down to a low rumble as the baby-shower crowd gathered around her.

Disaster averted. For now.

Medusa's sister winked at me. "Great idea, doctor."

I dropped my hands to my sides. "You've got to be kidding me."

The gray woman stood next to her, nodding. "I'll certainly be summoning you when I have a bun in the oven."

Medusa huffed, her red eyes dimming back to brown as Lakhesis and Atropos eased her into her rocking chair. "I want to meet my baby. Besides, I feel so large and round. I am done with being pregnant."

Atropos patted her on the arm. "Every woman reaches that point sooner or later, dear."

The gorgon wasn't convinced. "For the love of all that is unholy, can you just put me into labor?" She ran her hands over her protruding belly.

"No, you will not," I warned the Fates. We didn't need to rush the child of the damned.

Lakhesis leaned close to Medusa. "We'll talk about it after she leaves."

Great.

At least they'd gotten Medusa a glass of punch. She needed to stay hydrated.

Galen came up next to me. "Let's get the hell out of here," he said, his voice low.

"Right," I said. I'd done enough damage for one day.

Besides, I needed to talk to Galen. Alone.

Even without the prophecy, I was having second thoughts about this entire thing, and particularly Medusa's ability to stay calm during delivery. I didn't need anyone getting turned into stone, least of all me.

"You need to come to the MASH 3063rd to deliver," I told her. "If we have any complications"—like me turning into a terrified limestone statue—"that's the best place for treatment."

Medusa snarled in her throat, but she didn't argue.

Thank goodness.

I edged around the baby shower crowd. "Call me if you need me," I said. Then, turning my attention to the

Fates, I added, "No early labor. It won't be good for the baby." Or humanity.

Their overly innocent expressions didn't fool me for a second.

Galen and I were on our way to the door when I saw Klotho hovering at the edge of the impromptu party, studying baby-to-be's book collection. Her gaze caught mine. Her skin was sallow, her nose hooked.

"Hold on a sec." I steeled myself as I made my way to her side.

The Fates were tricky. I knew that. But I refused to think there was no way out of this.

"Don't you just love what she did with this room?" Klotho said to me, fingering the bookends, as if that were the point. "Such craftsmanship." She lifted a skull Medusa had decorated with rough-cut jewels and a pink silk scratch guard.

"It's great," I said automatically, watching the wrinkled corners of her mouth turn up. I blew out a breath. I wasn't sure if I'd get an answer but I had to ask. "I know what I did. I messed with the prophecies."

She ran a bony finger over a dead eye socket. "Exactly what are you admitting, healer?"

Nothing she didn't know already. "How do I fix it?"

She tilted her head. She knew.

Damn. These creatures really did have power. I'd never thought about the Fates or what these three could do until this latest prophecy had come in.

Maybe it was a coincidence that Medusa had asked for a special child moments before the oracle came down, but I didn't think so.

She studied me. Up close, she smelled like dried

cloth and sand. Wrinkles carved deep into her skin, her eyes a vivid green. "You wanted to make a difference." She touched a hand to my arm. Her skin was papery. I could feel the bones underneath.

My lungs tightened and I found it hard to draw a breath. "I don't want to be responsible for damning anyone."

Her eyes narrowed. "You don't get to choose," she said, turning away.

I started after her, but Galen intercepted me. "Let her go."

He was right. Nothing I could say would make a difference. This was all a sick game to them.

We had to get out of here and figure out what we were going to do about this prophecy.

We made our way down the long marble hallway. I was pretty proud that I matched his stride. Of course, I was taking two steps for every one of his, but still.

"At least we have the bronze weapon," he said.

I snorted. "I'm still trying to figure out how an angry, half-crazed dragon is going to save us all from the child of the damned."

We found ourselves back in the sitting room where we'd had the party. The gray woman's spider necklace inched up the wall.

I didn't see any way around it. Medusa's child would be born. I'd always thought the prophecies would bring us peace. I never thought that peace would be achieved by damning everyone. I didn't even know how one child could wipe out both armies.

We couldn't let it happen. Still, "I can't kill Medusa's baby."

"I know," he said, heading for the main entryway, cluttered with fallen heroes. I looked into their dead eyes, stepping over broken columns and abandoned swords. "We'll find a way to make this right."

"Are you sure about that?" I asked, as he lifted me over a particularly big slab of stone.

His fingers tightened on my waist as he set me down safely. "No."

Oh, good. Now all we had to do was find our way home on the back of a fire-breathing chimera. Of course at that point, I would have climbed on the back of a velociraptor if it meant getting out of here.

The beast stomped and belched flames as we approached. Show-off.

I glanced back at Medusa's lair as the sun set behind it and hoped Marc had at least gotten our bronze weapon under control. We needed something to go right.

The ride back was bumpy, and dark—save for occasional snorts from our ride. We made it back to the tar pits at around midnight.

It was pitch-black as Galen slid off and quickly dragged me down after him. I was still getting my legs steady as the chimera bellowed and dashed out into the desert. Its cries echoed, growing more distant.

"You okay?" Galen asked. I was pressed close to him and didn't make any effort to move.

I cleared my throat. The truth was, I needed his touch. Like it or not, Galen's strength, his presence, his love was one of the few things I could count on in this war.

Especially after a day like this one.

I buried my cheek against his shoulder, felt the roughness of his uniform against it. "Thanks for coming today." Looking back, I couldn't imagine going through that alone.

He held me, and I savored his warmth, his steady breath. "I've always got you, especially where big bad beasts are concerned."

"Not just with the chimera," I said, needing to make it clear, for him and for me. I drew back, willing him to see the truth as I spoke it. "It felt good walking in there with you." And I'd sure as hell needed him beside me on the way out.

The stupid thing was, I'd been so worried about what we'd do when the time came for him to leave again. But now, we had days, hours maybe, until the axe came down and all I wanted was him.

Galen was my rock, my partner, the person I'd want beside me if I had to go to hell and back.

He touched my chin, his fingers caressing the soft spot behind my ear. "Now she admits it," he said, with a touch of irony.

A tingle of guilt flitted through me. "I may have been dumb, but at least I've been honest," I said, drawing my hands up his chest.

His chest rumbled under my fingers. "Too honest."

"Says the former demigod of truth."

His breath quickened under my palms as I unzipped his top zipper. "It's not like we have to be at death's door in order to get through to me," I said.

He chuckled low in his throat. "It helps."

Yeah, it did. The tar pits bubbled softly behind us.

My insides quivered as he pressed a hand to my back and drew me closer. I nipped at his collarbone.

I could be bullheaded and I could be an idiot, but after what I'd seen tonight, I'd have to be crazy to turn down my chance with this man.

It was nuts. I'd been so worried about the future and what everything meant, but I'd never stopped to realize that maybe all we'd have was today.

The prophecies were made to serve the gods, not us.

All we had was each other.

Galen's lips trailed down my neck and over my collarbone. Liquid fire shot through me as he caressed my breasts.

I didn't know how much longer I'd have with him—how much time either one of us would have to be whole and alive. Here. But I was done wasting it.

"Where's your tent?" I asked, desperate but sure—more sure than I'd been in a long time.

I gasped as his thumbs grazed my nipples. "Two down from yours," he said, voice tight.

Too far.

It was dark. We were alone.

He was the one I could count on, the man I could trust. He'd be there to keep me safe, to keep me strong and sane, and love me for as long as he could. I just wished we had longer.

His breath came in raspy puffs as I undid the zipper near his waist. I was really beginning to dig flight suits.

I dropped light kisses on his mouth. "I don't ever want to lose you."

He slanted his mouth over mine and kissed me hard. He tasted so good. "Then don't," he said against my lips. He threaded his fingers through my hair, drawing me back for a long, lingering kiss.

I ached for him, needed him like my next breath.

Before, I could say that I made love to him in the heat of the moment. That it was a reaction. That I did it out of hurt or fear or hell, out of lust.

But now, I wanted it to be a choice.

War was a waste. Death was a waste. But this, I would not throw away. Never again.

"I love you, Galen," I murmured against his heated skin.

He rested his forehead against mine. "I've never wanted anyone but you."

He groaned as I ran a hand over his rigid length. "Let's go somewhere else." He spoke as if the words were being pulled from him.

But I wasn't going to stop. This was right. And we were going to be together, here, for as long as we could.

I dropped to my knees, sinking down into the soft sand, tugging his zipper along with me. His stomach trembled as cool air touched his skin.

He was luscious. Powerful. Mine.

I closed my mouth over the head of his cock and heard his intake of breath, felt a slight shake in his knees. This man faced down demigods, beasts, and immortal warriors. Yet he shook for me.

He wanted me.

I ran my tongue around the head of his cock, tasting the saltiness of him before plunging down and taking as much of him as I could.

Hades, it felt good. I was powerful. Needy. And not afraid to take what I wanted. I let go and savored him—us—for the first time in I couldn't remember how long.

He wound his fingers through my hair, caressed my neck. He cursed when I cupped his balls. "God, I never thought I'd have you like this again."

His flight suit hit the ground and he stood before me completely naked while I worked his cock. He was beautiful. Fantastic in the dim light of the moon. I drew the pleasure from him, gave to him in the most primitive way I knew how, until he bent at the waist, his fingers running through my hair.

"Hold up. I don't want to . . ."

I sucked harder.

He cursed and came hard in my mouth.

Afterward, he took two steps. Then with a grunt, he sat hard on the sand next to me.

"I need to start working on my fantasies," he said, out of breath.

"Oh, yeah?" I asked, practically purring as I ran a finger down his chest.

He looked at me sideways. "Thanks to you, I'm adding tar pit seduction to the list."

I kissed him softly once, twice. He must have tasted himself on me, but he didn't care. He teased me with his tongue, his hand wrapping around the back of my neck, his fingers digging through my hair.

I pulled back, my lips a breath away from his. "I wanted to make love to you slowly. It just didn't work out."

He kissed me once more, the smile lingering on his lips. "Well, maybe this time it can."

chapter eighteen

We considered locking Rodger and Marius out of my tent, but instead we somehow managed to make it back to Galen's. There, I did my level best to show him exactly how I was going to savor every minute of time we had together from this moment on.

We stumbled against the wall of his hutch. He nipped at my neck, caressed my breasts. "My turn."

"If you insist." I gasped as he stripped me.

Okay, so the man didn't waste time.

I wound my hand around a canvas shade, trying to get some support. "I have to warn you that as your doctor, I don't recommend too much strenuous physical activity until you're completely healed."

"I've never been the best patient," he said, his large body bare, his hands stroking, touching, turning me into a puddle of aching want. I heard the shade rip.

He kissed me long and hard. I held him tight, savoring the feel of him naked against me as he teased me with his tongue. I ran my nails down his sides and felt him tense. Ground against him as his cock swelled against my stomach.

We battled, hot skin sliding against hot skin. We tasted. We tried to make it last. I knew I needed to imprint every moment with him in my mind. If this really was the end of it all, I wanted to savor this. Him.

His muscles clenched and his hips thrust against mine.

He kissed my neck as I breathed hard against his cheek. "I need you," I whispered. "Now."

We moved to the bed, where we began an immediate battle for who was on top. He won, and sank hard into me.

It was incredible.

I arched my back as I took him to the hilt. It felt so good, having him. Loving him. He slid his hand between our bodies and his thumb found my clit.

I gasped into his mouth as the sensations crashed over me.

"I love you." He groaned against me, his speed increasing. His thumb circling. He knew just how to touch me, to love me. He drove into me until my excitement spiraled out of control and peaked in waves of pleasure.

He convulsed and spilled inside me, burying his face in the crook of my neck.

It was amazing that this was mine. He was mine. We held each other for a long moment, savoring the contact and the warmth.

I kissed his sweat-dampened skin. "I love you."

He drew away, tucked a wayward strand of hair behind my ear. "Stay here with me tonight."

I couldn't think of anywhere else I'd rather be. He drew the covers over us as we crammed onto his tiny cot. It squeaked as we pressed together, tight and loving and perfect.

We woke, still snuggled together. "I'm glad we have another day," I said, kissing him on the chest. I'd never take that for granted again.

His fingers stroked my shoulder, tucked a wisp of hair behind my ear. "It may not be the end," he said, clearly not convinced. It was bad when Galen of all people found it hard to see the light.

I glanced at his bedside clock. "I'm due on shift soon."

He helped me find my uniform. Watched me get dressed—and yes, I teased him a little. Might as well make him look forward to my return.

He kissed me good-bye. It felt so surreal, and so right at the same time.

To think, he was living only two doors down from my place. We'd certainly have to make good use of that.

I headed home to grab my shower kit and a fresh uniform. I should have told Galen I'd stop by his place after my shift. I nudged my door open. If I had time, I'd let him know on the way over to the hospital.

What I didn't expect to see was Leta perched on the iron stove inside my tent. "Petra," she said, as I jumped in shock.

"Of all the—" I scanned the room. She was alone. "What are you doing here?"

She should be with Marc, hiding from the investigators, getting better, or doing whatever dragons did. And she should have realized that the cast-iron contraption wasn't furniture.

She slid off the stove and stood in front of me. Her scrubs were rumpled and her hair tangled around her shoulders. She let out a rumble in the back of her throat. I glanced behind me and I wondered just how much of the dragon she'd succeeded in burying today.

She took one step toward me, then another. "I looked for you all day yesterday."

And she'd better not shift in my tent. "I had Medusa's baby shower."

She snarled, a lock of hair falling over one eye. "The child of the damned shall damn us all." Her speech was stilted, as if she were still getting used to speaking instead of growling.

"Thanks for reminding me." If this was her idea of small talk, she had a lot of work to do. "Listen, I'm on shift in a few," I said, edging toward my cot and reaching underneath for my shower gear.

She stood over me, completely crowding my personal space. "It is about Marc."

I straightened, and took a step to the side so she wasn't completely in my face. "Is he okay?" She better not have taken a bite out of him.

Her chin trembled. "I don't know. He confuses me." She stared at me, not even blinking. "I like Marc."

Okay, this wasn't weird. "Liking Marc is fine," I said, opening the door for her, hoping she'd take the hint that we had to keep moving.

She didn't. "What do I do?"

I paused with my hand on the doorjamb. "You're asking me for love advice?" On my ex? "There has to be another dragon you can talk to. What about Stephens the mechanic?" He was a dragon. "Or that tall EMT. What's his name?"

She looked slightly panicked at that. "They are men. This is girl talk."

Lord. "Well, find a girl dragon."

"Where?" She frowned. "There is my grandmother. But I do not think I am strong enough to reach her with my mind."

"Have you tried?" This could be a good training exercise.

Tears welled in her eyes.

Oh, hell. I sat down on the edge of my cot, motioning for her to take a seat on Marius's footlocker.

I touched her arm. It was rock-solid muscle. "It's okay to feel something for him." I made sure to catch her eye. "He's a good man. Dragon," I corrected quickly.

Her voice caught in her throat. "I had a vision Marc was very angry with me."

"He can be impatient," I told her. "Tell him to put a sock in it."

She grunted, but I saw how the corners of her lips turned up.

"Try to talk to your grandmother." She needed the support. And it would give her confidence to do something to help herself. She had to be a powerful creature, or else both sides wouldn't want her so bad.

In fact, I wondered if she might be able to see anything about the child of the damned. "Tell me, Leta. How long have you had these visions?"

"All my life," she said, back straight, holding herself proud. "I am a bronze dragon. We all have the gift of sight, but it is especially strong in me. My grandmother believes it is because I am a true telepath."

Yes. It was why Galen had been sent to steal her.

I watched her, trying to think about what we could do with this. "Telepathy just means you get messages without words." *Just.* I would have laughed at my words if I wasn't so interested in hearing what she had to say.

She twined her fingers together. "All bronze dragons can predict small things about their own futures. But I see well beyond myself. I also receive messages from other realms. My gifts work in tandem."

"Can you see what will happen with this latest prophecy?" If we had some warning, maybe we could figure a way out of this.

"No." She sighed. "I am damaged too badly. I no longer get to choose what I see."

I was disappointed, but I couldn't help feeling sorry for her at the same time. "Did the old army ever use you?"

From the way she stiffened, I could tell it was a painful question.

"They asked me what I saw," she said. "I would lie and tell them I saw myself missing my marks as a suicide bomber."

"I'd lie too." It sickened me to think she'd even have to do that.

She looked at me, sad. "Most bronze dragons are incapable of lying."

She really was different. "I'm glad you can," I told her.

Leta shrugged. "After a time, they declared me unfit

to kill and instead attempted to breed me against my will."

I was so glad Galen got her out of there. "I'm sorry."

"I don't want your pity." Her eyes shone with defiance, and something else. "I survived. When Commander Delphi came to me, I knew he was my way out. He offered to take more, but the others were too afraid."

That sounded like Galen.

"You saw your survival?" I asked.

She looked uncomfortable. "I saw a successful escape for most. If they had attempted," she added. "I saw them scattering. But I could not tell them. None of them knew my power to see beyond myself. There was no time to find them all and they would have been shocked if I spoke to them without words. If I revealed my true gifts, and even one had stayed behind . . . or if my secret had gotten out . . ." She shook her head. "I sacrificed their freedom," she said, her voice barely above a whisper, "so that I could stay hidden."

"You did the best you could," I told her. The war was bigger than one dragon escape. But even I was ashamed to think it. I'd seen what happened to dragon bombers. How many of them could have survived? How many fewer emergency burn victims would we have had without them?

She crossed her arms over her chest. "My telepathy is a hidden power, one that could have damned me if the old gods had learned of it." She glanced up. "Your army will put me to death as well."

She was right. "I know all about hidden powers," I said.

A moment of understanding passed between us.

Merde. Two misfits walk into a tent . . .

The question was, what were we going to do about it?

I drew my fingers through my hair, trying to make sense of it all. "So you see the future—"

"I dream it," she corrected.

Okay. "You dream the future and let me guess—you're stunningly accurate."

She winced, as if what I'd said pained her. "No. I am ill. I know that. I understand it affects the visions. But I saw my escape. And I saw you before I knew you. I saw you leading an army."

I sat back. Impressed, but well, not really. "I'm not a soldier." There was no way in hell I'd have any desire to lead an army into war. Maybe Leta's visions were a little messed up. "I'd rather leave that kind of insanity to the generals."

Her gaze bored into me. "That's what Marc said. He said you'd sooner cut out your tongue than order a charge. But the visions have only gotten stronger. I don't think it is a mistake. And now there is a baby. She will help you lead the army."

I about choked at the absurdity of it. "I am not taking a baby into a war zone." In fact, I advised new mothers not to even take babies into a mall for the first four to six weeks. We were talking about the battlefields of limbo here.

"You will take the child with you," she continued.

"No. See. I'm not even all that great at holding babies." I delivered a few in residency, and handed them right over to the nurses to weigh and measure. I wasn't

about to carry one around or take one into the desert
or—

Leta pointed a finger at me. "She will lead you. And
you will lead them!"

"Did you know it takes babies at least six months to
speak and then it's usually small words, like "ma-ma"
or 'dog.'" Nothing to inspire an army.

I felt like I was talking to the iron camp stove.

She snarled at me. She honest-to-God showed her
teeth. "You do not believe me."

Cripes. So much for our moment of understanding.
"I think"—I crossed my arms over my chest—"you
think you saw it."

She stood and began pacing. "My grandmother
would believe me. She would understand."

"Then talk to her." It was obvious she needed more
than I could give.

"Maybe." She stared out at the sun beating down
over the tar swamp. "She is all-wise," Leta said, turning to me. "She knows about me. I worked with her
before I was taken. I didn't dare contact her before I
was rescued. I wasn't strong enough to control my powers. Marc says I'm not strong enough now."

"Yes, well, Marc not believing isn't exactly news."

Leta stared me down. "These visions won't stop.
They are important. I am here for a reason, and not just
because your Galen saved me. I am here because I'm
somehow connected to you."

I wanted to protest, but sadly, it was starting to make
sense. Leta was my bronze weapon.

Okay. I began pacing myself. "If you contact your
grandmother, do you think she could tell us how to

deal with the child of the damned?" There had to be
more than what she saw.

Leta nodded. "She is the only one I trust."

"This is coming to a head soon," I said. I didn't want
to scare her, but she had to know what we were up
against.

If we could figure out what to do about the child of
the damned, we might have a chance. There was only
one more after this. One more thing we needed to do to
stop this war for good.

Then Leta would be free. Galen could be with me.
We could go home.

"Do it. Contact your grandmother," I said. She
stopped at that. "You're here for a reason. You're a telepath, and you've been hiding your gift."

"There is another problem," she said slowly.

I fought to keep my face impassive. Why couldn't
we just deal with one issue at a time?

"It's been years since I used telepathy," Leta said.

I planted my hands on my hips, thinking. "It's got to
be way easier than visions, right?"

"It is a natural skill for me," she said, wringing her
fingers. In the short time I'd known her, I'd never seen
her so unsure. "I've been so scared to use it. I don't
know if I can talk to her anymore, or if she can still
hear me. Maybe I really am alone."

I took her hands and stilled them. "She's listening. I
don't think we ever stop listening for the people we
care about, even when they forget to speak to us for a
long time."

She blinked hard several times. "I don't know what I
would say."

"Ask for her help. Tell her you've met the healer who sees the dead. Tell her you are the bronze weapon. That the child of the damned will be born soon. Ask her how we can defeat the gods. Today."

We stood together as my words settled between us.

We were really going to do this—we were at war with the gods. A shiver ran through me.

Leta gripped my hands tighter and closed her eyes, holding them tight as concentration furrowed her forehead and brought beads of sweat to her hairline. She squeezed my fingers harder and I felt the air around us shimmer with energy.

I closed my own eyes, willing her to succeed. Opening myself up to the possibility of this dragon speaking to her kind, clearly, confidently. I pictured her open to the universe and the creatures it contained. I saw her as a pure and perfect communicator. I had no power to give to her, no magic to send her way, but at that moment, I lent her every bit of my will and desire.

Our palms grew slick. I heard her labored breathing and tried to infuse her with calm, with clarity. I willed her to speak.

She jolted and her eyes flew open. "They heard me!"

"How do you know?" I asked, steadying her as she stumbled backward.

Her eyes were wide. "They talked back."

"Wait." Dread slicked through me. "Who are 'they'?"

Leta's nostrils flared. "I made a mistake."

My heart threatened to pound out of my chest.

She wet her lips. "I thought I was talking to her. I gave her the message: 'You are the healer who sees the dead. I am the bronze weapon.'" She looked lost.

"And," I prodded, resisting the urge to grab her by the arms and shake her.

She drew a hand over her mouth. "And I accidentally sent the message to everybody."

For a second, I couldn't breathe. "What do you mean, everybody?"

"Just the dragons," she said quickly.

I jerked to my feet. My secret was out. I'd kept my ability hidden for almost a decade and now my secret was out. "How many dragons?" I demanded.

She tore her fingers through her hair. "Seven hundred and eighty-three. They know I'm *the* bronze dragon. The gods are going to come after me."

"Me too!" Terror ripped through me. I couldn't even think. "Are you sure you did a 'send all'?"

"Yes," she said, her voice breaking into a snarl. "I didn't mean it. I wasn't thinking clearly enough and it just happened."

I had to get out of here. Only there was nowhere to run. Once the gods found out, I'd be doomed.

"Tell them it's a secret," I told her, although I knew the chances of seven hundred and eighty-three dragons keeping a secret was about nil.

"Take my hands," she ordered, grabbing them before I had a chance to offer.

She clung to me and we both closed our eyes tight. I shoved every bit of desperate hope at her as I felt the air around us sizzle, and I hoped and prayed and willed her to somehow make this right.

Her eyes flew open. "Okay," she said.

"Do you think they heard?"

"I don't know," she said, shoulders jerking as she

broke away from me. "They were all yelling back." She clutched her forehead.

"Okay, well, maybe they hadn't heard clearly." Or maybe they wouldn't tell. Or maybe I was just screwed."

A sharp rap sounded outside.

I nearly jumped out of my skin until I saw it was Horace. "Petra, we have an emergency."

Leta and I shared a glance.

He yanked open the door. "Medusa is in labor and she won't come into camp. We've got her in Father McArio's tent, but she's not doing well at all. They need you there. Now."

chapter nineteen

I pointed to Leta. "You stay here." I never should have talked her into broadcasting to the dragons. I knew she was still recovering her powers. But damn it, we didn't have time to wait. She'd looked good. She was talking fine. Damn it! I glanced up at the cloudless sky, half expecting the gods to come crashing down on top of us.

And now we were out of time. I headed back out, buckling my watch on my wrist.

"Horace," I said, leaning back inside for my stethoscope, "I need you to go to the recovery tent. Get me a half-dozen surgical masks, two gowns, towels, hot water, an emergency field kit, a fetal heart rate monitor, and a Snickers bar."

Yeah, I felt kind of bad using Medusa's medical condition to get a Snickers bar, but cripes, it had been a long week.

And I needed breakfast. Or lunch. Or whatever meal we were supposed to be having.

The sprite sped away and I began jogging toward Father McArio's place, with Leta on my heels.

"What are you doing?" she demanded, nearly running into some supply clerks walking the other way. They looked overly pleased with themselves, and barely minded the jostle. I wondered what they'd been doing with our inspector friends.

Leta kept pace with me. "How are we going to fix the problem with the dragons?"

"Hell if I know." I ventured another glance at the sky. At least we hadn't been smited. Yet.

There was nothing to do, except, "You want to help deliver the child of the damned?"

She snarled, baring her teeth. "I will shift into a dragon and devour her!"

"Nope. You're out," I said, leaving the path, dodging graves as I headed through the cemetery. I'd have Horace send a nurse up.

I tried to think who. Most of the medical staff had been squeamish of the gorgon even in the early stages of her pregnancy, when she'd been happy. Nobody even pretended to get excited when she'd dropped by with thank-you finger cookies. Yes, the ingredients had been suspect and I didn't actually eat them either. Still, the nurses could have at least pretended.

I held up near the entrance to the minefield.

Yes, Medusa's child was bad news, but it was an innocent baby. It was my duty as a doctor and a decent person to give that child the best possible start in this world.

Then I noticed Leta was still next to me. "This is as far as you go."

She visibly paled. "You can't leave me to face Marc alone. He will be enraged."

And then some. He'd told her point-blank she wasn't ready to use her powers and we'd gone ahead and tried it anyway. In our defense, we were desperate.

We had to find something—anything—to turn this situation around. Besides, when you got down to it, at least it was our butts on the line and not his.

"Talk to him." Marc was a smart guy. And a dragon. "I also want you to find Galen. Let him know Medusa's in labor."

She hesitated. "You love him, don't you?"

"Yes," I told her. *With all my heart.*

She watched me for a long moment. "Will you hide with Medusa if the gods come for you?"

"Leta." She knew as well as I did. "There's nowhere to hide."

By the grace of all that's good, I made it through the minefield and down the path to Father McArio's without tripping any pranks. We didn't have time for me to be wrapped up in a giant spiderweb or fend off dozens of Hickey Horns.

His sculpture garden gleamed in the high midday sun. Father liked to work with junk metal, and he had quite a collection of pieces. Most of it consisted of birds and other winged creatures that appeared as if they'd take flight any second. As I drew closer, I saw dozens of very alive, very sinister-looking black vultures.

They rested on the sculptures and all along Father McArio's roofline, their bald heads and narrow gazes following me. I didn't let my guard down for a second, which meant I nearly tripped over the metal sculpture of Pegasus, lying battered on the ground. It seemed Medusa still held a grudge.

I opened the door to the hutch, sending a multicolored Talavera cross slapping against the wood. "What have we got?"

Father stood up from the stool at Medusa's bedside. She was lying on his cot, with pillows piled behind her and at least two quilts over her.

"I'm burning up!" she said, flinging it all off. The gorgon's breathing was labored, the snakes on her head twining as she turned to me. "Doctor! I need you." She gripped Father's arm as he tried to move away. "Get me another Popsicle."

It was stifling in there. Fitz the hellhound had abandoned his post at Father's side and was nosing frantically for my attention. "Has your water broken?" I asked, edging past the snorting beast.

She nodded. "Right in front of some hotshot hero who thought he was going to chop my head off." Her taloned fingers trailed down her green-scaled torso, coming to rest on her bulging stomach. "Do you know how embarrassing that is?"

I doubt he'd lived to tell about it. "How far apart are your contractions?" I asked, unwinding the stethoscope from around my neck.

She rolled her eyes. "I don't know." She groaned as I pulled up a stool and listened to her heartbeat. "Time has no meaning on the Isle of Wrath and Pain."

Fitz's cold nose hit my elbow. Yeah, well, this place wasn't exactly sterile.

Medusa was a little out of sorts, but that was to be

expected. Her chest sounded fine. I'd have liked to have taken her blood pressure. "What do you say we get an orderly up here and take you down to the clinic?"

"No!" She turned on me, her eyes ringed with red. "I am not going to expose my baby to dragon pox."

"You don't have to worry," I told her. "It's just a camp rumor." Started to keep the inspectors busy.

She hissed. "Of course dragon pox is real. I looked it up on the Internet. Symptoms are elevated breathing, thirst, dry eye, itchy arms . . . paranoia. I think I might already have it!"

"Gorgons can't get it."

"Supe MD didn't say that."

Lovely. Another Internet diagnosis. I tried another tack. "You may have some of those symptoms," I told her, "but I gave you a full checkup at your baby shower and I can guarantee you, you don't have dragon pox."

"And I'm not going to get it either."

"Fine." Damn it, where was Horace? "We'll deliver the baby here."

She'd had a normal pregnancy. I wasn't expecting any problems. I ignored Father as he went a little green around the gills.

He recovered nicely, though, handing Medusa a Go-Gurt.

"What is that?" I asked as she ripped open the wrapper.

"It's a Popsicle," he said, with an overly bright smile on his face.

"O-kay."

"All the pregnant women get them," Medusa said, slurping. "I read it online."

I traded a glance with Father, who was nodding frantically. "So you get them too." Right. Okay. Because I was willing to bet there wasn't a Popsicle within a thousand miles from here.

Frankly, I was wondering how Father had gotten yogurt.

"Is there anything else I can do to make you more comfortable?" Father asked. A wicked gleam shone in Medusa's eyes before he waggled a finger at her. "No heads of your enemies on pikes."

She sighed, settling back on the pillows. "It's not like I wanted all of my enemies."

"I know," he said, adjusting the blankets over her rattlesnake tail.

Medusa dropped her Go-Gurt, her teeth set in a snarl as she gripped her belly. "Eeeeeee-yeeee . . . . !"

I timed her contraction as the lanterns above our heads swayed. The paperweights on Father McArio's desk rattled, as did the pens in a St. Louis University mug nearby.

The blankets twined in her tail crinkled and began to fall apart. I watched, rooted to the spot, as they crumbled to dust.

"Gah!" She flung herself back down on the cot.

Holy hell. I shook my head. "Forty-eight seconds," I said out loud, still not quite believing what I saw.

I'd tried to learn as much as I could about gorgon birth, but this wasn't in any of the manuals. I sure hoped we weren't in for any more surprises.

"Did that happen before?" I murmured to Father, as he found a broom and quietly went to work on the mess.

"Yes," he said. "I have to give her credit, though, she

tried to go easy on my Notre Dame stadium blanket." He smiled at a lumpy greenish mass in the corner.

Maybe I'd have Horace bring me a pair of fireproof gloves. Just then the sprite banged in through the door, followed by two more orderlies with delivery supplies, baby monitoring equipment, and even one of those portable baby warmers.

"Thanks, Horace," I said, as they started setting up.

"I'm not staying," he answered, handing me a Snickers bar. It was obviously melted. We were in limbo. I didn't care.

I shoved it in my pocket for later. "Did you get me a nurse?"

"No," he said, in a way that brooked no argument. Damn. I wasn't going to talk about this in front of Medusa. "What about Rodger?"

"In surgery."

"Send for Galen."

"Absolutely not!" Medusa shrieked. "I came here to see the professionals. Anyone else will be turned to stone."

I rested my hands on my hips as Horace and the orderlies fled. "Did you have to do that?" I asked Medusa.

"Power has its privileges," she said simply.

Nice.

She unwrapped another Go-Gurt while I pulled Father aside. "You're staying, right?"

He glanced over my shoulder. "As long as our patient doesn't seem to mind."

"Good. Listen," I said, unsure how to say what I had to tell him next. "Leta let my identity slip. And hers. She told every living dragon in limbo."

"No," he said softly.

"Yes." He touched my arm and I almost wished he hadn't because it made me want to sit down and cry.

It might not even matter anymore because I was about to deliver the baby that would damn everyone. It seemed everything I tried to do to make things better only made them worse.

Father shook his head. "I don't know what to tell you."

I shrugged off his grip, needing a little levity. "Fine load of help you are."

It didn't faze him. "I do know that things happen for reasons that we sometimes don't understand."

I smirked. "After everything we've seen here . . . You really believe that?"

"Yes," he said, positively unwavering. "And there's a reason you seek out my help. Deep down, you believe it too."

I shook my head. I'd give my life for a pinkie's worth of his faith. "Father, I—"

"Eeeee . . . !" Medusa shrieked behind me.

Father lurched backward. I went sideways. The ground shook so bad I had to grab on to the tent pole to stay upright. The cart rolled into the heart rate monitor and both of them crashed over.

"It's coming!" she screamed as winds tore through the tent.

Merde. I hoped it was just the child of the damned and not the gods coming to smite me. The canvas crackled. Fitz was barking wildly. The door rattled on its hinges. Light poured in from around the corners as everything rumbled and shook.

"Hold on, Medusa. I've got you!" I said, taking one hard step after another into the driving storm. Dust stung my eyes and I forced myself to keep pushing forward even as the gorgon clutched the sides of the cot. She ground her teeth, the snakes in her hair standing on end.

I knelt in front of her and fought her gauzy skirt. Father averted his eyes as I made my exam.

"I can see the head." She was fully dilated. Two or three good pushes and we should be good.

The winds died down and she leaned forward, panting. Sweat slicked her forehead and arms. "You can see my baby?"

I fought a grin. "She has hair like her mother."

Medusa choked on a grin.

"We're going to push on the next contraction, okay?" She nodded.

"Father, can you get me some fresh towels? And your welding gloves," I added, not taking my eyes off my patient. "You can do this, right?"

She blinked twice. "I want an epidural."

"It's too late for that, but the good news is this baby is coming fast."

"My baby," she said, panting.

"Yes," I said, reaching up to squeeze her hand.

A knock sounded at the door and Horace burst in.

"Did you bring Rodger?" I asked, trying to see behind him. I'd even take Nurse Hume at this point.

"No." Horace eyed Medusa like she was going to fry him on the spot. His attention shot to me. "We have bigger problems. The investigators are on the way."

"Here?" Panic shot through me. "They're coming here?"

Horace nodded frantically. "Thaïs is with them."

This was it. Only I couldn't leave. I couldn't do anything.

"Run!" Horace shrieked before he zoomed away.

"Eeeee . . ." Medusa clutched her belly.

"Get me the gloves," I said, hurrying toward her.

Winds streaked through the room. I clutched onto the bottom of the cot as it began sliding sideways. Father gripped my arm, shoving the gloves into my hands as the back wall of the tent blew out.

I shoved the gloves on as Father worked to keep the cot upright. Medusa screamed and sunlight blazed down as we lost the roof.

"She's coming!" I screamed over the din. Baby snakes snapped at my gloves as I supported the head. "I want you to push!"

Medusa's tail slammed against the side wall, taking it down. "It hurts!"

"On the count of three!" I told her.

"Ow-ow-ow!"

"One." The cot lurched toward me as the bottom right leg snapped off. Father shoved a shoulder underneath, keeping it steady.

I could almost see the shoulders. "Two."

"No!" she screamed.

Father reached out to take her hand, his shoulder still bearing the brunt of the lurching cot. Her talons dug into the skin on the top of his hand, drawing blood.

Driblets of sweat ran down my back. "Three!"

Medusa's shriek shattered the lanterns.

I forced my hands steady, as my pulse pounded in

my ears. "Push!" We almost had the baby's shoulders free.

"Duck!" Father hollered as one of the boards from the ceiling swung down, crashing into the freestanding heart monitor.

Fists pounded on the door, never mind that we had two entire walls blown out. "Investigators. Open up!"

Fuck.

Not now. Heart in my throat, I ignored them. "One more push."

"Argh!" Medusa flung her head back, her tail blasting through what was left of the side wall. "You said that the last time!"

"Go!" I ordered.

She stiffened, her growl shaking the tent.

Crash. The door fell in.

chapter twenty

Wind shrieked through the space. Thaïs stood front and center, flanked by two heavily armored investigators. The operatives wore head-to-toe red, with polished boots and the crest of the gods on each shoulder.

Sweet Jesus. I couldn't deal with them right now.

My gloved fingers supported the baby's head as a tiny asp from her hair wound around my thumb. This was what mattered. This baby. This life. I locked eyes with Medusa. "I've almost got her."

"Halt!" Metal screeched against metal as one of the investigators pulled his sword. I glanced up. The other whipped out a roll of parchment from his coat, his back ramrod straight, his jowls sagging. "We have a warrant."

"It's going to have to wait," I called above the winds, my clinical armor threatening to crack as Medusa geared up for another contraction.

She sat up on her elbows, body clenched, breath tight. "Get out!" She glared at the intruders, her hair twining.

"Out! I command!" Her jaw clenched and her irises reddened.

Oh, no. Not now.

"Calm down!" I warned her. Stress was bad for the baby and there was no way for me to monitor what was happening with my equipment in pieces on the floor.

Medusa's face was a mask of rage.

Padre and I shared a terrified glance. "Look away," I warned.

He jammed his head against his chest and shut his eyes tight. I did the same, bracing myself as bright heat seared through the tent. My breath felt humid, my hands stiff as I kept them steady for the babe. If anything happened to her, I'd never forgive myself. I took deep, measured breaths, tasting the acrid stench in the air, trying desperately to stay focused despite the unmistakable crackling of flesh turning to stone.

My mind swam and my muscles ached as the heat died down.

"What is this?" Medusa demanded.

Neck stiff, I lifted my head to find the gorgon frowning at me.

She heaved, her face set in a snarl, but at least her eyes were back to normal. "Intruders are not in my birth plan."

Mine either. I could only imagine the mess behind me, but I didn't have time to look. The baby was coming fast.

"Okay," I said to the gorgon. "Are you ready?"

She clutched the rails of the cot and looked at me like I was the one shooting curses out of my eyeballs. "It. Hurts."

"I know. You're doing great."

I flexed my fingers. "One more time," I said, as Father grappled with the bottom of the cot.

Medusa bore down with all her might. "Arrrrgggggg!"

"Good, good, good!"

I exhaled as the babe slid free, into my waiting arms. I turned her around, cradling her as she wriggled, her tiny fists closed tight. My heart did a flip-flop when she looked up at me with the biggest, most beautiful violet eyes. Her nose was a button, her little lips perfectly bowed. A baby asp gave the teeniest tiniest hiss as it curled around her cheek.

The winds had stopped, the air had stilled.

"She's perfect," I said.

I wrapped her in a clean towel. I didn't trust my legs, so I walked the baby up on my knees. Gingerly, I eased the baby into her mother's arms.

Medusa gasped. "She is perfect, isn't she?" She snuggled the babe against her breast, murmuring and cooing.

I stayed there and checked to make sure mom was doing okay, but her gorgon body was already healing fast.

Muscles stiff, I stood and eased off the welding gloves.

"Keep them," Father said, as he noticed the afterbirth sizzling at the tips. I dropped them where his trash can used to be. Then Father and I backed off to give Medusa and her baby some privacy.

I ventured a glance at the ruins of the doorway. The three intruders had been turned to stone. Only one of them had had the sense to duck. The other held his sword, ready to skewer us. And Thaïs, in stone as in life, sneered like the world had somehow forgotten to bow down and worship.

"Are you okay?" I asked Father. I saw that he'd managed to steady the cot with the remains of the heart monitor. Smart man. I hadn't even noticed him doing it. Then again, I'd been distracted.

"I've never seen a birth," he said, grinning ear to ear. "It's a miracle!"

I shook my head. "It's usually more organized."

Then again, this was war. We were grateful when our patients lived, when we could send them back to the front to be shot at again. I'd never delivered a baby down here. I felt a burst of warmth.

This was the first time I was dealing in life instead of death.

I had to think it meant something for our future that a child could be born here, among the chaos. I glanced over at Medusa, murmuring kisses on the wee one's forehead. This baby might be epic, but so was every child. This was a new life, a fresh start. A person with infinite possibilities ahead of her.

This was the moment when one child really could change the world.

I watched a little snake tail escape her makeshift blanket and curl around her mother's arm.

This child—every child—was a gift. Innocent. And I refused to believe that something so beautiful could bring total disaster.

The sun hung low in the sky.

Father and I wandered past the smashed medical equipment and debris, to where his desk used to be. All of the walls were blown off his hutch. We'd lost the roof too.

Fitz whined and trotted in circles. Father bent down to hug and calm him.

"I'm sorry, Father." Sorry for him, for me. For this war and everyone in it. I took a step and nearly crushed his seminary graduation photo, under smashed glass. I retrieved it for him as Father stroked Fitz's head and let the hellhound lick his cheeks.

"Pictures. Stadium blankets. They're only objects." Father glanced around the ruined tent. "Although I admit I was growing a bit too fond of them." His mouth twisted into a small smile. "It's people who matter."

I couldn't agree more.

We stood inside the wooden frame of the hutch and looked out onto the minefield.

A light breeze nudged sheets of tattered canvas across the junkyard. The sun sent rainbows skittering down the broken windshield of a wrecked Humvee.

There was nothing to do now but wait.

I stiffened when I saw movement behind the burned-out ambulance. "Padre," I warned.

He tried to nudge in front of me, which was sweet, but futile. Nothing would be able to protect me from the gods.

My palms slicked and my breath hitched.

I'd always known this day would come eventually.

If this was the way the gods wanted it, fine. I could deal. As long as they didn't hurt anyone else, especially the baby.

There was only one of them. Although one was all they'd need. I wondered what kind of torture they'd chosen. Maybe I could bait this god and trick him into smiting me on the spot.

He was strong, sturdily built, and . . . wearing a brick-red flight suit. Sweet heaven. "Galen?"

My head felt light when he emerged from the mess.

Damn. It felt like I'd aged ten years since I'd last seen him. I flung my arms around him and kissed him soundly on the mouth.

"Thank God." I nipped him on the mouth. "It's." I kissed him again. "You." He felt so solid against me, so right. I was a wicked, stinking, gooey mess, but I didn't care.

His hands tightened on my hips. "A man could get used to this."

Father grinned and clapped Galen on the shoulder. "Good to see you, son."

"I heard Thaïs was heading this way and thought there might be trouble," he said, glancing past me to the ruins of the tent. "Clearly you've taken care of it."

"It was actually a rather uneventful birth. Except for them." We stopped in front of the statues of Thaïs and the two investigators.

"Yes," Father said. "What are we going to do about this?"

Galen inspected Thaïs's outthrust jaw and superior sneer. "Do we have to do anything?"

"Call me crazy," I said, "but I think HQ's going to notice."

Medusa waved at Galen. "You came!" she exclaimed, as if he'd dropped by for a hospital visit.

"Wouldn't miss it," he said, moving to her side. He pulled up Father's discarded stool and sat to hold the baby. "Congratulations. She's beautiful." Galen cradled her while Medusa reached out to stroke her hair. "What's her name?"

"Emma," she said, growling gently. She glanced at Galen. "You don't think that's too common, do you?"

"No," he said, as the baby gripped his finger. "I didn't meet anyone on the Isle of Wrath and Pain named Emma."

He looked so natural with the child, like a proud uncle. Pride swept through me, followed by a pang of regret. Galen would never know what it was like to have a child of his own. Neither would I.

We had no future. Unless we could somehow fix all of this.

After a while, Galen gave Emma back to Medusa and we moved away to give the two some privacy while she nursed.

Father had gone to fetch the new mamma something to eat.

We moved to the sculpture garden. I didn't want to get my hopes up, but it was hard with Galen right here, with me. So near I wanted to touch him, hold him.

We'd been through too much to let it end this way.

The child of the damned shall damn us all.

I ran my fingers across a particularly beautiful dove, poised to take flight off a twining metal olive tree. Father had given it a glittering yellow glass beak and pink-tipped wings. "I refuse to believe it," I said to him, low so that Medusa wouldn't overhear. "Baby Emma is a gift, not a curse."

Galen stood opposite me. "Exactly. And I'm not sure what it means."

It was the first time Galen had denied one of the prophecies could come true. I didn't point it out. He knew.

Medusa and her child snuggled together, eyes closed. Several of the baby snakes had even curled to sleep. A few slithered lazily over Medusa's hand, mouthing at her fingers.

I didn't like waiting. There was too much at stake. I ran my hand harder against the sculpture, nearly slicing the pads of my fingers. "We need to strategize. Somehow, we need to change fate. Maybe it has been done before. It's not like gods would broadcast that."

We both glanced back at mother and child.

"Fitz." Medusa frowned, her eyes half open.

The baby's rattlesnake tail had escaped the blanket and the hellhound was licking it.

"Ew. Fitz," I said, going for the dog.

The baby threw her arms out and laughed.

The hairs on my arms and the back of my neck stood on end as the air sizzled around us. "What the—" I stopped in my tracks as I heard the distinct crackling of a portal firing up.

Galen grabbed my hand and we both watched as a bundle of color spun in a compact spiral just beyond the minefield. It lingered waist-high, spitting energy and light.

It flickered at the edges, and it was small, but it was there. In fact, if I wasn't mistaken, this was the same portal that had brought me to this cursed place.

Holy shit. "That's the way to New Orleans," I said, voice cracking.

I stared at Medusa, and the child she held. "Only the gods can open portals. This baby's half damned."

"Half god," Galen said, his voice tight.

Medusa winked. "I'm not telling you who I slept with."

I wanted to kiss her. Good thing I was too shocked to move.

Galen's hold on me tightened. "Portals take you anywhere you want to go."

The gods had kept them hidden from us. They'd trapped us here, isolated and unable to escape. Until now.

I turned to Medusa. "Make her laugh again."

She smiled at my wide-eyed wonder and tickled her baby's rattlesnake tail. Emma giggled and we were hit with another blast of heat as a faint red portal revealed itself directly over us.

Galen and I shielded our eyes. "Where the hell does that go?" I croaked.

"It's a pathway of the gods," he said.

As I live and breathe . . . "We definitely want to avoid that one."

Galen watched it, as if he expected it to smite us any second. "Yes, we do."

I couldn't believe it. I was staring at our way out. "How did the gods even hide the portals?"

"Like this," Medusa said, snapping her fingers. At once, the pathways disappeared.

"No!" I cried.

"Don't yell in front of my baby," Medusa scolded, as if she were the calm one. Luckily, little Emma was grinning up a storm. The gorgon let out a contented sigh and continued. "Portals are always there. The gods just mute them so mortals like you don't do anything stupid."

"But your child can unlock the portals." Reveal them.

Medusa tucked Emma back into her blankets. "I told you she was special."

"'The child of the damned shall damn us all,'" I murmured under my breath. "But it's not us. We're not the ones being damned," I said, the burden of it lifting.

"They were talking about the gods," Galen said.

It made sense. The oracles served the gods after all.

I hadn't known just how resigned to death and damnation I'd become until I realized that it wasn't true. We could live. We could fight.

Or we could go home.

The child of the damned would damn them and their plans. *She'd revealed a way for us to go home.*

Galen stood as tense as I'd ever seen him, full of wound energy and strength. "We can leave," he said, the possibility of it washing over him.

Yes. "With two opposing armies." This could get interesting. The portals were weak. The logistics were a nightmare. And the gods would fight us. I knew they would. But this was our chance and I'd be damned if I wasn't going to take it. "Here's what we need to do. We need to start sneaking people out of camp. Tonight."

Galen looked at me like I was nuts. Which, okay, maybe I was. "You don't think they're going to notice when people go missing?"

It could get dicey. But, "We're one prophecy away," I said quickly. "We can cover."

Galen swore under his breath. "It's a risk we'll have to take." But his lips tipped up and soon he was smiling. We both were. "First, we'll get the dragons out," he said. "That means Marc, Leta, and anybody else in camp who may be targets."

"Right. Then we'll find a way to expand. Open portals in the other camps." I didn't know how, but we had to figure it out. This was it. Our chance. "I can't wait to get out of here," I said, throwing my arms around his neck. We could do this. I knew it.

"I love you," he said, grinning as his lips brushed mine. "We will get out of here. Together. And when we do, I'm going to show you exactly how much."

I kissed him slow and sweet, ignoring Medusa's groans.

We broke away to find the gorgon rolling her eyes. "Ah, what do I care? I'm Greek," she said. "It's not like I haven't seen it before."

chapter twenty-one

Father returned to us with four plates of chipped beef Wellington from the cafeteria.

We ate standing up, and it tasted fantastic, which meant I was starving. After we finished, Father gathered up the plates. I wasn't sure why he focused on neatness in the middle of the wreck that had been his home. Maybe it was just his way to cope.

Meanwhile, Medusa eyed the statues.

Galen caught her watching. "We've got to get rid of those before she knocks the heads off," he murmured. "How about I take care of that while you get cleaned up?"

I eyed the change of clothes and shower kit Father had brought me. "Is it that bad?"

Galen barked out a laugh. "I'm not going to answer that."

"Ah, so the big, bad special ops soldier is afraid of something," I said, gathering up my things while he began tossing a few loose boards out of Father's jeep.

Padre hooked up a trailer and positioned it next to the statues while I headed off.

Luckily, Father's shower was still standing. Most likely because he'd connected it to an old water tank, about twenty feet into the minefield. I cleaned up and put on my fresh clothes.

Medusa and the baby were asleep when I got back.

Galen was talking to Father.

"Done so soon?" I asked. Those statues had to be heavy.

"More or less." Galen shared a conspiratorial glance with Father. "I couldn't take them to camp."

True. He didn't need that kind of attention. Besides, I supposed it would be hard to explain three flesh-to-stone injuries without talking about the birth we'd conducted outside the clinic.

"So what did you do with Thaïs and company?" I asked.

"We left them in the overturned guard tower," Father said. "You know. The one with the colony of saber-toothed sand lizards."

No kidding? "I've never heard of that prank."

"Oh," Father remarked, rather innocently. "The point is, we didn't think anyone would look there."

I'd have to agree with him on that one.

At least we had the investigators off our case. For now. We'd have to bring them back eventually, but there was no need to rush.

"Come with me," Galen said, taking my hand.

"Is Father going to be all right here?"

"Go." Father shooshed us along. "I've got this handled."

Twenty bucks said he was the first person to say that about Medusa. Still, I wasn't about to argue. Instead, I let Galen lead me down the path to the rocks.

I felt better than I had in a long time. Free. Like things really could work out. Medusa's baby was beautiful. She'd opened up possibilities I'd never dared imagine. For the first time, I let myself hope.

"Galen." I stopped him at a small clearing before we descended down to the rocks. "I love you." We'd come so far since we'd been here last. And we'd done it because we loved each other, because we trusted each other and worked to make things better.

He brushed a kiss over my lips. "I've always loved you," he whispered, his mouth against mine. His fingers threaded through the hair at the back of my neck and drew me closer.

He kissed me and my eyes slipped shut. My heart pounded and I felt it in the back of my knees as I opened my mouth to his.

My fingers tightened on his shoulders and I moaned as he kept up his delicious assault, his tongue battling with mine. He was erect, as excited as I was, and I ground against him. He felt so good. So hard against me. And I knew exactly how it felt to have him inside me.

I went for his zipper and ended up running my hands down his arms instead. God, I loved his arms. He broke away and kissed my cheek, my chin. He ran kisses over my neck until he found the soft spot behind my ear. I practically purred with it.

"This is where I belong," he murmured between kisses. "Here. With you."

I touched my hand to his temple, drawing it down

his cheek, and saw the raw love in his eyes. "I know. I want it too." More than anything. I knew exactly what he was feeling—the joy, the love, the knowledge that this was good and right. That for the first time, we had a chance at true happiness.

And here—now—he deserved to know exactly how much I loved him.

He cupped my breast, his fingers finding the nipple, eliciting a gasp from me. I ran my hands down his arms, over his back. I gripped him and pulled him tighter to me.

"You taste so good," he murmured, pulling away, kissing my breast through the thin material of my tank top. He lifted it off so I was standing in front of him, nude from the waist up.

"We have to get out of here," he said, voice rough.

Only then did I realize that we were indeed still standing on the path to the rocks.

"This way," he said, leading me toward the minefield, past a wall of plywood, to a small blue telephone booth.

I'd never seen it before. "They don't have telephones in limbo."

"Not anymore," he said, drawing me inside, bracing me against a cool metal wall. The sun was going down. It was getting chillier. Although I had a feeling I wouldn't be worrying about that.

"I left my top on the path." I gasped as his mouth closed around one nipple. I leaned my head against the wall. God, it felt incredible.

"It's in my pocket," he murmured, moving to the

other breast, but by that time, I'd forgotten what he was talking about. I just wanted more.

His hand slid down under my scrubs to where I was slick and wet and dying for him.

Oh, yes. Right there.

One of his fingers circled my slit, teasing me. I drew in a hard breath, clutching his back as he touched me and stroked me and made me lose my mind. His fingers moved in rhythm with his mouth and I felt myself gasping, tensing. I felt so empty and I wanted to tell him to hurry the fuck up only I didn't want him to stop.

I was drenched, throbbing. Focused on the delicious tightening between my legs. I wanted his cock there instead of his fingers. I fumbled once more for his zipper and ended up hitching a leg over his hip instead. I was desperate, needy. I wanted more.

He gave a low chuckle, kissing up my neck as his fingers worked their magic between my legs.

His warm breath tickled my ear and an orgasm flooded through me. My bones went weak and my cry of ecstasy was swallowed up by our little room, our escape.

He rested his forehead against mine, telling me how much he loved me, how beautiful I was, how much he needed me, while he kept touching me until the last streaks of my orgasm sparkled through me.

I watched him as he shrugged out of his flight suit and boxers. He was perfect. Rippled and muscular. Restrained and loving. And oh, my God—hard as a rock. He gave me a small, sweet grin that quickly turned into a groan when I wrapped my hand around his cock.

My nipples tightened against his chest hair as he

kissed me. I ran my hand up the length of him, then abandoned it, running my fingers through his hair as I kissed him for all I was worth. I poured all of my love, faith, and strength into that kiss. Because he believed, I believed. Galen was my rock. The one man I could count on, now and for everything we would face.

We'd do it together.

I savored the surety of his arms around me. His hard determination. The way he rubbed against me, my breasts crushed against his chest, his cock against my belly.

It seemed he was as desperate as I was, kissing me, holding me. He shifted and the thick, wet head of his erection pressed against me.

"Now," I murmured, rubbing myself against him, wetting him with my juices.

I was so slick, so ready as he pulled back and looked into my eyes. I saw the love reflected there, the trust—the knowledge that we were meant to be together.

My breath hitched as he slid into me, filling me perfectly.

He fought to keep his eyes open, groaning as he withdrew slightly, found the right angle and buried himself to the hilt.

He kissed my neck, my shoulder, burying his head against me. I braced against the metal wall behind me, grasping him as he stroked me in the most intimate way possible. Loving it as I felt the puffs of air as he gasped against the curve of my shoulder.

Sweat slicked between us, our heated strokes magnified in the small booth. I ran my fingers along his back, over his ass, and down his thighs. He tasted like salt and desire and I gave a small cry as his long, thick cock stroked me.

I grasped him, my fingers digging into him as he thrust faster. Every sensation heated inside me as he quickened and drove me harder. He knew exactly what I needed, what I wanted.

He knew me in a way no one ever had before.

"I need you." His warm kiss stroked my neck. "Always." He plundered my mouth, rocked my body, and with a sharp jolt, I came, kissing him hard, squeezing his cock as the pleasure of it broke over me.

He tore his mouth from mine, moaning, pushing harder, his entire body tense and hard as he rocketed to his own orgasm. I held him tight, reveling in his release, loving it as he gasped against my ear.

For a long time, I couldn't move. Didn't want to. I could spend the rest of my life curled around this man, his cock inside me, and I'd be just fine.

He kissed my shoulder, my neck, his cock softening inside me. I wished we could fall asleep this way.

His breath scraped against my skin. I felt his heartbeat, and mine, both pounding hard. "We've got to find a way to get this phone booth out of the minefield," he mused.

"Hmm . . ." I pondered the thought while stroking the muscles along his shoulders. "So now you have a phone booth fetish?"

He raised his head, his hair rumpled. "After that, who wouldn't?"

I kissed him lightly on the nose, held him close. "Thank you for being here with me."

His mouth tugged up at the corner. "Well, you know how I like to be around when all hell breaks loose."

As much as I loathed losing the moment, we really did need to get dressed. We gathered my scrubs and his flight suit, and stepped out into the darkening minefield.

The cool air hit me and I hurried into my panties, as Galen handed me my top.

"Aren't you getting dressed?" I asked, inching the T-shirt over my breasts.

"Sure," he said, eyes glittering with desire as I shimmied back into my scrubs. We'd have to do something about that later.

For now, it was getting late. The sky was streaked with red. I looked up as a large bird circled over camp. Two more flew in from the south.

Strange.

"What is up with the birds?" I'd seen vultures around camp, but this was something else. For one thing, they were huge. For another, they had tails.

"Those aren't birds." Galen stood naked, watching. His body tensed. "They're dragons."

Seven hells. He was right. If I looked closely, I could pick out the spikes at their backs, the way their tails curved.

Two more flew in from the east. "It's almost like they're assembling." Right over the MASH 3063rd. As I spoke, I saw more coming in from the south.

"Get your shoes on." Galen was already zipping up his flight suit. "There's no hiding now."

chapter twenty-two

We made good time through the minefield. Still, as we ran, at least a dozen more dragons zoomed overhead.

I fought between keeping my eyes to the ground, watching for trip wires, and glancing anxiously at the sky. It was incredible. "Where are they all coming from?"

"The old army. The new army." Galen moved beside me, with the stride of a trained warrior. "This is a disaster."

Every MP within a fifty-mile radius would be able to see what was going on.

And there was no way the gods weren't going to notice.

I'd never needed Galen more than I did now. He was with me in all things. Which meant we had two choices. We could end this war together, or we'd die together. I wanted more than anything to fight for this man, for what we could have.

And it was even more than that. I wanted to give Rodger his family back. To pull Father back from the edge of hell. To let Marius spend eternity the way he wanted, even if it meant he'd spend the rest of his immortal life lounging around on black leather furniture in a trendy loft with those ridiculous mirrored walls and ceilings. They deserved to be happy. We all did.

I wanted to give my friends and everyone who had fought so hard the one thing that we hadn't dared hope for—peace.

I didn't know why the dragons had come or what they could possibly do to battle the gods, but I had to think it had something to do with my bronze weapon.

"There she is," Galen said, as we reached the edge of the minefield.

He pointed down through the cemetery, to the massive dragons clustering at the very center of the camp. They were red, green, gold, black, orange, yellow, their scales glittering against the setting sun. Leta stood in the center of it all, her eyes wild, her chest heaving.

Dragons trampled the bulletin board to matchsticks and crushed the torch stands along the paths. MASH staffers crisscrossed the camp and gathered around the edges of the assault.

A black dragon near the edge belched fire and hit one of the light poles. Black smoke curled into the air, as flames shot up like a giant torch.

Galen and I dodged graves and tried not to lose our footing as we careened down through the cemetery.

I spotted a green horned dragon at the back herding several dragons who had broken out and started running toward the helo pad.

We were in real trouble if the dragons got spooked or decided to go on a rampage. I hoped with everything I had that our new guests weren't as fragile as Leta had been when she first came to us.

Holly and another nurse stood shocked outside Recovery, as a giant black and gold flecked beast strolled down the path like she owned it.

We kept running.

"It's the revolution!" Leta bellowed, when we reached her.

No. I gripped her shoulders. "You've got to get them out of here."

Leta's eyes glittered and her red hair tangled wildly. "They stay. This is your army. I am the bronze dragon. I'm not going to cower or hide. Never again."

Wrong answer. I held her tighter. "Look, I'm glad you can control yourself now." At least when it came to shifting. "But you said it yourself. Telling them about us—both of us—was a mistake."

We could only hope we survived long enough to undo the damage.

She jerked out of my grip. "That was the old way. This is the new one. Maybe we did not plan this, but it is done. These dragons risked their lives to come here. They are not victims anymore and neither are we."

Galen cursed under his breath. "You're going to get these people killed."

Leta glared at him. "These dragons are dead already. They were marked for extermination the moment they chose to leave their posts and come to us."

The dragons kept landing. They still wore the collars that kept them more animal than human, but they had broken free. I couldn't believe this was happening.

The dragons spilled past Kosta's office and into the field beyond as more and more dark forms appeared on the horizon. I spotted the colonel outside, barking orders to Shirley, who frantically wrote on her clipboard while trying to dodge a wayward tail.

No question about it. The revolution was happening. And it was going to fail. There were tens of thousands of humans and other shifters with no telepathy, people who had been trained to kill on order. People who would put down the revolt, who would strike down our chances—and their own—of ever going home again.

"I heal people," I ground out, as two more dragons landed. "It'll be a cold day in hell before I'll tear them apart." This wasn't a battle and we didn't have an army. What we had was an unplanned, chaotic mess.

I spotted Marc. He looked tired, worn. His cheek was bruised and his lip was split open. "Please tell me you've been fighting this."

"I did," he said, his breath coming in harsh pants. "I have." He stood between us looking from the dragons to me. "But I think I was wrong."

"You're insane."

"We didn't choose this, Petra, but it's happening," he said. "Right now. You can't back away and you can't cover your eyes. You just get to decide how you're going to stand. And let me tell you this: if the gods are going to slaughter us, I'm going to go down fighting."

Fuck. "I get your need for revenge." I craved it as well. And the dragons had even more reason than I did to stand up. They didn't need to be kept like animals. They didn't need to be used as weapons. They were hurting. So was Marc. I got that.

This war had cost Marc everything—including me. But drawing weapons against the gods was suicide.

Especially when there was another way. "Medusa's baby can open portals."

Marc stared at me. "Sweet Jesus."

"We can send them home so long as the gods don't notice the portal we now have floating over the mine-field." I shielded my eyes from the dust as a dragon landed hard right next to us. "I think they're going to notice this."

I could see Marc's mind racing. "We have to get them out of camp."

"Good idea, and while you're at it, find a way to sta-bilize them so we don't send a horde of half-wild drag-ons into New Orleans."

"Let's go," he said, leading us through the mass of bodies.

The dragons had lit fires on the communications poles, casting sharp light and shadows onto the crowd.

I looked to Galen. My rough-and-ready warrior stood tall, shoulders back, the entire left side of his face cast in shadows. A sheen of sweat slicked his skin, and he could have used a shave.

Leta snarled when we caught up to her beside the VIP tent. "We are your weapon. Use us."

She didn't get it. None of them did. My teeth clenched. My body shook. "I never wanted a bronze weapon."

I'd never asked for it. And it would be a cold day in hell before I'd use it.

Leta bared her teeth. "This is your destiny, not your *choice*." She advanced on me, ready to pounce. "You owe it to me and to them to—"

"Get back—" Galen ordered, grabbing her, holding her at a distance as she lunged at me.

Four MPs shoved through the crowd. I was almost relieved until two of them took Galen by the arms.

Colonel Kosta stood behind them. "Galen of Delphi, you are under arrest for dereliction of duty."

Galen shoved a raving Leta back as he struggled against the massive pair of Cyclopes. "You think now's the time?" he barked.

"He's helping us," I explained to the commander. "Yes, he doesn't belong here, but don't you think we have bigger problems?"

The commander eyeballed me, the scar on his cheek puckering. "I don't have a choice."

"Shirley," I pleaded to my friend behind him. Not like she could do anything, but Jesus Christ.

Just then I spotted Horace darting over the crowd, torch in hand. "The new prophecy is in!"

The dragons let out a mighty roar. Heat blasted us as they spat fire into the air. Horace landed next to Kosta and cleared his throat. The embers floated down while the PA system crackled to life.

We endured the screech of feedback before the microphone clicked. "This just in from the gods," Horace announced into the mic.

Leta yanked it out of his hand. "I have something to tell all of you. It's about the prophecies."

Oh, no. Oh, shit.

I tried to tear the microphone from her hand, but she

was too strong. My skin was rubbed raw as she yanked it away.

"Petra is the doctor who can see the dead," she announced, prideful. Suicidal. "I am her bronze weapon. And now Petra will use the dragons to defeat the gods!"

The hell I would.

The ground shook as countless dragons roared and stomped their feet. I glanced frantically to Galen, who looked like he could chew nails.

Horace fluttered next to me, visibly pale. "Is it true?" he asked, his voice echoing out over our unit.

The microphone screeched feedback. It was picking up everything. The entire camp was looking at me. I didn't know what to say. This was not how I wanted to tell everyone. Hell, I didn't want to tell anyone.

I didn't know if I could lie to them anymore. They deserved better. My throat tightened and my voice caught. "It's true."

The entire camp went quiet, stunned. Shirley stared at me, openmouthed. Even Kosta looked surprised.

Horace cleared his throat. "I don't want to freak anybody out, but we just got word that the armies are massing directly east of here."

That sent the crowd into a fervor.

"When were you going to mention that?" Marc snapped.

"I'm trying," Horace shot back, one wing fluttering harder than the other one, tilting him off balance. "That's not even all of it. The last prophecy is in."

Fuck. This was it.

Galen reached for me, but the MPs blocked him.

I was shaking, tense.

Not only was I outed, but chances were, my life was about to go to hell. After this, there was nowhere else to go. It was win or fail.

Horace's hand shook as he read from a piece of paper. " 'As armies collide . . .' "

The dragons gave a deafening roar until we were all screaming for them to stop.

Horace yelled over the din. " *'The healer will face the gods . . .'* "

My chest tightened in shock. I knew this day would happen. Still, I wasn't ready for it.

" *'. . . and leave this world forever.'* "

"What?" I sputtered. The armies were going to fight and I was going to face the gods—and I was going to lose?

As armies collide, the healer will face the gods, and leave this world forever.

It had to mean something else. Maybe. *Please.*

The prophecies were never one hundred percent clear.

What if I didn't have to die? What if I could just sneak through a portal and leave this world?

But no, I couldn't run away and leave my friends to deal with the fallout. The prophecy said I had to face the gods. I didn't see Zeus opening any portals for me, slapping me on the back and letting me go. There was only one way to end things and it wouldn't be good.

The camp had gone deathly silent. Even the dragons stood mute. We were going to fail.

We always had hope before, a reasonable belief that maybe, just maybe, we could pull this off.

Now?

We were so close to the end. I was going to have to sacrifice myself. I'd have to die. I turned to Galen. At least he looked as furious as I felt.

"This is bullshit," he said, shocked.

After everything we'd done. After all we'd sacrificed and worked for, hoped and dreamed, it was going to end like this.

There were no guarantees we'd even succeed. We only knew that I would die a horrible death. Or more likely, be taken by the gods for eternal punishment. It was wrong and terrifying and impossible to avoid. I knew by now that there was no other logical way for this to end.

"Jesus." I felt light-headed. I needed to breathe.

"We'll figure this out," Galen said, even as he was held powerless by the guards. He was strong and loyal and determined. He was the bravest man I'd ever met. But even he couldn't stop this.

No matter what we'd shared or what we felt for each other, I was going to leave. I was going to die.

I couldn't imagine facing the gods with my secret. I hadn't wanted anything other than to live my life. Be normal. Have friends and a mortgage and a shot at something more. But that wasn't going to happen now.

The dragons roared and collided around us as the ground trembled. The skies opened up and I felt sick to my stomach.

"It's all over the news," Horace said, his voice grave. "The gods want to get one last battle in. They're going to decide everything before peace strikes."

They were going to wipe us out.

Okay. I could do this. I found Marc next to Kosta. "Get the dragons out. Everyone at the 3063rd too. Father will show you where."

I turned to Galen. It was hard to see him through the tears crowding my eyes but I could see his anguish as well, the scattered hopes. I regretted every last second of pain I was causing him. Felt awful that I'd never get to hold him again. That I'd never have a life with this man. I'd never get to love him the way he deserved. "I love you," I told him. "I always will." Nothing could change that.

"Petra—" He looked like he was going to say something, stop me. His face was a mask of pain. "I love you."

I smiled. Couldn't help it. It lit me up every time I thought of how much that man loved me.

Just as quickly, despair settled in once more. I gave one last nod to my friends and colleagues, the people that had been my family down here. The ones who had made it bearable. I had to do this for them.

Get on with it, Robichaud.

I forced myself to move, to leave them. I walked past the VIP tent and headed straight east, out of camp.

They let me, their silence speaking volumes.

There was nothing else any of us could do.

My boots crunched against the sandy red soil as I reached the edge of our unit and kept going. Now that I was past the dragons, I could see the hulking forms of the mass of troops dead ahead.

Every step brought me closer to death, dismemberment, eternal punishment.

At least my death would mean something. I'd gain an end to this conflict. I'd free my friends.

I'd seen a lot of people die for nothing in this war. Hell, I'd prepared myself to be one of them. I'd walked through the MASH 3063rd graveyard and known that's where I'd spend the rest of eternity, forgotten.

At least now my death would buy freedom for everyone trapped down here.

Yes, this was the end. But damn, what a way to go.

chapter twenty-three

The heavens had opened over the massing armies, bathing the entire landscape in an eerie pink light. It was like dawn, only it was unnatural.

Wrong.

But soon—when I'd done my duty—we'd have peace.

Galen would be released. My friends could go home. The dragons would never have to fight again.

When I died.

The gods knew how close we were to ending it all.

I could feel their energy crackling in the air.

Lightning struck and loud booms sounded as the gods transferred troops and artillery.

I focused on putting one foot in front of the other. The path curved to the left, but I kept going straight, through the stark desert, toward the thundering armies.

Images scattered in the distance, and when I drew closer, I saw that there were dozens upon dozens of spirits waiting for me. I recognized some, like the visiting doctor who had lost his life to a poisoned weapons wound. I saw Charlie. He gave a small wave; I nodded as I headed toward the battle.

I didn't understand it. They could have left at any time. They didn't have a stake in this. I fisted my hands in my pockets. Then it hit me.

Charlie and the rest did have a right to be here. They'd waited for this, for justice, for the end of the war. I might not be able to make what happened to them right, but I could give them the peace and the rest they'd been waiting for.

Trudging on, I saw Klotho herself standing alone in the desert. I'd almost mistaken the Fate for a ghost. Her gnarled hand clutched a length of weaving twine and her thin, wrinkled lips pressed together as she watched me.

"You did this," I said, as I approached her.

"No," she said, the wrinkles in her face deepening as she narrowed her eyes. "You did." She pointed a ruby-ringed finger at me. "You wanted to make a difference." Her voice grated like the sands of the desert.

"I gotta stop saying that," I muttered.

Behind her, the armies faced each other over an open field. Both sides were so massive, I couldn't begin to count the soldiers, or even see where the lines ended. It was a wave of people, of fragile lives, on each side.

The skies crackled as more men, more weapons were added to the never-ending sea of bodies. Immortal armies built up incredible amounts of energy. It was a side effect of the enormous power of these soldiers. It could melt engines, jam guns, short out modern weapons systems. The electricity crackled over my skin and made my head swim.

At the center of the armies was no-man's-land, a

break of desert no more than fifty feet wide. Menhit, Egyptian goddess of war and massacre, stood with Mars, the Roman god of war.

More gods and goddesses descended from the clouds.

I'd never been this close to the battle lines. The gods were treating it like a show. Like the gladiatorial contests from ages ago—only on a much larger, deadlier scale.

I walked straight for the Great Divide. I'd tell them who I was. I'd turn myself in. I'd bring an end to this insanity.

The energy of the Great Divide was deafening. I'd better not get fried before I could get close. Warning cannons boomed as I walked down, right into the break between the armies. It was like the road to hell.

It pressed down on my chest, stealing my breath. As long as I could breathe, think, put one foot in front of the other, I'd keep going.

The gods didn't even notice me until I drew within five feet of Menhit. She wore a cape made from the pelt of a lion, bedewed with glittering jewels. She turned her high-cheekboned, haughty gaze my way and the crushing fog of the Great Divide lifted.

My limbs trembled and my heart lodged in my throat. Still, I spoke as loudly as I could. "Stop." It didn't even sound like my own voice as I called out to the god, "You've got me. I'm the healer who sees the dead."

And then all hell broke loose.

Sandals pounded the ground as gods landed left and right. Their energies hit the Great Divide with enough force to give me whiplash. In an instant, I was surrounded.

My ears popped and my head lightened.

Menhit shoved through some of the lower goddesses and stood directly in front of me. She leveled the blade of her sickle at my throat, the razor-sharp edge scraping my skin.

"I don't have time for this, mortal." She lingered over the last word with a sneer.

I didn't dare move as Mercury landed next to her. Then Abnoba, the Celt, along with some goddess who wore nothing but feathers.

"Move the blade back," the feather goddess rasped. "They die when you slit their throats."

Menhit sneered and drew back the sickle.

"Holy shit," I said quickly. And not just because of the sickle.

Right there, over Menhit's shoulder, I saw a beautiful Chinese goddess wearing silver robes. Around her neck was a silver chain that held a disc of the moon.

And she was dead. A ghost.

Major gods couldn't die—or so they'd always told us. I didn't know what to think. Maybe there was more happening here than any of us had realized.

But I couldn't think on that now. I had to prove myself.

"You." I pointed at her. "Chinese moon goddess. What is your name?"

It startled her. But she didn't respond.

Menhit paled. "Who are you speaking with? You make no sense." She scoffed, raising her sickle once more.

My jaw slackened. "You can't see her?"

The moon goddess began to leave.

"Wait!" I stammered. What was her name? I knew I should have paid more attention in mythology class. "You! With the silver robes and the twinkly eyelashes and the hair piled up on your head and that, that disc moon necklace!"

She froze.

"What do they call you?" I looked directly at her, begging, pleading. If she disappeared, I was screwed. She glanced furiously around her. Yes, the gods looked right through her, but, "I can see you," I said, willing her to believe me, to stay with me.

She blinked.

"Tell me," I rasped.

"Heng-O," she said

Oh, thank God. "Heng-O," I repeated. "She's right here," I told them. "She's dead."

Thunder boomed as a Chinese god pushed his way to the front. "You lie." He sneered, eyes wild. "Heng-O is at home."

No she wasn't. She was right next to him.

Heng-O pulled her robe to the side and I saw the deep gash to her chest. Poor woman. She'd had a painful death.

"She's been stabbed in the heart." And not that deeply. I'd saved Galen from a similar wound.

A lump formed in my throat. She clutched her hands to her chest and gave a small bow. I brought a hand to my own heart in solidarity.

Who knew it took so little to kill a god?

"You high gods aren't truly immortal," I said, to myself as much as them. I looked the Chinese god in the eye. "You can kill each other."

No wonder they'd conscripted humans, shifters, demigods, and everybody else to do their dirty work. "You don't want to fight each other because you could actually die."

The gods broke into chaos.

I tried to step back, but there was nowhere to go as accusations flew.

Pretty soon, I realized that the gods weren't arguing over her murder, how her husband most likely had killed her, or how the crime should be punished. They wanted to know how a mortal could find out about the death of a god.

All eyes turned back to me.

"She *is* the healer," the Chinese god snarled. "We should sentence her to the eighteen levels of hell." He paused, then added, "To the grinding rooms."

"No," said a blond goddess wearing ox horns. She fisted her hands in anticipation. "The healer will drive my plows for eternity, while eagles peck out her eyes."

"Oh, that is so tacky," said a goddess wearing a wreath of peacock feathers. "We should tie her to a rock, split her open, and let hummingbirds make nests in her innards."

I couldn't believe these people were for real.

I felt a steadying hand on my shoulder, turned, and saw—"Galen!" Shock slammed through me. "You're here." What was he doing here? It didn't make sense. But at the moment, I didn't care. Relief wound through me along with joy that he'd do this. That he'd be here for the end.

He gave a small smile, as he caressed my cheek. "I don't want you to face this alone."

I hugged him tightly. "You got away."

"I'm pretty good at sneaking around."

I let out a snort. Giddy. Scared out of my mind. And just when I'd wrapped my head around Galen being there, Marc and Leta walked up behind him. "You."

The corner of Marc's mouth tipped up. Leta had her eyes closed. I could only guess she was projecting what was happening here. They were supposed to be escaping.

Through the clouds of dust on the path, I could see a shadow, like a new army of people marching up the Great Divide. As they drew closer I could make out the familiar faces of my friends, my colleagues at the MASH 3063rd. They were supposed to be sneaking through the portal. But they were here.

They were all here.

Marius walked up, hands on his hips, staring at the gods and not quite believing. Kosta drew up next to him, with a half-panicked Shirley clinging to his arm. Jeffe pawed nervously at the ground.

"What are you doing here?" I'd wanted them out, gone. I needed to do this alone. Although, damn, it felt good to have them with me, if only for a little while.

Rodger walked up from the back. Oh, no. He had a wife, pups.

He cleared his throat, his hair standing on end and eyes wild as if he were seeing me for the first time. "I can't believe you're the one who sees the dead."

"Yeah," I replied, unable to think of another word to say.

We were facing down two massive armies, plus the wrath of the gods.

Yes, I'd asked my friends to hide a dragon, but I never thought they'd go this far.

More fanned out behind Rodger—the guys from the motor pool. The nurses. My friends stood by me, and for that I was deeply touched. They were the reason I was doing this. For them and for countless others like them.

To the right, on the front lines of the old army, I spotted Oghul the berserker. I hadn't seen him since he'd saved my life all those months ago. He wore leather armor studded with animal teeth. His long, curled moustache twitched as he stepped into the Great Divide.

He gave me a bow, mounds of colorful beaded jewelry hanging from his neck. You could have knocked me over when he drove a fisted hand to his breastbone and stood by me.

These people were stupid. They were my friends and I loved them but holy hell. "You have to go back before anybody gets hurt."

Galen stood by my side, as did Marc, Oghul, and Kosta. The rest crowded behind us. Jeffe buried his head in the small of my back. They were scared out of their wits. So was I. But incredibly, they were here. They were daring the gods to smite us all.

I turned to my friends. Damn it all. "You don't have to do this." They could run, live, get the hell out of this death trap.

"We know," Lazio said, trying for a cocky grin. "Too bad we never listen."

There was a great gasp among the crowd—mortal and immortal—as Mars, god of war, rose up. He wore ancient Roman battle gear. Thick black hair cascaded down his back. Thunder rolled and the clouds spat rain as he snarled.

"How dare you?" His voice boomed. "How dare you stand against the gods?"

Oh, shit.

His face held rage, violence. "Your lives are insignificant. You have no power to change the future. You exist to do our bidding and *you have failed*."

For a moment, nobody moved. Galen took my hand, his fingers tightened against mine, and I had the cowardly urge to sink into the ground.

But running wasn't an option anymore. The gods had me. There was nothing I could do, other than sacrifice. And hope my friends would be smart enough to get out of the way.

Then a young blond-haired god pushed his way out of the front lines to the left. An angry red scar sliced the side of his face and spikes jutted out from the rondels on his shoulders. For a moment, I thought he was one of Mars's enforcers, the one who would arrest me, take me, do whatever the hell they were going to do to me. But my heart nearly stopped when I realized who it was.

Dagr, god of fear. I'd rescued him from an enemy camp, tried my damnedest to save him from the Shrouds. I'd had him in my ICU where he'd talked about wanting to be a hero.

This wasn't the way to do it.

He stood directly in front of me, rivulets of sweat running down the sides of his face, and I waited for the axe to fall.

"No one touches her!" he declared.

The gods let out a collective gasp and I would have done the same if I'd had any breath left. This god—one of them—scooted Marc out of the way and stood beside me. He was so close I could feel the power radiating off him. "Hell of a way to make an impression, doc," he muttered.

It warmed me. It inspired me. And it scared the hell out of me because Dagr had just taken this to an entirely new level. I had no idea what the gods would do to me now.

Dagr was the one who'd escaped us all those months ago and found his girlfriend, the virgin goddess of hope. Well, I heard she wasn't a virgin anymore.

Then I saw her—Cavillace. The raven-haired goddess stood behind Mars, with a baby in her arms. The little one was the god of peace. And with them on opposite sides, I doubted poor Dagr had ever gotten to meet his child.

Tears filled his eyes as she stepped around the god of war and ran to us. She embraced Dagr. He held her tight. Then pulled away tenderly, as she let him hold his baby for the first time.

The gods stood facing us, thunderstruck.

I knew the feeling.

We should have been fighting by now.

Instead, we had hope. Literally.

"Okay," I said, having no clue what to do next.

Galen watched in stunned surprise. Rodger was handed the god of peace while Dagr put a lip-lock on his girlfriend. Holly stood grinning like a fool. And me? I had friends.

For so long, I had thought I was alone in this world.

It was easier that way, to refuse to believe anyone else could care about me. I thought it would hurt less to live like that. But I was wrong. I needed these people. We needed each other.

"What is this?" Medusa slithered up next to me. She scanned the battlefield, the asps on her head twisting and hissing. "The battle should have started by now."

I stared at her for a second. "What are you doing here?" I knew gorgons recovered from birth well, but she was carrying a battle-axe and she had her baby strapped to her chest.

"I am defending you," she said, placing herself between me and the gods. "Why are they staring at us?"

"Get back," I said, reaching out to touch her shoulder and then thinking the better of it. "Not with Emma." We didn't know what the gods were going to do. We couldn't risk a baby.

Medusa glared at me, as if I dared question her parenting skills. "You try finding a sitter at the last minute." She hoisted her axe onto her shoulder. "Nothing will touch me." She tossed a glance at the people behind us. "I can't make the promise for the rest of these fools."

They might be fools, but they were my fools.

The gods were smiling now, which was a pretty good indication they'd come up with a fantastic way to axe the entire lot of us.

Everyone was looking to me for answers, but I had none.

Mars glared down at us. "You are nothing. You are dust under my sandals. Even if you turn against us, you will never defeat us in battle."

Lighting streaked against the sky and the ground under us buckled. Dragons soared overhead.

"Bring it on!" Leta screamed behind me.

And a great war cry went up from the armies.

chapter twenty-four

"Get the babies out of here!" I ordered. I didn't care if they were immortal. Hadn't I just seen that even high gods could die?

Rodger handed the baby back to Cavillace, but she wasn't listening to me at all. She'd spotted the other new mommy. "She has so much hair!" the goddess said, admiring Emma's full nest of asps. She held out the child of peace to meet the child of the damned. "Baby!"

Cavillace smiled. "See how she wriggles so vigorously."

Medusa nodded. "Yes, well, she does take after her mother."

The babies reached for each other. That was all it took for the child of the damned. Emma squealed in delight.

The sky crackled as portals fired up. Bundles of color spun on all sides of the armies and even in the lines. Soldiers shrank back from the whipping energy and light. The portals whirled harder, expanding outward until dozens upon dozens of them hovered just above the desert floor. Each of them could easily fit an entire squad at a time, plus dragons, centaurs, and any other kind of war beast.

They were beautiful.

They churned, hot and red. And I swore I could hear the gods, the heavens, and both armies let out a collective gasp.

I couldn't believe it myself. The portal in the minefield had been weak, solitary. These were enough to move an army.

A million eyes turned to me.

But I hadn't done it.

"Medusa?" I said, still trying to wrap my mind around it.

The gorgon shrugged. "So she likes other babies."

Right. Sure. I let it go. Because right then, I knew how I needed to take my stand.

I'd be willing to bet my life that every soul on this battlefield would rather drop weapons and leave. I knew I wanted to go home.

It took me a second to find my voice, but when I did, I turned to Leta. "Can you get a message out?"

"Yes," she rumbled. "Are you ready for the battle to begin?"

Her and battles. "No." Tears filled my eyes and I felt my throat clog. I needed my bronze weapon for something else. "Tell them they can go home."

The dragon was speechless. Another miracle. "I don't understand," she stammered.

"I'm done here," I told her. The armies had raged. I'd faced the gods. And now? "I'm going home." If the gods wanted to smite me, they'd have to follow me to New Orleans. "Anyone who wants to stay and fight can have at it. The rest can go back to their families. The portals will take them where they want to go."

Leta's eyes swam with tears.

I placed a hand on her shoulder. "Tell them they are free."

These warring soldiers were good people who had been trapped for too long. My friends too. The gods were willing to see each and every one of us die to prove a worthless point in a senseless war.

But not anymore. We deserved to go home. All of us.

She nodded and began to broadcast. I turned to Rodger, who threw his arms around me. "I can go home! I can see Mary Ann. She won't even know I'm coming!" His eyes darted from portal to portal. "Are you sure this is going to work?"

"They can take you anywhere you want to go," I told him.

But he was already talking to himself. "I can put the kids to bed tonight. Gabe's been reading this Smile story about braces. He has to get braces." Rodger snarfed, half crying, half laughing. "I'm going to have to pay for braces."

Soldiers on both sides of the Great Divide left their battle lines and began walking across the divide. A half dozen at first, then more. They greeted old friends, or simply offered a hand to people just like them, who happened to have been drafted onto the other side.

A few of the minor gods began yelling out orders to cease. Some went as far as to grapple with soldiers crossing the lines, but there were too many of them and it was too late.

The portals whooshed as soldiers began going home.

I hugged Rodger.

He patted me on the shoulder. "You'll make it out to California, right?"

"Sure," I told him, hugging him one more time, squeezing him tight. "Get out of here."

He winked and headed for the nearest portal. He gave one final wave before he stepped through.

"Halt!" Mars bellowed. "By the power of Zeus, I command you to take up arms!" A smattering of a cheer went up somewhere, but that could have been from the entire company of centaurs who charged through a portal at once. "Who is with me?" Mars bellowed, holding his sword in the air.

No one.

Mars lowered his weapon, staring right at me.

A bolt of lightning shot from the night sky and Zeus himself descended. Even the troops at the portals hesitated and craned their necks to see the king of all the gods. Word was, he hadn't even picked a side. He just liked the fighting.

"Why are you dismantling the armies?" he boomed.

Mars snarled while Menhit's mouth opened and closed like a caught fish.

"They will not fight anymore," she finally said.

Zeus sighed. "Then you will fight," he told her.

The Chinese god behind her frowned. "It is no fun to be stabbed or shot. We could die."

"They will not obey," Mars ground out. "And if we smite them all, then there will be no one to fight."

I turned to Leta. "Are you broadcasting this?"

"Loud and clear," she said.

That's when it hit me. The gods needed us—the humans, the shifters, and the demigods who fought for them. Only we'd been subjugated for so long, we forgot *we* held the power.

There was no epic battle if we refused to fight it.

"We can smite her," Mars said, pointing at me.

I froze.

"And make her a hero? A legend?" Zeus bellowed. "No. The healer will live a piddling, mortal life and die in obscurity."

That sounded great to me.

"This war is over," Zeus declared. "We have fought well."

Leta gasped and there was a great rattling as the collars began dropping off the dragons.

One by one, they shifted back into their human forms. The joy, the relief was palpable as they were brought back, whole and unharmed.

The gods watched Zeus, clearly unsure of what would happen next. Hell, I didn't know either.

The Chinese god crossed his arms over his chest. "Clearly, we have planned this all along."

"Yes," the feathered goddess said, gathering steam. "This was obviously a test to see if the people would stand behind us and our chosen healer." She pointed a finger at me and I wasn't about to argue. She threw her hands up in the air. "The people passed! The healer can live!"

I couldn't believe it. I looked to Galen, relief flooding me. These gods were insane, but I didn't care. I might actually get out of here.

A cheer went up from the gods. It was echoed by the troops, but for an entirely different reason. They were cheering as they formed lines to the portals and left the gods and their war behind.

Jeffe clapped a bottle of nail polish into my hand. "Here. This is yours."

It was my I'm Not Really a Waitress. I waggled it at him. "You won this fair and square, buddy."

He shrugged. "Yes. But I cannot fit it anyway."

It was then that I saw the sphinx had crammed all of his poker winnings onto a hospital gurney.

"I thought I would use these things in the afterlife, but now I can take them home." He beamed. "That is good because in my country, it is customary to bring presents after a long time away."

I hugged him and rubbed his back, startling the sphinx. Still, I was pretty sure I'd heard him purr.

Grinning, I let him go and watched him amble toward the nearest portal.

"Look at this." Galen nudged me. I followed where he pointed and saw Kosta down on one knee in front of Shirley. Now that was one wedding I wouldn't miss.

Marius clapped a hand on my shoulder. "I'm going to take care of Thaïs before I leave."

"You don't have to do that," I told him. "It should be my job."

The vampire's long mouth turned up in a grin. "You've done enough."

I couldn't help but smile back. "Thaïs is going to be

pissed when he wakes up and there's no more fight-ing."

"Then that will be my reward," Marius said, before he grew serious. "Thank you, Petra. And you," he said, shaking Galen's hand.

"Are you ready?" Galen asked.

"Yes," I said, dodging the celebrating troops as we made our way to the nearest portal. Soldiers I didn't know, from both sides, were thanking us and clapping me on the back.

They didn't understand. I hadn't done it. They had.

Thunder rolled as Zeus surveyed the rapidly empty-ing field. They had no armies. They had no support. All they had was delusion.

The god raised his hands to the sky, throwing off thunderbolts. "It is to the benefit of all that the gods declare peace."

No one was listening. We'd already made it so.

As I neared the portal, I saw Klotho.

She treated me to an approving nod. "I love a well-woven cloth."

I smiled and gave her a bow.

I turned to Galen and saw the love and the warmth in his eyes. "I love you," I told him, kissing him, hold-ing him, savoring the feeling of having this man with me. Of knowing I could have a life with him at my side.

As armies collide, the healer shall leave this world forever.

And so the prophecy came to pass. When it was our time, we too stepped through the portal, and into our new life.

chapter twenty-five

A few weeks later . . .

The benefit of having a large Cajun family is that they had actually kept my house up while I'd been gone. My bungalow in the Garden District stood not much worse for wear on a street lined with palm trees and sprawling sawtooth and live oaks, with Spanish moss flirting with the wind.

They had taken the liberty of painting the shingles outside a bright yellow, and my shutters green.

I didn't care.

I had Galen sprawled out on my blue couch in the living room, and me right there on top of him.

He was running his tongue along the tip of my ear—much to my squirming delight—when the doorbell rang.

I was perfectly happy to assume it was yet another well-wishing relative welcoming me back from the Peace Corps, or to lecture me for not writing, but Galen was always the type who had to know exactly what was going on.

He craned his neck to look out the front window. "Delivery."

I let him answer the door while I grabbed a pair of scissors from the cutting block in the kitchen.

My kitchen.

My house.

I stood for a moment and took in the country wallpaper—which now seemed too quaint. In my defense, it had come with the house. I'd never really stopped to notice it before, but now I did. My place, my home was a precious thing and I wasn't going to take it for granted again.

I'd raided my magnolia tree outside and every room had fresh flowers. There was fruit in a bowl in the kitchen. Real fruit, not the dehydrated kind. My windows were open to the breeze that smelled of spring in New Orleans, not the red dust of limbo or its bubbling tar pits.

"Deep thoughts?" Galen asked, plunking the box down onto the white kitchen island.

"Good ones," I said, smiling as he moved behind me to wrap his arms around my waist and plant a kiss on the side of my neck.

I scissored through the shipping tape, scooped through endless packing peanuts, and withdrew a purple velvet bag with a note attached.

Used this on Nerthus. Don't need it anymore.
B.t.w. Congrats on the end of the war!
Eris

"Son of a . . ."

"When did you meet Eris?" Galen asked, taking the package.

"It's a long story," I said, as Galen withdrew a bronze knife. It was as long as my hand, with a compact handle and a triangular blade. I picked it up. It was army issue, and very, very familiar.

"Ha," I said, "it's yours now."

He smiled, inspecting the blade—perfect except for the sliver missing from the tip. "It can't hurt us anymore."

"None of it can," I said, as I watched him find a spot for it on my picture shelf in the hall.

As he did, I glanced over to see commotion on PNN. We'd muted the TV earlier, so we could focus on more pressing matters. But now—

"Galen, come in here." I turned the volume up.

Newscaster Stone McKay sat at his desk, looking even more tanned than usual. "PNN is first to report that a peace treaty has been signed between the old gods and the new gods." He smiled, showing overly white, perfectly straight canines. "The gods rejoice at their beneficence!"

And there she was, Eris, the goddess of chaos, smiling into the camera. She held a silver flame in her open palm, her arm bent, like a waitress holds a tray. A white barely there dress clung to her every curve. An array of tiny diamonds on invisible strings flickered over her neck and chest.

"Thanks, Stone." She brushed at the silky blond curls that cascaded down her back and curled over her shoulders. "The gods are truly brilliant," she said, as if it were obvious. "They decided—on their own—that our heroes had done enough fighting and dying for glory. The gods then brought the troops home in record time—the same day peace talks began, in fact."

She smiled into the camera and her skin itself seemed to glow.

There was no mention of the oracles or the struggle or the mass exodus at the end. And I didn't care.

Galen and I settled in together as PNN moved on to a light celebrity-style piece about the god of fear and the goddess of hope, and the first paid pictures of their darling little baby.

Galen ran his hands up my arms. "Did you see the postcard from Shirley?"

"Yes." I snarfed. I couldn't believe she'd talked Kosta into a weekend in Amish country. The salty commander had to be in love.

We'd heard from the others as well. Jeffe had made it back to his brothers and sisters in Egypt. Marius was scouting locations for a vampire pop music club in Las Vegas. And every time I opened my e-mail, I found pictures of Rodger and his kids. It's like he had to make up for the last half decade of his life. I didn't blame him one bit.

And in the interest of making up for lost time, I turned around and playfully shoved Galen down onto the couch.

He grinned. "I like a feisty woman."

"You haven't seen the half of it," I said, straddling him, rubbing my body along his like a cat.

I kissed him once, twice, reveling in the feel of him sliding his hands up my back and drawing me down to lie flush against him.

"What?" I asked, when he paused.

"I just can't believe any of this is real. That I went fishing with your cousins yesterday. That I'm out of the business of killing people."

It was amazing.

Perfect.

"You'll do well in private security."

"Nothing is going to come between us again," he said.

"Never." It felt wonderful.

He was my rock, my strength, my reward for going through hell and back again.

The phone rang, and we ignored it. I slid my hands up under his T-shirt, loving the feel of his warm, hard muscles underneath.

"Petra?" Marc's mom called out from my answering machine on the counter. I really needed to update my technology. "Petra. This is Lacey." She sounded choked up. Join the club. I'd called her when I'd gotten back into town, but I hadn't gotten a message like this from her since Marc had gone to war before me, since she and I had both believed he'd died. "I'd like you and Galen to come to dinner," she said. "We're all celebrating. Again. Marc and Leta will be there."

I could hear the joy in her voice, and the love. Marc was back. And luckily he hadn't completely shocked his mother because Leta had gotten him to reconnect with her while we were still down in limbo. It was something I'd always tried to do.

I was glad for them. And happy to have my own hero. I gave Galen a saucy grin as I looked down at him.

"I love you," I told him. I'd never love anybody else.

He gave me a lusty grin. "How about you show me how much?"

I did.

After all, we had hours before we had to be . . . anywhere.